"Impeccably assured. She knows as well as any of her contemporaries how to shape a narrative to the effect she means to achieve; she writes as easily about men as about women, as well about teen-age eroticism as about middle-age lust." —*Newsweek*

"We are swept away....Always formidable. Oates' sense of dramatic conflict has with practice become absolute."
—*Chicago Tribune Book World*

"A most welcome collection indeed. Oates builds these stories to powerful conclusions through the simplest yet most difficult means, employing a single sentence, a perfectly tuned phrase, or even just one word to convey a mood of intense restless eroticism."
—*Dallas Morning News*

"Displaying a disturbing, almost hypnotic power, [these stories] show Oates' ability to conjure up very quickly the dark side of our emotions." —*Publisher's Weekly*

"Forceful, beguiling, and pungent, these six stories form a book of powerful and emotional human conflict." —*Vogue*

belisk

A
Sentimental
Education

Stories

Joyce Carol Oates

A Dutton belisk Paperback

E. P. DUTTON INC., / NEW YORK

This paperback edition of A SENTIMENTAL EDUCATION first published 1982
by E. P. Dutton, Inc.

"In the Autumn of the Year" originally appeared in *Bennington Review* (April 1978), and
was reprinted in *Prize Stories 1979: The O. Henry Awards*.

"A Middle-Class Education" was published in a limited edition by Albondocani Press.

"The Precipice" originally appeared in *Mississippi Review* (Summer 1979).

"Queen of the Night" was published in a limited edition by Lord John Press
(Northridge, California), 1979.

"A Sentimental Education" was published in a limited edition by Sylvester and
Orphanos (Los Angeles, California), 1979.

"The Tryst" originally appeared in *Atlantic Monthly* (August 1976).

Published in the United States by
E. P. Dutton, Inc.,
2 Park Avenue, New York, N.Y. 10016
Library of Congress Catalog Card Number: 82-72047

ISBN: 0-525-48021-8

Published simultaneously in Canada by
Clarke, Irwin & Company Limited, Toronto and Vancouver

10 9 8 7 6 5 4 3 2 1

for Mary
and
Mike Keeley

Contents

Queen
of
the
Night

This is how Claire Falk's marriage of twenty-six years, which accounted for more than half her life, ended one humid Saturday afternoon in June: she blundered into overhearing a conversation.

It was one-sided, only one-half of a conversation, because her husband was on the telephone. And there were no words to it, no distinct recognizable words, because she was nearly out of earshot. She heard only sounds. Her husband's voice, curiously raw and aggrieved, a young man's voice, and yet *his*. She would know it anywhere.

He was arguing with someone. And then begging. His voice rose and dipped and went silent. Then began again: strident, passionate, craven, exasperated, frightened. A harsh, jagged, dissonant music Claire had never known in her own lifetime.

Or, if she had known it—it had been long ago, many years ago.

She shrank back against a wall, listening. Though she did not want, *really*, to eavesdrop. Even in this moment of shock, of sickening apprehension, she did not want to violate another person's privacy. But who was her husband talking with in that angry, intimate tone, why was he so upset, why so suddenly and uncharacteristically abject. . . . Claire half-wanted to go to him, to comfort him. It had been many years since she had had to comfort him.

He was silent awhile. Then began again, this time more evenly. He was trying to convince someone, his manner was more familiar: half-jocular, ironic, bullying. Yet he was still begging. It was the begging that was so ugly, so final: Claire knew what it must mean.

She knew, and retreated.

After all she was a woman of principle. Her instinct turned her away from what she might discover, what she might precisely discover, if she drew nearer, if she pressed her ear against the closed door: it would be *degrading* to eavesdrop now that she knew her husband was quarreling with a woman. She did not at that time think exactly of betrayal, in the sense in which she had been "betrayed," their marriage "betrayed." Her husband's passion excluded her. It had nothing to do with her at all.

She left the house. Retreated. He had not expected her home for another hour, she had made a miscalculation, a fatal blunder. Consequently nothing would be the same again. Now is life very real, is it very convincing?—so Claire Falk queried herself, half-ironically. When she was alone she often spoke to herself in silence and her voice, her tone, at such times was oddly cynical, even impersonal; not exactly a woman's voice. It was frequently reproachful as if it considered her something of a fool, yet it was sympathetic, good-humored, forgiving, if she stayed with it long enough. How much reality can you credit to all this?—so the voice drawled, referring to the street, the busy intersection which she was approaching, a child pedaling energetically on a bicycle, the filmy sky, the day, the world itself. But despite the voice's smug cynicism Claire was trembling, she was really in a state of mild shock, she hardly knew what she was doing. Afterward, when such extreme emotions, centered on her first husband, were to seem merely curious, she was to remember that blind panicked walk that would take her some three miles from home. She did not know what day of the week it was, what time of the day, what she had been doing all afternoon, why she had imagined it important. Her life had come to a stop.

She survived the blow, barely. How must she have looked that afternoon, a woman in her fifties, well-dressed, very pale, blind and disheveled and in a great hurry. . . . She must have been a spectacle, people must have stared at her. But she saw nothing. She saw no one. There was a wide street busy with traffic, and the corner of the park, there were a number of people playing tennis, there was the cemetery where for weeks now the groundkeepers had been on strike and weeds grew abundantly. She found herself huddling in the doorway of the little stone chapel in the cemetery. It was raining, when had it begun to rain? The drops were cool on her overheated face.

You had no idea that your husband was in love with another woman, they would ask, watching her closely.

I had no idea.

There wasn't anything . . . strange . . . ?

I had no idea.

Stubbornly, angrily. But then her jaw would quiver, her voice shake. In the doorway of the chapel she crouched like an animal, her back against the heavy oak door. Now you can cry if you must, the voice instructed her, impatiently, but nothing happened. Her forehead and cheeks were damp, it was only the rain, which was now being flung against her. An indignity. But somehow consoling.

Such things are blows, after all, people would say. There were many divorced women now. There was a small army of divorced women in this very part of the world, in the wide circle of friends and acquaintances and business associates Claire and her husband knew. A kind of death, people said. Losing a loved one in any way—it's a kind of death. A terrible blow to one's ego, to one's sense of self. So the familiar words went, the litany of clichés. She would hear them all many times, she would not turn away in contempt or anguish or amusement. Chagrined, she would recall that she herself had mouthed such platitudes in the past before she had known what they meant—before she had even guessed at their incontestable truth.

You had no idea, Claire . . . ? Really? So her sister would inquire, staring at her.

I had no idea.

With Ronald it was so obvious, you know, you remember all that year I was calling you late at night, I must have made your life miserable, you must have dreaded picking up the phone. . . . But *you* hadn't any idea, any suspicion?

Nor had she wept. Weeks after that Saturday, months afterward, on the morning of the divorce, on the evening of the divorce, she had been grim and subdued and even a little ravaged but tearless. Not out of defiance or rage but out of a queer impersonal conviction that had come to her . . . that had come to her from nowhere, as she crouched in the stone doorway, her face streaming with rain, her clothes soaking. The conviction had to do with the fact that tears were pointless. What had happened was an event, it was out of her control, in a sense not her responsibility, not her fault. Her husband had evidently fallen in love with another woman. A younger woman, of course. Younger by twenty-five years. *He* had acted, he had turned from her, he had not so much violated their marriage as simply forgotten it. And of course it was not true, as Claire told her friends, that she had "no idea": she had known very well that the two of them were emotionally estranged, no longer really intimate, uninterested in sexual love, uninterested in seeking out the causes of their indifference. She had known very well that they were friends rather than lovers, they were courteous with each other, but not *always* courteous. . . . Yet the marriage had seemed to Claire an absolute unalterable fact, an impersonal condition in which she was to continue to live, neither happy nor unhappy: simply as Claire Falk.

The divorce proceedings were impersonal too. And tedious. Even with the reformed divorce law Claire found the experience tedious, and any emotions she might have felt—after all, the Falks were dissolving not only a marriage but what added up to a small but complicated business partnership involving property, investments, works of art, two cars, a son in his mid-twenties who was studying international law in London—were flattened, drained away. There were too many details, too many fussy points, her husband's attorney and her own were better suited to deal with them, let them deal with such things while she went her own way. She would acquire an apartment, of course the house must be put on the market and sold quickly; though her husband—guilty, embarrassed, proud—had very generously offered it to her, without qualifications. Once she was out of the house and living in an apartment, perhaps one of those large, airy, very modern high-rise apartments along the river . . .

Her son flew home, to comfort her. To accuse his father. But the drama did not really interest her, she found herself embarrassed in her son's presence, as if he were mistaking her for someone else: another, weaker, far less intelligent woman. Has he always thought of me like this, she wondered. His mother. A woman who is his mother, and that only. . . . With him she managed to be "hurt," to express the usual ritual bewilderment. (Why, when things have been going so well, when we've been so happy together, twenty-six years together after all. . . .) He had her long blunt nose and squarish chin and somewhat bold, intimidating stare, and that pronounced widow's peak that had caused her grief as a young girl but which, in later years, she was rather vain about. Unlike her he was tall, and his complexion was coarse. Still he was an attractive young man. Too fussy, too solicitous of her feelings, in a way too inquisitive (for there were private matters Claire would never discuss with anyone, not even members of her family), but an attractive man, a boy who had turned out well.

Could you call him off me? her husband pleaded.

Amused, Claire assured him that their son wouldn't stay long. He had made plans to spend a month with her but of course he would grow restless, he'd soon return to London, they had only to be patient with him. He thinks I am grief-stricken, Claire said with an ironic twist of her mouth. Eventually I will convince him otherwise.

Twenty-six years, now being put behind them. And apart from the burden of the legal problems, and certain flashes of memory that evidently overtook them both (neither Claire nor her husband were sentimental people but they were susceptible, at times, to queer unanticipated painful stabs of nostalgia), the experience of closing off that passage of time, declaring it no longer valid, was not a very difficult one. One lives, after all, day by day; petty problems are more exasperating than large ones; there was no time for Claire's skeptical voice to quiz her about love, the meaning of love, whether it *had* any meaning, when she was arranging with a realtor to put their house on a crowded and grotesquely inflated market.

It *did* hurt, of course, to learn—by way of an acquaintance—that her husband believed he was in love "for the first time in his life." This, at the age of fifty-five. After those twenty-six years. But was the statement, the flamboyant deluded hope, very original . . . ? Claire laughed her infrequent ribald laugh, and said that adultery must have unhinged him. The illicit meetings, the scrambling in corners, the deceit, the silly tiresome guilt. The physical exertion involved in keeping up with a woman that young, and no doubt very experienced.

But even that hurt, that wound, faded. In the judge's chambers she and her husband were polite with each other, they made every effort to smile when smiles were not inappropriate, they were very civilized and responsible adults. Their attorneys, the judge, the recording clerk, the young woman whom Claire's husband was to marry the following week —all must have been impressed with the Falks' behavior.

In truth, Claire had been strangely hopeful about the young woman. Her initial resentment had long since faded, she felt only a curious hope that . . . that her husband would not shame himself, make a fool of himself. For she too was involved. Intimately, and publicly. If the young woman were a disappointment, if everyone talked about them, her husband's new bride, the folly of the alliance, what it must mean about Claire herself as a wife, as a woman . . .

But the girl was not a disappointment. She was not extraordinary, certainly no beauty, Claire could not reasonably feel a tug of envy of her, not even of her youth, which seemed merely shallow; she was attractive, and soft-voiced, and obviously ill at ease, and probably not *very* bright —but she wasn't a disappointment, to Claire's relief. The new Mrs. Falk would not publicly shame her.

And yet—how flattering it would have been, she said, joking, to friends, to her sister, if he had managed to set himself up with a truly beautiful, a truly remarkable woman. A politician friend of theirs had done exceptionally well, though he was in his late fifties. . . . On the other hand, another friend, newly divorced from *his* wife, had made an utter fool of himself by marrying a vulgar simpering divorcée with two small children, who quite clearly wanted only his money. So Claire's husband had not done *too* badly. At least I don't have to feel sorry for him, she said. I can begin the process of forgetting him.

As a young girl Claire had not been especially attractive. The bones of her face were strong, her nostrils flared as if she were impatient, thinking her own rebellious thoughts, cryptically amused, censorious. Her thick dark hair and her deep-set intelligent eyes were her most striking features. As she matured, however, the very uniqueness of her appearance came to have a value; she was set apart from other women, conventionally pretty women, and dependent upon her mood she was sometimes exceptionally beautiful. Who can say, who can judge, she often queried herself, studying that face she was linked to for life, examining it for blemishes or signs of aging, idly, without the anxiety other women commonly feel. By a quirk of fate she was photogenic, and a little vain; but not *really* vain, since she measured such things as a woman's sexual attractiveness against other, more abiding qualities, or were they achievements, or possessions —marriage, family, friends, a home, a fairly busy life, flexible bonds with the community. She did volunteer work for the symphony, for St. Patrick's General Hospital, for the Art Students' Guild; for a while she had been thinking quite seriously of buying into an unusual clothing boutique with the wife of her husband's most frequent golfing companion, but in the end the project had fallen through, no one knew quite why. She handled many of their finances, prepared a good deal of their income tax information for their accountant and tax lawyer, did research on certain investment properties, even wrote, from time to time, freelance articles for her suburban newspaper. (She had hoped while in college to become a journalist, not knowing at the time how difficult, how exhausting, and how ill-paid such jobs were.) Now is all this relevant to your present situation, she quizzed herself, or is it to be brushed away, forgotten with all the rest . . . ? She stared at herself unsmiling. It was remarkable how little the divorce had affected her, how alert, even youthful she still looked. (And another birthday drew near: another!) She had a very pale, opaque skin, a certain heavy and slumberous look, disturbingly erotic; or so someone had told her. Her husband, perhaps. Or a half-drunk admirer. Though she was not overweight there was a solidity, an almost leaden substance to her, as if she were not flesh—not entirely. Something sculpted. Marble. Alabaster.

As a young wife, newly pregnant, she had been eerily lethargic, slow-moving, given to long periods of daydreaming. Her husband would call her back. Sometimes rudely, she thought. Jealously. What are you thinking of, where has your mind gone, he wanted to know. But she could not answer, she could not say. In later years, particularly in the year before the telephone conversation, she had found herself drifting off again. . . . She would stand immobile, as if listening to sounds in the distance, or to a near-inaudible music. Claire, what are you thinking about? her husband would inquire. When you stand like that, staring off like that, what are you thinking of?

Nothing, she said, roused, and a little embarrassed.

But it isn't possible to think of nothing, her husband said.

Now he was good-natured about her moods, her habits. They were harmless, after all. Hardly a threat or a challenge to him. Of course he was in love, and like a young besotted lover he could think of no one else but his love, though he made an attempt to be attentive, even generous; Claire had not understood at the time but she had felt the force of his good-humored, somewhat distracted curiosity.

My mind just slipped away, she said.

Yes, but where?

An immobile, impassive woman, with a striking profile, a head of thick dark hair wildly streaked with gray. Something glacial about you, something remote and forbidding, the young man who was to be her second husband said, shyly, yet half-mockingly. It was clear that he was in awe of her. Fascinated by her. ". . . Queen of the Night," he whispered.

"What? What did you say?"

He caught his lower lip between his small crowded-together teeth.

"Oh nothing. Some nonsense that crossed my mind."

a small inexplicable thrill of concern that he was barefoot despite the chill.

His long slender feet danced bluish-white in the dusk.

There was a party of "adults" and a party of "young people," some of them very young indeed—fifteen or sixteen. Claire did not approve, really. The two parties overlapped awkwardly, as if by accident. Her sister, vodka martini in hand, introduced her to the guests: a Democratic congressman, someone in the hotel business, an editor for the *Miami Herald*. "My sister is a freelance journalist," Claire's sister said before Claire could silence her.

The party had no center. There must have been hosts—the couple who owned the enormous sprawling stucco-and-glass house—but Claire never met them.

Her niece Maryanna appeared, hair loose to her waist. She was nineteen years old and had dropped out of the University of Miami in order to join an amateur theatrical group; she was training to be a mime. A pert, pretty girl with small high breasts and small buttocks snug in a pair of bleached blue jeans, Claire's only niece, at one time quite a favorite of hers. But all that had changed. Why it was that Maryanna didn't care for her Aunt Claire, why she never smiled *quite* warmly enough, Claire could not fathom. Certainly she had always been kind to the girl, especially since her sister's divorce, and generous with gifts.

"How nice you look tonight, Aunt Claire," the girl said, raising her droll eyebrows.

Maryanna's friends hung back, as if conscious of being obtrusive at the party. Certainly they had not been invited—but then who *had* been, in this confusion? The young blond man edged forward, barefoot, graceful. The lenses of his eyeglasses were round and fairly thick, and magnified his beautiful eyes. He stared at Claire openly, taking in her fashionable new gown, which was coarse-knit, ivory and cream-colored and a pale russet-orange. The skirt was made of several layers which fell unevenly, rather rakishly, about her ankles.

"My name is Emil," he said softly, licking his lips.

His hand was small-boned, light as a bird; the flesh was uncommonly soft. Though their two hands were joined for the space of some seconds during which they gazed raptly at each other, there was little pressure, hardly any force at all.

He introduced himself as a "polymath." His pale hair stirred in the oceanward breeze, his eyelids and his fingers fluttered, Claire found him

charming—though rather absurd of course—as he elaborated his talents:
he was a poet, a playwright, a composer of "musical theater," a linguist,
an economist, an actor, a director, a historian, a former track star (in
high school—long ago, in Paris, Illinois), a watercolorist, a potter, a
flautist, a pianist. He was to have been a concert pianist, and the piano
was still his first love, but the designs and blackmailing tactics of his
parents and various instructors had forced him to reject the entire
business; it was sordid, the competition was sinister and antimusical. Did
Claire agree?

Delighted with him, Claire found herself laughing in agreement.

Some minutes later the two of them were strolling along the beach,
carrying their drinks. Emil had even offered to carry Claire's heavy purse
of glazed wicker into which she'd thrown, earlier that day, all sorts of
things—hand lotion, moisturizer, a bottle of Bufferin, a four-ounce
bottle of expensive French perfume, her checkbook, her traveler's
checks, a pair of plastic sunglasses with oversized blue frames. As they
walked Emil kept up a constant stream of chatter: anecdotes about a few
of the people at the party, speculations on the future of Florida, and of
the United States, and of Western civilization in general, his theories
of art and culture and morals and religion. Evidently we are in the "Tin
Age," the last of the cycles before the entropic collapse of the universe.
Languages begin to fail. The gestures of affection and love begin to fail.
Individuals take to shouting at one another but still cannot make themselves heard. Frustrated, they take refuge in the senses, they attempt to
communicate through the body—through love, or brutality; but of
course they fail. And all subsides into its original chaos.

"Really?" Claire laughed.

Then he was complaining bitterly about the poor public and critical
reception he and his group had received back in October when they had
presented their own production of Webster's *The White Devil*, con-
ceived in a Brechtian style, with appropriate music. Tickets had been
only one dollar, yet very few people had come; and some rude, ignorant
fools had even left during the performance, which badly upset certain
of the actors. Including Emil. ". . . just don't make the *attempt* to hear
what we're saying," he mumbled, edging around in front of Claire,
gazing at her appealingly. "Then they wonder why we shout, they
wonder why we're forced to behave like children. And it's very difficult,
you must realize, to retain a child's innocence and arrogance at the age
of twenty-nine!"

His pale jester's face was drawn up into a look of—was it sorrow, was it a small boy's naughty glee—and there was a hint of complicity too. Claire grinned at him, refusing to be moved, to be obviously "charmed."

She sipped at her drink, which she no longer tasted. "If the universe is running down," she said, raising her voice gaily to be heard over the sound of the surf, "none of this matters, does it?"

"Oh hell," Emil said flatly, his shoulders slumping, "the universe *won't* run down. It never *has* and it never *will.*"

They had walked some distance, the party was far behind them, Claire's feet in her expensive sandals were wet and sandy, the moon had become filmy, eerily beautiful, nothing mattered and everything mattered. The palm tree leaves made papery, restless sounds in the wind, and of course the surf pounded and pounded and spilled itself frothily up onto the beach. Am I drunk, Claire asked, allowing her attentive, admiring young escort to slide an arm through hers when she stumbled in the sand, is any of this real, does it *matter . . . ?* Emil's daring made him tremble. She could feel him trembling. But her own body was suffused with a sudden vitality, an uncanny strength that had lain in trance for many years. The body's life is a matter of power, she saw, and one of the manifestations of this power is—simply—to recognize it and pay homage to it.

Emil was dissatisfied with the Miami area and had plans, tentative plans, to hitch a ride out to Key West. Where he had friends. Someone to put him up for a few weeks. Though possibly he might go elsewhere —he really didn't know.

"Emil—you hear such stories about him," Maryanna said.

"What kind of stories?" said Claire.

The girl's limbs were covered with a soft brown-blond down, like the down of a baby animal. Except for her lower legs, which she had shaved, and which were hard and muscular and very tan. She did not like her aunt, that was clear. And now she had a reason for not liking her.

"What kind of stories?" Claire persisted.

"Oh—drugs and dealing and—that kind of thing—" Maryanna said irritably. "Borrowing money and not paying it back. Lying. Playing people off against one another. That kind of thing." But then she added, glancing at Claire, as if she suddenly feared this information might find its way back to Emil, "I don't know: you hear stories about everyone. Most of it's bull. I really *don't* know, you'll have to ask him yourself."

Claire laughed in surprise. "But I won't be seeing him again, I'm leaving next Monday."

"Next Monday?" her niece said, raising her eyebrows. "Oh, that soon? Are you leaving that soon? . . . But it's so cold back north isn't it?"

She bought a car, one of the smaller models (she had, of course, a car back home), and she and Emil took turns driving. It was not a difficult trip—a few nights on the road, interstate highways that were dry well up into southern Pennsylvania, and after that adequately plowed. Emil had drawn up a "verbal contract": though she was paying for his meals and lodging and the gas for the car, he fully intended to repay her within six months, as soon as he was settled with a job. He had connections in Boston. But he wouldn't mind even manual labor, for a while.

In a Sheraton Hilton "motor hotel" somewhere in the hills of Virginia they shared a bed for the first time. (They had taken adjoining rooms.) Claire in an ivory negligee—a beautiful thing, and rather costly, bought as a Christmas present for herself back in a Miami Nieman-Marcus—opened the door to Emil's timid knocking, and saw with pleasure the awe, the confused love, in the young man's eyes. "Oh God," he whispered, as if for an invisible audience. And she *was* beautiful at the moment—her own reflection had startled her. Calm and impassive and hard and yet lovely, classically lovely, with her dark eyes and strong bones and pursed, contemplative lips. She felt no passion herself but might gaze upon it, unjudging, tolerant.

"Do you think—? Is it—? I mean— Could I, just for a while—"

He began to stammer. Claire touched his lips with her forefinger.

As a lover he was quivering and self-conscious and far too quick, too clumsy. Claire held him, feeling unashamedly maternal: she murmured words of love and encouragement and praise to him, and stroked his shuddering sides, and his sweat-slick back. Ah, the poor boy was so thin! —so painfully thin. His ribs protruded, his collarbone protruded, his grinding pumping hips were hardly larger than a child's. Though his shoulder and arm muscles were hard. And his thighs. Claire held him, and laughed with delight of him, and told him she had never been so happy in her life—which was, of course, untrue: but then such things are uttered, at such times.

"Do you love me?" he whispered.

His body still trembled, he had to press himself against her, burrowing his face into her shoulder. He was very warm, and slender as a fish, quivering with life, altogether delightful. While making love to her he had whimpered, like a child in pain, or a child terribly frightened, and Claire had found herself excited by the sounds, the high-pitched half-conscious sounds, which stirred a memory she could not grasp.

"Do you love me?" he whispered.

II

They were married the first week in March, at a private ceremony, and celebrated alone afterward with a champagne breakfast at the city's most elegant hotel. And then on their honeymoon: to Nassau: which was supposed to be different enough from Miami to make the effort worthwhile. (It was not *very* different, but then what can one expect from a winter resort?) Emil was an energetic, attentive, high-spirited young bridegroom, apt to mock his very enthusiasm by droll grins and self-mimicking routines, though it was obvious that he loved Claire very much, and was still somewhat intimidated by her. He liked to attribute to her certain not-quite-natural powers: she could "read" his thoughts, she could pitch him out of a black mood by "focusing" on him, she could draw him to her, to make love to her, by her gaze alone, fixed on the back of his head. On the wide white beach he never tired of oiling her body, or arranging the beach umbrella so that the shadow fell over her face; he never tired of running little errands—getting lemon ices for them at midmorning, and drinks at noon, and beer at odd times. (Claire developed a taste for beer, it must have been because of the sun and the beach, a certain dryness in her mouth, a near-perpetual thirst. They discovered a very interesting Japanese beer, new to them both, which was expensive but well worth the price.)

The only problem was, Emil could not tan: his pale, near-translucent skin simply pinkened and began to smart.

"Just look at you!" he wailed, sitting slump-backed beneath the umbrella. "You're so dark! You're dark as a native! Perfect! You radiate heat and warmth and health and sanity, your body is obviously *wiser* than mine though you don't belong to the daylight any more than I do. . . . Oh God, how I envy you, it just isn't *fair.*"

His nose was burned, and began to peel. Which humiliated him. Which he would not allow her to joke about.

"I feel like a freak. I *am* a freak. Go to the dining room by yourself, you obviously can't want a creature like me to accompany you," he said.

She overheard him speaking in a peremptory way to one of the tennis instructors, a young man his own age, and was startled at first—and then rather thrilled—by the tone of his voice. He could be firm, even somewhat bullying, out of her presence. Though with her, of course, he was always puppyish, boyish, tremulous, uncertain.

"You *do* love me, you *do* love me?" he asked repeatedly.

"I'm your wife now, of course I love you," Claire laughed, stroking his hair, his shoulders, his sides.

"You won't throw me aside someday, the way you snatched me up?"

"Don't be absurd."

"I'm not absurd," he said petulantly. ". . . Am I absurd, Claire?"

"Hush. Why don't you sleep."

"Will you sleep too?"

"Of course."

"You won't stay awake, will you?—and look at me?"

"Hush now. It's very late."

"You *won't* stay awake, will you? After I've gone to sleep?"

"No. Of course not."

"Shall we fall asleep at the very same moment?"

"That's rather difficult, isn't it, Emil?"

"But don't you even want to try!"

Then he would drift off into sleep, his eyelids only partly closed, his pale, almost white eyelashes fluttering with the nervous intensity of unwilled sleep. At such times her heart would expand with love of him —of his awkward, almost crude innocence; and she would kiss his parted lips gently, and murmur a blessing.

"Love, love, love. . . ."

Though her realtor had received an offer of $275,000 for her house and the 2.3 acres that went with it Claire decided not to sell after all.

Emil saw the house and exclaimed, "Oh Jesus. Is *that* . . . ?" And so she decided not to sell.

Why bother with the fuss of locating an apartment, and moving her things, and selling much of her lovely furniture? She could not even remember the reason she had wanted to move, had it had something to do with her grief over her first husband's adultery, and her wish to put all memories of him behind . . . ? But now all memories of him *were* behind.

When Emil questioned her about him—lightly, playfully, not at all jealously—Claire had to think before replying. What sort of man was he, this Falk? "Oh, I think basically—basically he was a man of limited imagination," Claire said slowly. "But very solid. Very reliable."

Emil snickered. "He wasn't worthy of you, obviously!" he said.

"He didn't exactly *know* me."

Her husband's closet, empty; and filled now, or partly filled, with Emil's clothes.

"We'll have to buy you some things," Claire said. "You seem to own only summer clothing."

"Yes, it *is* winter up here, isn't it? I'd almost forgotten what winter was."

A houndstooth English jacket, a pale orange blazer, a camel's-hair coat, fur-lined leather gloves made in Hungary, fur-lined leather boots made in Italy, a half-dozen sweaters, a dozen shirts. A smart plaid vest. A suede suit. Trousers of various textures, various hues. A blue terry-cloth bathrobe to slip into when he was still wet from his shower.

Clowning, he went to stand in the plate-glass window of the men's shop in the Fairway Hotel, positioning himself like a manikin. He was wearing the suede suit, without a shirt. His slightly hollow hairless chest shone.

The salesman managed to laugh but Claire, unamused, spoke sharply.

Whereupon her young husband turned away at once, flushing, hurt, and fled—simply ran out the front door. Claire called after him but he didn't look back.

He was gone, that time, overnight. She stayed up until two and then decided that she would sleep, she wouldn't martyr herself for him; she made herself a rum toddy and fell asleep on her bed, beneath a quilted afghan. Where Emil found her the next morning and awoke her with a wet puppyish kiss.

He crept under the afghan, burrowing into her arms.

"Forgive, forgive. Forgive little Emil."

His breath stank, there was an odor of something dry and harsh in his hair, perhaps smoke; and the stubble on his chin chafed her sensitive breasts. But she held him, and rocked him gently, and forgave him.

There were temper tantrums, there were shouting matches. Claire had never guessed herself so easily enraged. Once she even began to strike Emil's tear-stained face, screaming at him, and he tried to catch her wrists, ducking backward in alarm. He *was* frightened of her, she saw with amusement. But how silly! . . . As if she didn't love him more than life itself.

After the quarrels there were drinking sessions, occasionally. And frequent bouts of lovemaking. And once Emil fished out of a knapsack in his closet something for them to smoke in a pipe—hashish, it was: but Claire demurred. She had read somewhere . . . No, she was afraid.

"But don't you trust me, Claire, dear?"

"It isn't that, Emil."

"Yes. But *don't* you trust me?"

"I simply don't want to. I don't want to."

"You hold yourself back from me, judging me. You're always judging. You don't *trust* me."

"Of course I trust you. I love you."

"But you hold yourself off from me, behind a glass case!"

Once, after the most protracted and childishly abusive of their quarrels—he called her a witch, she called him a male slut—they made love on the first-floor landing, gasping and clutching at each other. It was the first time Claire allowed herself to feel passion, to draw the tiny spark of pleasure up, upward, into something resembling a flame, and by the time she came to her climax she was groaning and shouting and tearing at him, her face distorted, her mouth gaping and ugly as a fish's—and still the sensation billowed onward, higher and higher, more and more violent, until she thought she would lose consciousness. *I love you, I love you, I love* . . .

Afterward, dazed, she hardly knew where she was, who this thin shuddering creature was lying on top of her, dripping sweat. Who, why. . . . What had led her to . . .

She began to cry. Her body shook. Everything was naked, exposed: her soul, her brain, her nerves: she had been destroyed, she had been

turned inside out: and yet she was living, still, convulsed with sobs of
dismay and incredulity and gratitude.

Emil said nothing. He eased himself from her and lay for a while,
holding her as she wept and murmured to him, *Love, love, I love.*
. . . He held her loosely, one arm beneath her shoulders. Until it became
numb. Until the position became distinctly uncomfortable. Then he
eased surreptitiously away. She would have called out for him but she
was too sleepy, too exhausted. Why was he abandoning her. . . . Why
was it so cold. . . .

A long time later she heard, or believed she heard, someone talking.
Muttering. She tried to rouse herself but her head ached. There was a
person drawing near, there were footsteps, silent, she must have been
lying on the floor, on the carpet, but where?—why? Someone laid a
blanket atop her, tucking it under her chin.

"Sleep it off, love," came a small cool remote voice.

Afterward, Claire was intensely ashamed of her behavior: that ugly
grasping maniacal passion. Her body had gone mad, that was all. And
the spell of weeping. . . . She had wept and wept like a giant child though
she had sensed, even at the time, in her half-conscious drunken state,
her young husband's secret contempt.

She would have liked to vow to him—I will never be that way again.
I will never submit the two of us to such an experience again.

She would have liked to beg him—Please forget! *Please forget!*

He hid himself from her, daydreaming. A book in his lap. A notebook
opened on the table before him, his pen turning idly between his fingers.
And sometimes he sat at the piano, depressing the notes so slowly that
they hardly sounded.

There was sheet music in the piano bench—why didn't he play
something? Her son Ted had taken lessons at one time, many years ago.

"I can't play with anyone else listening, I'd be too self-conscious," he
said.

"But I *won't* listen. I'll be upstairs on the telephone."

He shrugged his shoulders indifferently. In recent weeks his face had
become drained of all expression, he no longer clowned and carried on,
he never teased her. When he raised his glasses to rub his eyes Claire
saw that he looked drawn and tired, much older than his years. There
were white crinkles about his eyes like tiny lines etched in the skin.

"You're bored," Claire said recklessly.

"Of course not," he said at once.

He adjusted his glasses and stared at her, blinking. His cheeks colored faintly as if he had been caught out in a lie.

"Of course you *are,*" she said. "And it's quite natural. There isn't enough for you to do here. Wouldn't you like to continue with your theatrical work? There's an experimental theater in the city, I was reading about it in last Sunday's paper, it sounds exactly like something you would . . . But why are you staring at me like that? You *were* interested in the theater when I met you."

"Was I?"

"Well—weren't you?"

"I never liked working with other people. In such close quarters. Subordinating myself to others' ideas. . . . You wouldn't understand," he said, yawning.

"Then what would you like to do?"

"Nothing."

"What?"

"*I do what I am doing.*"

"Yes, but what *are* you doing?"

His pale lips stretched into a wide rapid humorless smile.

"You're too solicitous of me, love," he said softly. "I'm quite all right as I am. I'm perfectly happy. Idyllically happy. . . . I'm waiting."

"Waiting for what?" Claire asked sharply.

He shrugged his shoulders again. Even in his handsome new clothes he looked scrawny and unkempt.

"Would you like to take piano lessons again?—with a good pianist? You could audition at the conservatory."

"Too late. Too old," he said, drawling. He stretched his fingers at her. "Stiff joints."

As the months passed Emil rarely slept with Claire for an entire night: he slipped quietly away as soon as she slept, or as soon as he believed she slept. Once, startled out of a half-sleep, she asked him where he was going and he mumbled guiltily that he couldn't sleep right now—he was too restless. But why can't you sleep? she asked, pulling at his wrist, smiling. Come back to bed, I'll hold you, you'll be asleep in ten minutes.

He hesitated. Then said, "I'm afraid—well—your snoring keeps me awake."

"My snoring!" Claire said, deeply hurt. "But I haven't been asleep.
. . . I'm sure I haven't been asleep. . . ."

He shrugged his shoulders and did not contradict her. But he did not
return to bed.

Later that night Claire *did* wake herself with a hoarse loud snort. She
woke, startled, to find her throat parched and painfully dry. She was
grateful, then, that Emil wasn't with her.

He got into the habit of wandering about the house downstairs, late
at night. She could not hear his footsteps, exactly—he was barefoot, and
of course he moved lightly—but she could feel a subtle, almost imperceptible vibration in the house. He sprawled on the couch in her former
husband's study and in the morning she saw the piles of books he had
pulled off the shelf and had presumably leafed through. Hawthorne's
Tales, The Iliad, Great Philosophical Ideas of the Western World,
Flaubert's *Bouvard and Pécuchet:* books her husband had acquired over
the years, had never read, and hadn't bothered to take along with him.
Emil wrote in his notebook, tore the pages out impatiently, discarded
them. But when Claire uncrumpled them she saw that he had written
only nonsense scrawls, or had covered a page with doodles of misshapen
people and animals. In one, a woman with gigantic breasts and a ribald
leering smile strode forward, a half-dozen heads hanging from her right
fist, held by their hair. In another a man had turned into a phallus—
or a phallus had turned into a man—and stared upward with a melancholy expression.

Emil began to sit at the piano for hours, reading music, touching the
keys listlessly. Occasionally he struck loud angry chords and the sound
was astonishing: though Claire might be far away upstairs the sudden
noise would alarm her, her heart would lurch in her chest. Sometimes
he played rushed, uneven arpeggios, cursing when he hit a wrong note.

He became obsessed with Chopin, and bought all of Chopin's music.
The preludes, the nocturnes, the mazurkas . . . even the polonaises.
. . . This is the music in which death speaks secretly, Emil said, but you
never know *quite* where. He leafed through the études, he tried to play,
attacking the keyboard fiercely, then letting his hands fall on his knees.
He couldn't play, he said petulantly, with someone always listening.

Claire returned from shopping late one afternoon to find Emil at the
piano, exactly as he had been when she had left hours before. His face
was pinched, his mouth puckered. Before him was a Chopin nocturne.
In a flat but amused voice he told Claire that he had been trying to play

the concluding cadenza, a single cadenza, for an hour and a half. Over
and over he played. Each time he made a mistake he forced himself to
begin again. It was discipline, it was punishment. He *would not stop*
until he played the cadenza perfectly, as Chopin himself must have
played it.

"Attention, love!" he said briskly. He flexed his fingers and wriggled
them like a clown.

Claire opened her mouth to protest but he cut her short. And began
the cadenza again, an octave above high C: his fingers moving so rapidly,
so surely, that Claire stared in astonishment. The notes were struck
softly, softly, and then gradually harder, building to a delicate crescendo
and then almost immediately diminishing. Though Emil's head was
tilted back and his eyes were half-closed the tendons in his throat were
rigid and Claire could nearly feel his impatience, his terrible rage. She
stood waiting helplessly. There was nothing to do but stare at those
blurred fingers. He *was* an accomplished pianist, evidently. . . . Then
he began a rapid, complex run down the keyboard, and still his fingers
moved with an incredible rapid grace, an almost inhuman grace, and
Claire held her breath, her own nails dug into her palms, and then—
and then of course he struck a wrong note—

He did not scream, he did not bring his fist down on the keyboard.
He merely sat there grinning. His breathing was quick and shallow, she
could see his thin chest rising and falling, and very nearly feel his
murderous heart.

Swaying, she brought her hand to her forehead.

"Oh please don't, please don't. . . ." she whispered.

"Don't *what,* dear Claire?" Emil asked sharply.

"Don't, don't. . . ."

He regarded her with silent contempt, and then laughed shrilly, like
a child on the verge of hysteria.

"Don't *what?* Continue to exist?"

He glided, he slid, he plunged into dark moods. Would not sleep,
would not eat. Would not leave the house. She came upon him slouched
in his underclothes on her husband's old leather couch, staring out the
window. How could he lie there so motionless, what was he brooding
about, where was his mind . . . ? If she spoke his name he often did not
respond at once. If she touched his shoulder he shivered; or, rather, his
flesh shivered. Slowly, reluctantly, his spirit eased back into his body and

he looked up at her, his eyes narrowed, the white lines edging them
pinched and severe.

"Emil? Is something wrong? What are you thinking about?"

"What am I thinking about? . . . Nothing."

She was in danger of bursting into tears. But instead she laughed, a
harsh mirthless laugh. And then, flushing deeply, went silent. "But I love
you," she said in reproach.

He smiled faintly, quizzically. Love? She loved him? But what was
love, where precisely was it? What did it mean?

"Well. I love you too," he said finally.

The moods lightened. He consented to be bathed by her, and to allow
her to shampoo his hair. She was gentle, loving, sometimes playful. She
stuck her soapy fingers in his ears and wiggled them. She tickled the crisp
pale hair beneath his arms. Without his glasses his green-gray eyes were
small and close-set and their gaze seemed comfortably blurred.

Now his spirits rose and he was Emil again, the old Emil. But then
they sank. Hour by hour, quite perceptibly, they sank. How much can
you believe in, Emil said, yawning, indicating with a dismissive wave of
his arms the house, the grounds, the sky. How seriously can you take all
this? Even when you own it.

Don't, Claire whispered.

She had always thought of depression as a simple pathological state,
the consequence of self-indulgence and sluggishness; neither she nor her
husband—her former husband—could tolerate it in others. Now, holding and rocking in her arms her stricken young lover, she wondered if
it was in some way a sensitive and even intelligent response to certain
. . . to certain implacable truths.

Yet she loved him, and she would nurse him back. And so it came
about that his spirits *did* rise. . . . He had become interested in real
estate, in property investment, and she gave him brochures to read, and
articles torn out of *Fortune* and *Business Week;* she loved to answer his
questions, which were often naïve, but sometimes surprisingly astute.
Tax depreciation. . . . Insurance. . . . Tenants' rights. . . . Perhaps they
should buy property in the Adirondacks, near Lake Placid? A summer
home? A small hotel? A block of shops? A restaurant? Or a small
apartment building here in the city, where Emil could oversee the
manager at close quarters. . . .

One night when he was especially euphoric he pulled her gently into
their bed, and began to make love to her. (In recent months they had

stopped making love. For some reason they had stopped. Neither mentioned it, of course, and Claire herself did not really think about it: if she began to think about it her mind simply went blank.) But then he paused. He drew away from her, half-sobbing.

"Emil . . . ?"

"I can't."

"Emil, please. It doesn't matter."

He lay very still. He rubbed the back of his forearm against his eyes roughly. "I can't, can't, *can't,*" he whispered.

"It isn't important," Claire said gently.

"Isn't it!"

She could not tell—was his tone sarcastic, was it utterly serious—but when she tried to stroke his face he turned aside and swung his feet over the edge of the bed.

"Emil—"

She grasped his arm but he twisted violently away. "Don't touch!" he said.

He rose naked from the bed and ran from the room. She heard his footsteps on the stairs. . . . For a long time she lay immobile, deeply hurt. She had never been so hurt in her life. We aren't really married, she thought. He isn't really my husband.

She woke before dawn, alone. The bedclothes smelled of sweat and were badly rumpled. When she went downstairs she found him asleep on one of the sofas in the living room, still naked, breathing hoarsely through his mouth. He slept with the single-minded intensity of a small child, his hands curved toward his chest, his chin damp with saliva. So deeply was he plunged into sleep that he fairly quivered with the experience. How profound, how very profound, was the element into which he had fallen. . . . She stood above him, noting his trembling eyelids, the pallor of his hollow, hairless chest, the small pale shrunken penis in the sparse bush of pubic hair. Emil. Her lover Emil. Her husband. He appeared to be dreaming. Certainly he was dreaming. His eyeballs jerked behind his eyelids, his fingers and toes twitched. She gazed upon him calmly. She was not at all jealous. He was dreaming, and she was not jealous: perhaps her shadow fell upon his sleep and it was she of whom he dreamed.

Yet it was unfair, it was unjust, that the man she loved so deeply could slip away from her, and plunge into an element that contained him utterly and set her apart from him. What are the secrets of sleep, who can account for the isolation, the selfishness of that solitude. . . . Odd, she had never cared about her former husband's interior life. She had never thought about it at all. In fact she had often been relieved when in bed he turned from her, overtaken by drowsiness, relinquishing her to her own solitude, her own small universe of dreams. But Emil was different, she would have liked very much to know what he was experiencing, whether indeed she was queen of his sleep or whether there, in that kingdom, he did not know her at all.

She touched his shoulder. But he did not awake: he moaned softly, and tried to burrow into the cushions. His long thin bluish-white feet kicked feebly. So she relented, and went upstairs, and came back with an afghan and a pillow to slip beneath his head. Again the sight of him mesmerized her. He slept so hard, so very hard, and he *was* her husband. It crossed her mind that she could smother him, with the pillow. If she chose. She was capable of a single great act of strength and he, surprised, bereft in that other world, would have been powerless to withstand her. . . . But of course she merely slipped the pillow beneath his head, and laid the afghan carefully on top of him so that he would not catch cold. His nakedness was so frail, so vulnerable, except for the premature lines etched rather deeply into his throat, and those small white lines in his face, it was a boy's nakedness, striking in its blunt innocence.

Not long afterward she telephoned her former husband at his office. His voice rose cautiously at first but when he saw that she wanted only to talk, and to talk about casual things—mutual friends, property they had once owned together, finances, city politics—he was cordial, and seemed quite pleased to hear from her. Claire knew that he had received a certain nasty letter from their son because a carbon copy of the letter had been sent to her, in the same envelope with a very nasty letter to *her.* She supposed that her husband had received a carbon copy of her letter; and since both letters questioned their respective characters, what poor furious Ted called their "moral degeneracy," Claire saw no reason to mention them, nor did her husband.

And how is—? her husband asked.

Lovely. Just lovely, Claire said. And you—?

Lovely, he said.

They were silent for a long moment. Then Claire's former husband told her of a new restaurant downtown that *the two of you* might check out sometime: it was overpriced, of course, but charming, with an impressive wine list.

We'll do that, Claire said, delighted.

She had wanted to ask him . . . she had wanted to ask . . .

Well, what *is* marriage, and how does one know when one is married? What *is* love, precisely? The questions were naïve and embarrassing, and yet they must be asked. Though Claire herself hadn't the courage.

She *hadn't* the courage, though she was over fifty years old and had lived, had lived, had lived forever.

Then the weather changed, and she and Emil flew to San Francisco for a marvelous two-week vacation—a second honeymoon, of a sort—and there acquired several fascinating jade figures, and looked up old friends of Claire's who were delighted to see them, not at all disapproving of the marriage as Claire had halfway feared. ("But you look radiant, Claire!" they said. "And Emil is so charming—and so deep, so obviously deep. You make a very attractive couple.") And when they returned, the house painters had finished with both the downstairs and upstairs rooms and everything looked lovely, clean and white and blank and new and lovely, and it would be a challenge, they both said, to acquire the right kind of art for the walls. . . . Claire spent much of her time shopping, and at her volunteer organizations; Emil joined an avant-garde theater group in the city. Sometimes they met for a drink downtown, at the Fairway, but often they didn't see each other until dinner, which was eaten late—never before eight o'clock. And there were times, of course, when Emil had rehearsals and wasn't back until one or two in the morning, and Claire, tired from her own activities, did not wait up for him.

It was a new season. A new autumn. Claire was elected first vice-president of the Friends of the Symphony. Emil's theater was to present a play by Lorca, the first of November. When his friends brought him home, when Claire came downstairs to join them for a drink, she saw the surprised, half-reluctant admiration in their faces: for of course they all gossiped about her, they speculated freely about Emil's "older" wife. But she had never looked more regal, more beautiful. Her skin bloomed darkly, her hair was now tinted a rich lustrous brown-black, fashioned to rise from her head in a winglike manner, exposing the prominent widow's peak. She wore unusual clothes: black trousers, a coarse-knit white sweater; many-layered muslin skirts in the latest style; simple wrap-around housedresses from Saks. She said little, and smiled little. Emil came at once to stand beside her. He was obviously very proud of her. When he introduced her to his friends she shook hands like a man, and fixed her severe dark gaze upon them one by one, and did not allow herself to be too easily won over. For she knew, she knew very well, that young people like these did not value easy conquests.

Sometimes, in the morning, Emil would stroll casually into her dressing room, toweling his hair, or wiping his glasses with a tissue, and he would say, very casually, that he had liked the outfit she'd worn the night before—was it new?—he didn't remember having seen it before. Or he would say with a droll twist of his mouth that one of his friends had fallen in love with her—had begged to be invited back sometime, maybe to dinner—what did Claire think? Yes? No? Occasionally he apologized for their having stayed so late, and having made so much noise. But Claire prudently did not comment. She would *not* comment.

The important thing was—he was busy, he was absorbed in his new life, he was happy. When he forbade her to see the play she was disappointed but did not persist. Your presence in the audience would make me self-conscious, he said. He forbade her also to read any reviews of the opening. She promised that she would not, but sought them out nonetheless in a nearby library: only one review, hardly more than a paragraph, mildly enthusiastic, complimenting the cast on their energy and zeal, and the set designer for his imagination. The names of several actors were mentioned but Emil's was not among them.

After the play's two-week run came to an end Emil often stayed out late, and quite frequently his friends brought him home very early in the morning. Claire came to detest a short burly-chested youth with red curly hair and a thick red beard, whose laughter was always dissolving into coughing fits. He was blatant, he knew himself good-looking, and very young—much younger than Emil. And another creature: tall and thin and delicate-boned as Emil, with a whispery, rather mocking voice, and a bad limp. And there were girls, women, interchangeable, always uncomfortably intense in Claire's presence: to hear them talk they cared about nothing except their "careers," their "work." Claire refrained from questioning them about their plans, their exact plans, for the future. Nor did she comment dryly that so much partying, so much alcohol and marijuana and exhaustion, would hardly help.

But Emil was happy with them, or at any rate diverted from his spells of melancholy. She was not going to judge him, she had come to love him too much, to exalt in him . . . in his mere being, his existence, as one might exalt in the fact of a work of art, or a superbly proportioned animal, or a comely child. She hardly thought of him as her husband. Husband—what did that mean? Its meaning was parochial, claustrophobic. He's like a child of my own, a second son—yet far more interesting than any child of my own, she thought with a curious satisfaction. And anyway one no longer wanted a *husband*, in the old sense. All that was dead, finished.

In mid-December Emil announced his birthday. It was that day, that very day. A small group of his closest friends, his favorite people, were coming that evening to help him celebrate, and he hoped Claire would not mind. They had been somewhat out of touch that week because of their conflicting schedules: for the first time in months Claire had had to attend a dinner, a fund-raising dinner for a local congressional candidate, and she hadn't returned home until well after midnight, and Emil mentioned the fact once or twice, always with a somewhat reproachful air. So they had been out of communication. It was not *his* fault.

"Your birthday . . . ?" Claire said, peering at him over her reading glasses.

"My thirty-fifth. What's wrong? Why stare at me like that? It's rude, it's eccentric. . . . Don't I deserve an occasional birthday, like the rest of you?"

"Your thirty-fifth . . . ?"

"Some of us age quickly," he said with a cheerful smile.

Somehow Claire had known beforehand that the party would be disastrous, and yet she did not forbid it; she felt too weak, too absurdly wounded, to protest. And then Emil did not quarrel fairly: he launched into one of his theatrical tantrums, or delivered a silly insulting speech at the top of his lungs, or threw things—pillows, vases, articles of clothing—onto the floor; or he went utterly cold, utterly silent, and regarded her with a pristine contempt she found terrifying.

Her heart ached, at such times. It was not farfetched to say that her very heart ached in her chest, between her tight constraining ribs. The real, the organic, the pounding heart and not a mere word, not a metaphor. . . . She grew short of breath, her body flushed with an obscure unspeakable shame.

She would stay away from the party. Would go to bed early. No: she would hurry out to the hairdresser's, and perhaps buy herself a new dress, something dramatic, stark, striking. So that he would gaze upon her with love and pride. But no. Perhaps it would be a better strategy to stay away from the party, and deny him the pleasure of seeing her. . . . Where is Claire, his friends would inquire, why is she keeping herself from us? Is she angry? Is she angry with you?

Even when the first guests began to arrive she could not make up her mind. She regarded herself in the mirror critically. She *was* looking rather tired, and there hadn't been a slot for her at the hairdresser's, and the shortness of breath stayed with her, vexing as an insect buzzing close to her face. "Come on, come on, get a move on, horsey," Emil said gaily, tossing gowns from her closet onto the bed, selecting a pair of high-heeled slippers, but she could not respond to his drollery and in the end sent him away. He made her a double Cuban Manhattan, one of their favorite drinks last summer, and brought it to her as a peace offering. She accepted it but decided against going downstairs. She *would* keep herself away, to punish him.

The party was extraordinarily noisy, and lasted until nearly four in the morning. Claire slept, and woke, and slept again; and still the sounds of gaiety continued.

And then it was silent, and Emil was pawing at her. He half-fell onto the bed, giggling. Before she could push him away he had torn her nightgown and turned her over roughly onto her stomach.

She smelled alcohol on his breath but he did not seem to be drunk: he was too euphoric, too manic. She shouted for him to stop—what on earth was he doing to her—his lean hard thighs gripping her hips, his fingers clenched in her hair. His words were incoherent, interrupted by giggles and brief spasms of coughing. "You like it! You know you like it! Hey, lady, you know you like it! Lovely big soft marvelous thing! A little whale—one of those little ones! They're so lovely! Oh, I love them! One of those—what-do-you-call-them—walruses—a female walrus on the beach! Oh, a cow! A walrus-cow! You know you love it, don't you!"

She forced him off—she *was* stronger than he when it was necessary —and struck him in the face. At once he shrank back. He half-fell out of bed. Holding his mouth in both hands he began to whimper.

"You hurt me. Oh, Claire, you *hurt* me. My lip is cut on the inside, I can taste the . . . ."

She pushed at him again and shouted at him to leave her alone, to get out of the room. But still he crouched there, naked, his chest hollow, his shoulders badly hunched. She saw two absurd tears running down his cheeks.

"Don't be ridiculous. Go and rinse your mouth, you aren't hurt, you're drunk and disgusting, you've been taking drugs, haven't you, though you know I've forbidden it in this house! You and your disgusting friends! Those preening exhibitionistic boys, those ugly slutty little girls, drinking my liquor and injuring my furniture and fouling my lovely house—"

"You don't love me," Emil whimpered. "You forgot my birthday."

"Coming up here half-crazy—saying those unforgivable things—You *aren't* hurt, go and rinse the blood away! Are you too drunk to move?"

"I was born thirty-five years ago and if you loved me you would celebrate that fact," Emil said. "I *was* born thirty-five years ago. . . . Just like anyone else. . . . If you doubt me I have papers, I can prove it. . . . I grew up in a real place, we were all perfectly normal Americans, I have snapshots, I have documents, I want only to be cherished, a real wife is supposed to love her husband more than life itself, I *was* born in the Midwest just like anyone else. . . . In Topeka, Kansas. It's still there, you can look it up! Look it up on the map! Oh, Claire, I hate the taste of blood, it *frightens* me so. . . ."

"I never want those hideous people in this house again, do you understand?"

"Oh, Claire, please—"

"Do you understand? Do you?"

"Yes, Claire, but please don't be angry, don't strike me again—"

She moved to take hold of him, the situation after all was more ludicrous, more silly, than serious, she would have to be the one to make the first gesture of reconciliation; but he misinterpreted her action and scrambled from the bed, as if deeply alarmed.

He backed away, still holding his mouth. Then grabbed at something to hide his nakedness—her ivory negligee, it was, lying where she had thrown it on a chair. "Don't—don't hurt me—don't be angry! I'll sleep somewhere else! I don't mind! I'm used to it! I don't mind!"

She could not determine if he was serious, or clowning—he was such a superb mimic, after all—but she made a gesture of dismissal and lay back, exhausted, in bed. Let him go, let him go, he was partly out of his mind, perhaps he was hallucinating, perhaps he saw someone else where she lay, some massive ugly creature that might actually hurt him.

He retreated. She tried to smooth down the covers, tried to slip back into sleep. But it was impossible of course. She kept thinking of him turning her so violently over, and riding her hips, her buttocks, his wild fists in her hair. How *dare* he approach her like that. . . . And what had he called her? A cow? A walrus-cow?

It struck her as amusing. She laughed, and then began to sob.

She wiped her face on the pillow. Well, it did no good to cry, she had not even bothered to cry that other time. . . . Something to do with a telephone conversation. A man locked in a room, on the telephone. Or had he been talking to himself. His words were inaudible, she had only been able to register the tone of his voice, they had put the oxygen mask on, in those days no one attempted natural childbirth, something astonishing was forcing itself out between her legs but it seemed to have gotten up into her chest, her throat, as well, and into her brain, so that she was being split in two. . . . No, that was another time. That was not this time.

What time was it?—ah, almost five o'clock!

A very dark rainy December morning.

She knew she must go to him, to her wounded young lover, but at first the effort was too much. She sat up, she moved her swollen legs beneath the covers, she pressed her hand against her chest to still her heart. Carefully. Carefully.

He would catch cold, downstairs. Without a blanket. Alone. Without her.

She would take something to cover him. . . . But halfway to the door of her room she forgot, and it would be a great deal of trouble to blunder to the linen closet in the dark, she couldn't find the light switch, the best thing to do would be to bring him back upstairs to her warm bed, if they both moved slowly enough the trip back up the stairs would not defeat them, perhaps they could lean on each other, he would forgive her for her bad temper, he would sob into her shoulder. . . .

She found him in her husband's study, on the leather couch, sitting slumped in the dark. By the window. Huddled close to the window though it must have been rather chilly there. She approached him slowly, not wanting to frighten him. He was hunched in her white robe, he had managed to thrust both arms through it though of course he hadn't taken the time to tie the sash. . . . She hoped he had not ripped the material, it was so delicate, edged with genuine lace, so very costly, so very becoming against her pale skin and dark eyes and hair. . . .

"Emil?"

For a moment it looked as if someone were outside the window, looking in. But of course it was only Emil's glimmering reflection.

"You *are* awake, aren't you? Emil? . . . Why are you behaving like this, why are you doing this to me?"

She approached him. She was barefoot herself, and shivering. Her discomfort translated itself into anger but she could not remember why she was angry, what logic there was to it, what justice. Though she knew there *was* justice.

He sat immobile, the negligee open to show his chest, his small protruding stomach, the insulting tangle of hair between his legs, his legs themselves, covered with a very pale down. Slack and indifferent and arrogant. Almost imperceptibly his head turned toward her. She thought, Without his glasses he can't even see me. . . .

"Why did you marry me if you don't love me, if you're going to behave like this?" she said.

Her voice was surprisingly harsh.

He looked toward her, evidently he saw her, but did not answer at first. Then he said, his lips barely moving, "You know."

She stood near him, but did not come close enough to touch him. She hoped he would not hear her painful rasping breath.

"Why did you marry me, if you don't love me? Don't you love me?"

She had not meant to beg—but there it was, in her voice.

A faint light from outside touched his face, which was a jester's face, narrow and shadowed and grave and unsmiling.

"Why do you treat me like this?" she asked.

"You know," he said in a neutral voice.

"But—I *don't*—"

"You know who I am," he said.

She dared come no nearer. Yet she could not turn away, she could not retreat. His hollow inflectionless voice was not one she had heard before but then he was so good at mimicry, at playacting. . . .

"I don't know," she said faintly.

"Yes, you do. You know."

They stared at each other for several minutes in silence. Then Emil rose unsteadily to his feet, the long ivory-pale gown falling gracefully below his knees; with a dignity that might have been ludicrous at another time he tied the sash, brushed his hair back from his face with a single rough gesture. Then came to her. He was very tall; because she was barefoot she had to look sharply up at him, it was kind of him to take her hand, and to hold it so firmly. The quarrel was over: why had they ever quarreled? She could not remember. She loved him so much. . . .

He led her into the living room, where a few lights were burning after all. Evidently the party was still in session . . . ? A number of guests remained. Odd, she had not noticed them, though they were making only a minimal attempt to be quiet.

"But Emil—" she protested.

"Hush," he said.

"But I thought we were alone— Can't we be alone—"

He led her into the room, and raised her hand to his lips in a ceremonial gesture. Everyone turned to them. Conversations were interrupted, there was an immediate and rather flattering silence. Claire, embarrassed at the eyes that were fixed upon her, half-saw that the room was larger than she remembered, and that more guests had crowded into it than she would have thought possible. In the darkness at the periphery of the room uncertain shapes moved, men or women Claire could not tell, and one figure with a pronounced limp stepped forward, and then paused, as if abashed by the sudden gravity of the situation.

"Queen of the Night," Emil said, kissing her hand again, and this time making a clownish lustful sucking noise with his lips, "I want you to meet my friends."

The
Precipice

Wesley Sterne has been beaten again. How badly? When did it happen? Where? . . . Rumors of a fractured skull, broken collarbone. Possible loss of an eye. But is he going to live? He won't be crippled, will he? Is he in Metropolitan General?

Questions fly around town. It's a small town, 45,000 people, everyone in the University Heights area knows everyone else, the wives, the children, Wesley's colleagues, the people on Wesley's block. Whoever did it has been arrested. A gang of them. Motorcyclists. They kicked poor Wesley in the face. Broke his nose and jaw. Knocked out several teeth. (But those were false teeth, weren't they—the consequence of a previous beating.) *Have* there been arrests, really? Where did it happen, out on the west side? A tavern on the west side? But what was Wesley Sterne doing over there?

Rumors of drinking. A quarrel with his wife, and an afternoon of drinking.

Rumors, telephone calls. Wesley's friend Burt Pitman, who was with him earlier in the day, who stopped for a beer with him at the Clover Leaf, they were on their way back from Burt's sailboat, they'd been on the river before it got too windy, with Burt's twelve-year-old boy who got a ride home from the marina with neighbors—yes, Burt had left Wesley at this place, this bar they sometimes went to, out by the Chrysler assembly plant, but only because he had to get home, his in-laws are visiting, he was already a half-hour late for dinner, it wasn't that he sensed there would be a fight and that Wesley would get involved, he didn't even know who had beaten him. He hadn't *left* him, really, it wasn't that way at all.

But was he drunk? Does he have a violent temper . . . ?

Of course he wasn't drunk, he had only a few beers. He never gets drunk. And he never gets angry: I don't think I've ever heard him raise his voice. He jokes, that's all. . . . Maybe his joking got him in trouble.

36

Is it true, his skull is fractured? There's a chance he might lose an eye?

The McIvers, who live in the redwood "ranch" house beside the Sternes' three-bedroom "colonial" on Brook Lane, whose son Bobby plays with their son Kevin: it must have been some sort of grotesque accident, everyone knows that Wesley Sterne is a gentle, civilized person, he's even a little shy, he blushes so easily, isn't he a pacifist, remember that story in the paper some years ago, Wesley organizing a demonstration against the Vietnam War, all the fuss, all the trouble he went through, and that dreadful mawkish interview—Wesley Sterne depicted as some sort of quaint folksy blend of Quaker and agnostic and Marxist and Spinozist. . . . And he wasn't drunk, certainly. He never gets drunk. And of course he and Lily aren't having trouble.

Someone said there was a girl, a young girl. And that the Sternes are thinking of separating.

Of course they quarrel occasionally, like all of us, but their marriage is one of the strongest, one of the most healthy. . . . There are just too many rumors, people haven't anything better to do than to invent rumors and spread them around.

Conversations on the street, in the I.G.A., in Mac's Milk; telephone calls. Calls from Wesley's friends, colleagues, students. A former student hundreds of miles away in New York City: has he died? Has he been murdered?

Lily isn't here, she's at the hospital. I'll tell her you called, Elizabeth Mason says. She is watching Kevin, who knows nothing about the situation except that his father won't be home for a day or two. A few days. It can't be that extraordinary since Wesley goes away occasionally by himself—he went to give a paper at a philosophical conference in St. Louis only a few weeks ago, in mid-April; he flew to Spokane for a weekend, to be with his elderly mother. If only people wouldn't fuss, wouldn't speak in hushed tones. . . .

Kevin is six years old, a very bright child. His father's fair, silky hair, his father's quizzical nearsighted gray eyes. Something of Lily's manner in his willfulness. Can that child be *stubborn . . . !* He's rumored to be precocious but not startlingly precocious, began reading at the age of three, began taking piano lessons at the age of five, that sort of thing, a high I.Q. inherited from Lily and Wesley, but not a genius: not a problem. . . . He knows something is wrong, obviously, from the way Lily behaved, Elizabeth says quietly, watching the child through a screen door. He is in the back yard, standing in an unchildlike posture, his

hands on his hips. Standing quite still. Staring at nothing. Thinking.
He's been too cheery, Elizabeth says. Bright and bouncy and aggressive
and cheery.

Wes isn't in any danger of . . . ?

Of course he isn't going to die, wherever did you get that from,
Elizabeth says irritably. He *isn't* that badly hurt, they say he'll be home
in a week.

And his eye?

What eye? . . . It's mainly some broken ribs.

But how did it happen? Was it really a fistfight? In a bar?

I have to hang up, Kevin's coming in, Elizabeth says. Why don't you
go down and see Wes yourself, if you're so curious? Go and ask him
yourself.

A warm swampy spring. A head of lettuce the size of a baby's skull
selling for $1.20 in the Kroger's on Grand Boulevard. A school millage
vote, defeated two-to-one. Over in Rutherford, thirty miles away, a
former student in the General Studies program who had once been
invited (but hadn't come) to the Sternes' house—Wes gives *so much*
to his students, where does he get his energy, his tireless idealism—tried
to hold up a variety store late one Saturday night, was trembling so badly
he pulled the trigger of his police service revolver and fired into a display
of candies, dropped the gun, and was shot down by the proprietor's
elderly mother who emerged from the storeroom with a double-barreled
shotgun. . . . The invasion of tiny black ants in the houses along Brook
Lane. An infinity of weevils in the Sternes' kitchen cupboard, their
home evidently in a giant box of oatmeal kept on the highest shelf and
more or less forgotten since Kevin decided he hated oatmeal.

Lily's husband beaten: the shock of the telephone call from police, the
shock of seeing him in the hospital, his face bandaged, his eyes hidden
behind thick swaths of white gauze. Lily, who had prepared a chilly
outraged speech, forgot everything she meant to say and began sobbing.
He was going to be blind! Her husband was going to be blind!

"Lily, is that you? Lily? Hey? Hey, Lily, come *on,* don't be like that,
I'm perfectly all right," he said, groping for her, the fingers of both
hands outstretched and trembling slightly. "Lily. Hey. What the hell did
they tell you? I'm perfectly all right." He laughed, huskily, hoarsely,
reaching out for her as she stood some yards away, sobbing bitterly, her
fists clenched, unmoving. She did not move to him.

Two days later she stood in the doorway of his room and overheard an exchange between Wesley and the elderly man who now had the other bed: a retired carpenter, retired decades ago, born in St. Petersburg in 1898, hospitalized now for a prostatectomy, white-haired, small-boned, slow-speaking but nearly as articulate as Wesley himself: what on earth were they speaking of, who were they quoting?

"Instinct and reason, marks of two natures," Wesley intoned.

"If there is a God, we must love Him only, and not the creatures of a day," the old man said.

"Man is in a dependent alliance with everything. . . . All is held together by a natural though imperceptible chain. . . . I hold it equally impossible to know the parts without knowing the whole, and to know the whole without knowing the parts," Wesley said slowly.

The old man paused. Lily peeked in to see him: his skin seemed papery-thin, a mass of tiny wrinkles. His eyes were closed. His lips moved, and then his voice was surprisingly strong. *"Between us and heaven or hell there is only life, which is the frailest thing in the world."*

Wesley said at once, *"We run carelessly to the precipice, after we have put something before us to prevent us seeing it."*

The old man said, *"A maker of witticisms, a bad character."*

Wesley said, *"By space the universe encompasses and swallows me up like an atom; by thought I comprehend the world."*

After a long pause the old man said, *"The eternal silence of these infinite spaces frightens me,"* and now Lily knew it was Pascal they were quoting, and the inchoate rage that had driven her all that morning drained away and her heart seemed to swell with love for—for both men —for the dying old man and for her husband who had made himself ridiculous once again, and had caused her such grief. She had rehearsed a brief speech setting forth the proposed details of their separation—had been awake most of the night rehearsing it—but now the speech too drained away, she forgot it entirely.

Thirty-two stitches in his forehead, very low in the forehead, snaking in and out of his pale eyebrows. A broken rib, three cracked ribs. Cuts, bruises. Nothing remarkable. And of course the plate in his mouth was smashed: the lucky thing was, he hadn't swallowed any of the broken pieces. It could very easily be replaced. It wasn't, after all, as if his own front teeth had been knocked out.

"The third beating in eight years," Lily says tonelessly.

"Nine years," says Wesley.

She stares at him, counting. Six, seven. . . . Eight. . . . She sees that his glasses are smudged, the lenses badly smudged, long ago she vowed not to be distracted by Wesley's thumbprints superimposed on his calm intelligent gray gaze, she must resist the impulse to snatch his glasses off and wipe the lenses herself. Her own glasses annoy her constantly, she is always wiping the lenses, holding them to the light and examining them and cursing under her breath when they are still smudged or shiny, nothing quite maddens her so much as lenses that are not perfectly clean. . . . "Eight years," she says flatly.

"But we were in Barcelona, that was the year after we left Columbus, remember, and I hadn't finished the dissertation yet, and . . ."

"Eight years, not nine. Don't try to distract me with peripheral details. You make yourself *ridiculous* with your old tactics," Lily says. She fusses with her cigarettes, slapping the pockets of her denim skirt, looking for a match, half-conscious that her mannerisms annoy Wesley, who was so strong-willed, so virtuous, to have given up smoking several years ago. She wants to imply that she is smoking now in his presence without knowing what she does precisely because she is so distressed by *him.* But she does not want him to guess that the action is not entirely unconscious. She is nervous, she is agitated, she slaps her pockets like a man, murmurs, Oh hell. . . . Where did I leave . . .

"I had no choice, in Barcelona," Wesley says stubbornly.

"You had a choice. You always have a choice."

"If I had had time to think, to make a choice, I would have been too terrified to hit that bastard," Wesley says, bringing his fingers together beneath his chin. "But I couldn't allow him to insult you. You know that."

"I wasn't insulted. I didn't even hear what he said."

"You heard him all right."

"I wasn't insulted."

"*I* was insulted for you."

Lily lights her cigarette and exhales the smoke impatiently. Of course they have had this conversation many times, it has even been a prelude to lovemaking, though not in recent years. Her mind jumps, skips ahead, she knows it is pointless to engage her husband in a debate in which they are more or less on equal terms, she can only achieve a moral triumph by the strategy of rejecting his position, his a priori assumptions. "The escalation from verbal abuse to physical abuse is unacceptable," she says.

"You have the intention of representing civilization but you end up on the side of its enemies. You fight an insult, you *become* an insult. . . . And you upset me so terribly. Oh God, do you remember! Do you remember! I fainted, the first time in my life, I fainted on those stone steps, I could have cracked my skull on those goddamn stone steps, and you—your mouth all blood, blood streaming down on your clothes!"

"I had no choice," Wesley says, his fingertips touching, his lips pursed contemplatively. "If I had known how strong he was, and how quick, if I'd known what he would do to my mouth with one blow—of course it wouldn't have made any difference. You know that. To hear the girl I loved insulted in public . . ."

"You didn't love me then," Lily says.

"Don't be absurd, obviously I loved you."

"You didn't seem to love me," Lily says.

"I had difficulty expressing myself in those days. I was very young, I was tongue-tied. . . . But it's obvious that I loved you, you knew that perfectly well."

Lily brushes at her eyes with the back of her hand. She is starting to cry. She is not going to cry.

"You asked me to marry you but you never said you loved me, and then you risked getting killed, you risked getting killed before we were even married," she says angrily, "before we were even *lovers.* That's the kind of person you are. That's the kind of myopic selfish fantastical person you are."

"I had no choice in Barcelona," Wesley says gently. He reaches out to stroke her hair. Long thick straight hair, dark. The bangs, cut evenly across her forehead, have grown a little too long, and are no longer exactly even. Lily draws back, shivering with something like moral outrage. Her eyes are angrily bright. "There are times when a man hasn't any choice, when he can't walk away from a fight. Even a man like me who isn't any good at fighting and who can't see across a room without glasses. You pretend not to understand, Lily, but I think you do understand."

"You're just ridiculous. It would be amusing if I weren't married to you. Your friends and acquaintances and students might think you're glamorous, it's all very exciting and dashing, a man who lectures on Spinoza's *Ethics* at ten in the morning getting his teeth knocked out in a barroom fight at seven that evening. I suppose you bask in your legend—"

"For Christ's sake, Lily, you know better than that!"

"—but I don't share in it, I don't share in the delusions that surround it, I can't live this way, I won't tolerate it. If you would only think of Kevin at those times. . . ."

"There haven't been that many times," Wesley says. "Three times in nine years. I suspect that the average man . . ."

"I didn't marry the average man."

"You don't seem to comprehend, I don't *want* to fight," he says, his voice rising like a boy's. "I don't *want* my eyes blackened and my ribs broken and my teeth knocked out, I don't *want* to be knocked to the floor and kicked while a little ring of curious onlookers gathers, and when the police come, when the police finally come, they're mad as hell at me for getting knocked down, and one of them does this classic routine, picking up my glasses, the frames are all bent and the lenses broken and a few shards of glass remain, it's all too familiar, only three times in nine years but it's too humiliatingly familiar, can't you understand?—can't you sympathize? I don't have any choice about these things."

"Then it might happen again."

Wesley swallows, staring at her. She sees that he is about to lie. He is about to lie, for her sake.

"Then it might happen again, if you don't have any choice," she says flatly.

"The thing is, justice must be . . . Well, there's a balance, I mean in the universe, a kind of . . . And then it gets . . . Suddenly there's an imbalance, Lily, and it has to be made right. We don't have any choice about these things."

"Can't you be a coward about it, then? Whatever happened at that bar—some twenty-year-old kid insulting the bartender—"

"It wasn't that simple, there were racial overtones—"

"Oh, I'm sure there were! I'm sure there were innumerable overtones! And nuances! But why can't you be a coward about things like that, why can't you back away?"

"I *am* a coward," Wesley says irritably. "Violence terrifies me, my knees buckle and I can barely—"

"Why can't you back away?"

"I've tried to explain to you. I don't have any *choice*. If another man were there who would take care of it, if he'd restore the balance, then I'd be happy to step aside—but I'm the one, I happen to be standing there, it falls to me, I am the witness, I can't pretend not to know what I know, I can't pretend to be blind."

"You don't think of Kevin. Or of me."

"I don't think of anyone, there isn't time."

"You don't even think that you might be killed."

"There isn't time."

"Blinded. Crippled. What if you were crippled, paralyzed, what if your life came to an end, so abruptly, so stupidly?" Lily cries. "Doesn't the *stupidity* of it make any impression on you?"

"There isn't time to think of such things, certainly not of consequences," Wesley says. "I know when I have to act. That's all. I *know.*"

"Then I don't want to be your wife," Lily hears herself saying.

"Don't be ridiculous."

"I don't want to live with you. It isn't worth it. And Kevin—it isn't fair to him. His father is a professor of philosophy, an intelligent, generous man, a civilized man, but he can't control his temper and he can't control his violence and he's going to be killed one day—"

"I'm not going to be killed, you're being melodramatic," Wesley says, trying to take her hand. "Hey. Aren't you exaggerating everything? I'm reasonably certain it won't happen again."

"But you have no choice, you keep saying you have no choice!"

"In Barcelona, in Saranac—obviously I didn't. The other day, I didn't. But I don't think it will happen again."

"You don't promise, though."

"How can I promise? I can't foresee the future."

"Do you *want* to get beaten, is that it? Do you *want* to get killed?"

"You know me better than that," Wesley says, blushing.

"A man who is so sensitive to physical pain, who can hardly force himself to go to the dentist—who could barely stand me prying that sliver out of his foot—maybe that's the sort of person who secretly wants to get hurt, who wants to get beaten to death—I don't know! I don't want to think about it any longer, I don't want to *live* with it!"

"We'd better stop. You're saying things you don't mean, now."

"For Kevin's sake—"

"Kevin is fine. Kevin is perfectly all right."

"After that fight at Saranac you said—you promised—"

"I didn't promise, I couldn't possibly have promised," Wesley says. "I said I wouldn't drink too much, that was all. And—"

"Now you won't promise? You can't?"

"How can I? Do you want me to lie to you?"

"Do you want me to divorce you?"

"Lily, this is ridiculous, *you're* the one who is being ridiculous, you hardly listen to what I say, you show no sympathy with my point of view—"

"You show no sympathy with *my* point of view—"

Wesley gets to his feet suddenly. "Look: I detest violence. I abhor fighting. And you know it. You know it perfectly well. The memory of those fights sickens me, the thought that certain people imagine me brave or dashing or a flamboyant character sickens me, but what can I do? I'll try to avoid the occasions, the places. . . . I'll try not to be a witness—"

"The occasions are everywhere," Lily says flatly. "The places are everywhere. A bar, a parking lot, in the street—what the hell. You create them yourself. You want to get killed."

Wesley pushes up his glasses and rubs at his eyes wearily. Lily watches him, faint with love for him, and with anger. She would like to jump to her feet and strike him in the face, on the shoulders. She would like to scream, and pummel him, drive him back into a corner: force a promise, a vow, from him. Even if it is a lie.

"You want to get killed," she says provocatively, staring at him.

He continues rubbing his eyes. The lurid scar over his left eyebrow appears to writhe. "If you say so," he whispers.

"You won't deny it? You won't defend yourself?"

"Since you evidently know me better than I know myself, how can I defend myself?"

"Then I'll leave you. I will. Kevin and I will leave you."

"You certainly won't."

"You can't promise it won't happen again?"

"I can promise that I don't think there is the *probability* of its happening again. But as for the *possibility* . . . I can't foresee the future."

"*A maker of witticisms,*" Lily says, "*a bad character.*"

Wesley adjusts his glasses and stares at her, hurt. "*Witticisms?* Me? Did you think that was meant to be a witticism? . . . I am incapable of making a witticism," he says, unsmiling, "on this subject. I think you know that."

"I don't know anything."

"You know when I'm telling the truth, when I'm appealing to you."

"I know when you're locked in your delusions."

"*Is* it a delusion? Do you really think so?"

He waits helplessly for her reply. It strikes Lily that he really wants to know: he really wants her to tell him.

"Oh God, I don't know," she says weakly.

Suddenly she is exhausted. She begins to cry but she is too exhausted to cry, her sobs are hoarse and dry, the guttural sounds of laughter.

92 Brook Lane. Buff-colored brick, not of the highest quality; and aluminum siding, white. Unexceptional house, unexceptional lawn. Lily Sterne in shorts and pullover blouses, her long coarse hair pulled into an unfashionable ponytail, her legs darkly tanned, is often seen working in the rock garden the Sternes inherited from the house's previous owners, though she has said she would like nothing so much as to have the whole thing dug out and replaced with ordinary sod. Wesley Sterne is seen fairly frequently, pushing a power mower, leaving unsightly swaths in the grass; occasionally he hoses down his car and washes it, in the driveway, like other young husbands in the neighborhood. He wears old khaki shorts, is sometimes bare-chested, a tall, graceful, slender man in his early thirties, with a quite ordinary build. He is not muscular, he does not even tan very deeply. There is always something bookish and self-conscious about him: even when discussing university politics with his neighbor Todd McIver, even when making sardonic jokes about the competency of the university's administrators, he is courteous, articulate, obviously aware of his words. He shies away from private matters. Perhaps he talks about such things with closer friends, for instance with Burt Pitman, but in general he is reserved; one can't get very close to him. Todd asked circumspectly about the "trouble" back in May, were charges pressed against the young man, were there witnesses willing to testify, what was going to happen . . . ? And Wesley Sterne only mumbled in embarrassment that of course he hadn't pressed charges, the entire matter was finished, over, he rarely even thought of it now.

"You're not going to press charges?" Todd asked, surprised. "But wasn't it— I had heard— The fight was unfair, wasn't it, didn't the kid hit you with a bottle or something—"

Wesley laughed, and shrugged his shoulders, and made a self-conscious swiping motion at his nose. "It worked out the way I might have anticipated it would," he said.

"But wasn't it unfair, didn't he—? Aren't there supposed to be rules of a sort, unwritten rules, governing such things? Of course it's far outside my area of experience, but—"

"He fought the way he naturally would," Wesley said, staring at the frayed toe of his tennis shoe, smiling queerly. His face had gone scarlet, it was obvious that he wished Todd gone, but was too polite to let on. "A bottle or not, a cleat-toed boot in the face or not, I can't imagine it would have made much difference. He was fifteen years younger than me and about twenty pounds heavier and he was fighting to win, not to be fair, and he knew how to fight to win, and nothing of what transpired is very remarkable. It's very commonplace, actually. And I wasn't hurt that badly. I really wasn't. This plate, you know, these teeth," he said, tapping at his front teeth with a gesture meant to be comic, "didn't replace real teeth anyway. . . . It *really* wasn't as bad as it might have sounded, people like to exaggerate."

"So you didn't press charges. So it just ends, like that."

"How else should it end?" Wesley asked, his face still dark with blood. "I haven't any ill feelings against him, as far as I'm concerned it was an accident, like a traffic accident, it wasn't necessarily anyone's fault, I certainly don't want revenge. When a fight's over it's over. The feeling goes, you know. You can't retain it honestly."

"I didn't know," Todd McIver said. "But it's interesting to be told."

Sometimes he sees it, sometimes it scuttles across a wall in front of him, or emerges around a corner: the shape, the being, of his opponent. And he pauses, mesmerized. Waiting for the thing to become clearer. To take on a more recognizable human identity.

Thick-bodied, strong, silent. Featureless. It *has* a face but the face is out of focus.

It is no one he knows. No specter out of his childhood, or out of his childhood imagination.

Sometimes, asleep, he struggles with his opponent. A man like himself but larger. Heavier. Silent except for his grunting, his painful breath. They wrestle together, both of them desperate to win. They fall to the ground, the impact knocks them senseless, they scramble up again, they rush at each other, grunting, panting, frantic to defeat the other, pro- pelled by a superhuman urgency. Once they fell in a shallow muckish pond choked with cattails and duckweed, once they fell heavily, some distance, to a hard, sandy surface, and their mouths were filled with sand

and their eyes ran with tears and each was desperate, desperate, to defeat
the other.

Wesley woke that time, gasping for breath. Did you have a nightmare,
Lily murmured, why don't you lie on my shoulder, come on, let's go back
to sleep. . . . Did you pull the sheet out, kicking around . . . ?

He burrowed against her, his face in her shoulder, one of his hands
cupping her breast, shivering, twitching with sleep: for he wasn't altogether awake, he wasn't altogether free of the dream.

Lie still, stop kicking around, let's go to sleep, are you all right now?
Let me get my arm under you: okay.

Sometimes he senses his opponent though he cannot see him. He
stands very still, hardly daring to breathe; hardly daring to think. *I am
in the presence of my enemy.* . . . He stands very still, his expression grave
and monkish and courteous. The knowledge that there were enemies,
there were certainly enemies, a man might go a lifetime without fighting
them or without even being aware of them but they certainly did exist:
this knowledge strikes Wesley Sterne from time to time, with the force
of a blow, an opened hand clapped smartly across his face.

He is mesmerized, he is transfixed.

Sometimes, at any time, during the day—waiting in line at the bank,
putting gas in his car at the self-serve station up on Iroquois, playing with
Kevin, chatting with Lily, having a drink at Tom and Liz Mason's,
shaving, sitting on the toilet, walking into his pleasantly crowded and
murmurous summer school class ("Introduction to Philosophy: From
Plato to Kant") in the old Haines Building that smells so wonderfully
of chalk dust and oiled floors and age—he is visited by the image of his
opponent, the almost tactile presence of his opponent, and for some
seconds he is shaken, speechless, so deeply and profoundly moved that
he cannot articulate, even to himself, even during his daily hour of
introspection and meditation, exactly what it is that has brushed close
to him.

Unspeakable. Unsayable.

Does everyone live like this, he wonders, drawing his breath in slowly.
Does everyone live in such secrecy. . . .

Watching Kevin and Bobby McIver splashing in the shallow end of
the McIvers' pool. Listening to Burt Pitman complaining: his wife has
heard a rumor, a malicious rumor, about him and the Fairlie girl, has
Lily heard anything, has Lily mentioned anything?—and the girl herself

has been saying some wild things lately, accusing him of hypocrisy, making threats. Spraying weedkiller in the back yard. Repairing the screen door. Shaking three Bufferin into his palm at midday when, after a few hours at his desk, working on an article for *The Monist*, his eyes ache and water, and his head throbs dully. (A new malady, perhaps related to the beating that kid gave him—that brutal son of a bitch. But Wesley doesn't want to run to the doctor, not so quickly. Give it time to go away.) Laughing at someone's anecdote in the Masons' living room, sprawled in a chair, Saturday night, drinking beer, utterly happy to be where he is, to be alive. Kissing Kevin. Kissing Lily. Gazing out with a feeling of confused paternal tenderness at the bowed heads of his students, who are writing their final examinations: how quickly, how very quickly, the six-week summer session passes! Sitting up late with Lily, drinking gin and tonic, eating cashews (absurdly expensive these days, $2.59 for a fairly small jar, but they were left over from a party and might as well be eaten), discussing their families, sifting through the day's news, the day's gossip, managing adroitly to avoid the subject of Wesley's "bad temper"—for though he really hasn't a bad temper, though he rarely gets angry at all, it has somehow evolved that his penchant for getting into fights is a consequence of some very normal failing, a very normal masculine failing: a "bad temper." And at these times, at all times, he is aware of the opponent, the enemy, a massive but shadowy figure at the periphery of his consciousness. He is aware too that he, Wesley Sterne, passes among his family and friends *as if he were one of them.* I do not mean to deceive, it is not my intention to deceive, he thinks helplessly. But the others are simply ignorant. Innocent. Unknowing. He moves among them as one of them, yet he has done things, and will perhaps do things in the future, that they cannot guess at.

The knowledge that he has *hurt* other men, and has been badly *hurt* by them. That they have fought—have struck one another. Why is it so profoundly disturbing, yet curiously satisfying, exciting. . . . He cannot say, he cannot analyze it. Of course he is irritated by the attention certain people pay him, and he always refuses to talk about that unfortunate incident in the Clover Leaf. In a milieu in which the average man is passive, perhaps even a little cowardly; in an intellectual milieu in which the average man is, at the most, aggressive in conversation, and ironic. . . . In such a world Wesley Sterne is quite naturally unusual, and small legends accrete about him, but he has no interest in these legends, he would be bored and embarrassed to hear them, he does *not* want that sort of foolish adulation, not even from attractive young women. Lily is wrong, he does *not* want such adulation. But though the excited interest of others offends him, and he never talks about his experiences, he nevertheless thinks about them almost constantly; he thinks about them, he tells himself, in order to comprehend their peculiar power over him, in order, perhaps, to free himself from that power.

Sometimes he is visited by a sense of almost unbearable elation. Knowing that he inhabits a place in the social world, knowing that he inhabits a marriage, an identity, a fate—and yet knowing that he is not contained by these circumstances, these accidents. His essence lies elsewhere, in another dimension, in unspeakable secrecy. And it is that essence that endeavors, as Spinoza saw, to persevere in its own being, quite beyond Wesley's conscious desire. And quite beyond his choice.

Wesley Sterne, playing baseball with his friends. Though they are not all his friends. July Fourth, Hammond Park, grilled hamburgers and steaks and beer, a great deal of beer, and a loose hilarious not-very-serious game of baseball; though, unfortunately, some of the players are serious.

Wesley Sterne, an average player. Unambitious. Swinging the bat, striking out. Swinging the bat, hitting a modest grounder out beyond third base. And then he is a second baseman, fumbling with the ball, throwing it to the catcher—easily winded, but not one of the worst players. Lily and the other wives applaud when he manages to do something right.

And then it happens, quite suddenly it happens, that a man on first base steals to second, and somehow runs Wesley down—out of sheer meanness—the sinewy little bastard is someone's brother-in-law, younger than most of the other players, younger by a decade than poor Wesley, and he has been drinking, and he is impatient with the game, and with the others' elliptical jokes and allusions—and so out of sheer bullying meanness he runs Wesley Sterne down, and Wesley goes sprawling, and his glasses fly off.

But it is an accident, of course. The young man apologizes heatedly. Helps Wesley to his feet, hands him his glasses, asks anxiously if he's all right—if he's sure he's all right. Wesley brushes himself off. He grins, abashed. Of course he's fine: it was nothing: he just sat down a little hard. But he's *fine*, really.

And not at all angry, evidently. Everyone notes that.

"Your husband is remarkably forgiving," one of the women says to
Lily, who smiles, stiffly, and does not reply.

The days pass, the summer passes, there are no events, no quarrels,
no tears, yet the marriage is deteriorating.

Wesley has unearthed his old piano books and is stumbling through
the first, and easiest, of Bach's Two-Part Inventions. Or he is hunched
over the bathroom sink, pressing a cold damp cloth against his eyes. Lily
is on the telephone. Lily is driving Kevin and four or five other children
to the zoo. There are picnics, day-long trips to the beach, the amusement park at Kelp Isle. At a going-away party for a young English
professor who has a Guggenheim Wesley notes that his wife has had too
much to drink and is arguing and laughing, too loudly, with someone's
husband who has had too much to drink. Much later that night she falls
half-undressed on their bed and begins to weep. "I'm losing everything,"
she says. "I can't hold it. My feeling for you. Even my feeling for Kevin."

"What are you saying?" Wesley asks, shocked. "You'd better get
undressed. You'd better get to sleep."

"I'm losing it all, I can't stop what's happening. . . ."

There are visits from in-laws, old friends from graduate school at the
University of Ohio, former students of Wesley's. Some of his former
students are still students, more or less, in their late twenties. Others
seem to have pulled ahead of Wesley: they have teaching appointments
at Mount Holyoke, at the University of North Carolina, at Oberlin. Lily
cooks for them all. She cooks spaghetti with Italian sauce, and chicken
with paprika, and chili, and an old favorite of the Sternes', shrimp creole.
She is tireless, she pads about the kitchen barefoot, a cigarette in her
mouth. Everyone loves Lily Sterne: she is so outspoken, so brash, so
funny, so kind and generous and vulnerable. It has been said of her that
she tries to raise new enthusiasms of her own—tennis, raw vegetables,
Amnesty International—to moral principles for the species, universal
laws, and that this inclination is *somewhat* annoying at times. But still
one can't help liking the woman, she is so genuine. So perfect a wife
for Wesley Sterne.

One morning in his office at the university he reads aloud, as if
discovering it for the first time: *In the mind there is no absolute free will,
but the mind is determined to this or that volition by a cause, which is
also determined by another cause, and this again by another, and so on
ad infinitum.*

Could the universe run backward, Wesley wonders, doodling on his
notebook. But would it still be the same universe, if it ran backward . . . ?

He makes an appointment with a psychotherapist, recommended by
a friend of a friend of Lily's. At their first meeting they circle each other
cautiously. Wesley is surprised at the cold haughtiness of his voice; he
holds himself stiffly, awaiting the cliché words—Oedipal, infantile, pas-
sive-aggressive. But the psychotherapist is not a Freudian, evidently. Nor
is he a Jungian. He appears to believe—so Wesley tells Lily, afterward,
making her laugh in disbelief—in the "new eclectic." The body gener-
ates energy, the energy must be released, if it is not released there are
"neurotic knots and snarls," the circuits must be kept clear, the emotions aired daily. It also helps to stand with one's knees slightly bent so
that there is a tremor in the knees and thighs: this is the life force
manifesting itself and is, evidently, a sign of health. Or a sign of life.

Wesley never returns to the psychotherapist.

He works at Bach and perfects the piece, and moves on to the second
Invention, in C minor. The voices are very interesting. The voices are
fascinating. They speak to each other through Wesley's quick nervous
fingertips: a statement and its echo, a statement and its qualification,
near-arguments, strident little turns and flourishes. And of course a
resolution. In Bach there is always a resolution.

At night he huddles in Lily's arms. He presses himself against her
warm fleshy unquestioning body. She is asleep and cannot know his
terror. He has seen the man's face: broad, doughy-pale, with small cruel
staring eyes, something slack about the mouth. . . . Despite his terror
he must run at his opponent, despite the inadequacy of his body he must
strike at his opponent with his fists. Ah, but then! But then! His opponent's massive featureless face absorbs Wesley's frantic blows. His opponent's thick, muscular torso cannot be shaken. The thighs, the legs:
unmovable. A giant. Unkillable. . . . Panting, sick with dread, Wesley
cannot defend himself against his opponent, who sometimes strikes a
vicious blow against the side of Wesley's head, and sometimes catches
Wesley in his great arms and slowly, slowly, begins the work of squeezing
his rib cage until the bones crack one by one.

Lily is rereading Proust, in the back yard. In the green plastic lawn
chair that is so tricky getting into. Wesley, who has never been able to
finish *The Remembrance of Things Past,* halfway thinks she is pretending to enjoy it, as she halfway thinks he has only pretended to give up

smoking. Kevin seems to be growing week by week. He needs new shoes, new play clothes. He has developed an odd new habit of grabbing his father by the upper leg and holding on tight, squeezing until Wesley cries out in surprise and annoyance. "Hey. Cut it *out.* That *hurts,* Kevin!"

Lily, who loves her husband very much, hears herself telling a woman friend of hers that she doesn't know if she loves him at all. The words are groping, experimental. A few days later at a party she hears herself telling someone's husband that she doesn't know if she loves Wesley or ever did: the reason being that she doesn't know him. He has other loyalties. He isn't really married to her. That ugly scar on his forehead, and a way he has of smiling and staring right through her, and absent-mindedly talking to Kevin as if he weren't aware of the child at all, the real child, looking up at him so anxiously. She doesn't know him, she isn't certain now that she ever did. They will have been married eight years on November 17.

Wesley discovers Lily crying in the kitchen. There are weevils in Kevin's favorite cereal, bought only a few days ago.

"I thought we'd gotten rid of those little bastards," Wesley says in astonishment. "I sprayed everywhere. . . . I thought we'd seen the last of them."

"But we haven't. We never will. They've infested the kitchen. They've gone underground."

"But they've been *gone* for weeks, since I did all that spraying. . . ."

"They've gone underground," Lily says angrily.

Kevin's fall on the playground one afternoon. On the filthy asphalt. A bleeding chin, bleeding upper gum. So many tears!—such alarm! Thank God, none of his teeth are loose.

"It was that Holloway kid," one of the mothers tells Lily. "That oversized dirty-mouthed brat, shoving the other kids around. He got behind the Barrett girl when she was swinging and practically knocked her out of the air, and he did almost the same thing to Kevin."

A clean-scrubbed face, some iodine, a double-dipped chocolate-and-marshmallow ice cream cone, and later that day Daddy's concerned attention.

"It hurts, does it? No? It doesn't hurt? Kevin's a brave little
boy. . . ."

Despite the frequent headaches he often feels a curious sense of
elation. The close presence of others who know nothing, who suspect
nothing. . . . The ring of onlookers who have no idea who he is. . . . It
is for their innocence he loves them, because of their innocence he
wishes to protect them, even from himself.

So he is not surprised, though he simulates surprise, when Lily speaks
vaguely of taking Kevin to her mother's the last week of August. That
big old rambling home on the Hudson River. And Wesley could finish
whatever he's doing—a review of a book, isn't it—for one of the journals. And drive up to join them on Labor Day.

"It doesn't mean anything," Lily says slowly. She is turning her
wristwatch around her wrist; the band seems to have lost some of its
elasticity.

Wesley smiles at her, swallowing. "Well," he says.

"I just think it would be a good idea," Lily says. They have never been
apart for more than a day or two since their marriage: and then only
because of Wesley's professional commitments. "I mean, to be apart for
a while. . . . A week, ten days, that isn't long. . . . It doesn't mean
anything."

Wesley nods, bringing the tips of his fingers together.

"All right," he says.

"You can join us on Labor Day. You can have the house to yourself,
stay up working as late as you want. . . . Look: it doesn't *mean* anything."

Wesley smiles thinly and peers at her through his glasses.

"Of course not. I know. After all—what *could* it mean if it contained
meaning?" he says dryly.

"Nothing means anything," Wesley says some days later. "Except
thinking makes it so."

Lily turns away.

"You know I love you," she says.

But what, precisely, is love. How are we to define it, let alone honor
it. Embodied in time, stuck in time. One loves people who are one's
contemporaries, people whom one has met: a narrow enough spectrum!

Alone in the house on Brook Lane Wesley *does* stay up late, though he is not always working. Sometimes he drinks, sitting at the kitchen table, in the dark, peering out into the amorphous back yard. By day there are weeds: dandelion, crabgrass. By day there are maddening burned-out spots. It is his lawn by day, his property and his responsibility. By night, however, it is something else entirely. . . .

That sense of elation, which alternates with a sense of despair, or is it, perhaps, a knowledge of despair: despair as the more fundamental, the more *reasonable,* of emotions. That elation comes and goes. He and Lily have talked on the phone, exchanging news, gossip, the usual thing, how is Lily's mother, how is Kevin, did he enjoy the flight, does he enjoy the swimming—the usual thing. No mention of separation, or divorce. Or love.

The shapeless night. Darkness as primordial: sunshine as a violation. Wesley thinks, scribbles notes, tears them up in the morning, resists dialing Lily's number because he has no idea what he might say to her.

Love. Loyalty. Fidelity. But time: isn't everything human embodied in time, stuck in time. What he wanted to pursue, what he believed himself fated to pursue, was something deeper, more profound than time. . . . It is often said that time isn't real, Wesley says to an acquaintance, they have discovered each other in the nearly deserted Campus Pub, they are pleased to discover each other so that they needn't stand at the bar drinking alone, it's often said fallaciously that time doesn't exist, but it seems to me, you're in, what?—history?—then certainly you agree—it seems to me that nothing is more real than time. I mean humanly real. Do you know what I mean? My wife has been rereading Proust, she reads the novels every three or four years. . . . I don't know why I mentioned that. . . . Yes: time. Everything pales before it. Drains away. The solidity of the world, the physical world. I don't mean to sound Platonic. I don't *care* for Plato, actually. But this thing about time: the strongest, most confident, most powerfully attractive people crumple. In time. How then is time *not* real. . . .

Do you think often about such things? his new friend asks, tipping the neck of his bottle into his glass. Though the bottle is empty. Though only a drop or two remains.

Why yes of course, constantly, don't you, doesn't everyone? poor Wesley asks.

The lurid scar quizzical as another eyebrow, his somewhat shaggy blond hair raised in awkward tufts. And he hasn't shaved for a few days.

. . . So word gets around, Lily has taken the little boy away, something is wrong, of course Wes would never say, he's an extremely private person, you can have philosophical arguments with him and joke outrageously but you can't be intimate with him, there is always a margin of detachment, of impersonality: the poor man, discussing Plato or whatever the hell it was, looking as if he'd just got out of bed, maybe sleeping in his clothes! Some very impressive-sounding gibberish about time, evidently the sort of thing the Philosophy Department specializes in. Then he says, the poor guy, doesn't everyone's mind work like my own . . . !

Word gets around. People drop by, out for evening walks; there are telephone calls; invitations to barbecues, swimming parties, the outdoor symphony at Rutherford. Graciously, unequivocally, Wesley Sterne declines them all.

The night, the hours of darkness. Oblivion. A quite ordinary window, a quite ordinary doorway: the means by which one steps forth, into absolute freedom, not knowing if there will be solid ground beneath one's feet, or whether one is stepping over a precipice. The flamelike elation, and then the systolic despair, a pulse beat, the blinking of an eye. He must go to Lily and Kevin, there isn't even time to get the car serviced as he has planned, if he leaves in the morning he can get there in a day, eleven or twelve hours on the road, he has made such desperate compulsive drives in the past . . . though not in recent years, not since his marriage. Or is it wiser, more prudent, to remain here. To contemplate. Meditate. A spiritual retreat, a time for close merciless introspection. . . . And Labor Day isn't until next Monday, Lily doesn't want him until then.

It doesn't mean anything, she said guiltily.

Of course. I know, he said. Deeply hurt he nevertheless forgave her: but could not resist hurting her in turn, by forgiving her so readily.

"Look: I'm coming up. All right? I'll see you tonight, I don't know exactly when. Don't wait dinner or anything, all right?"

"You can't make that drive in one day," Lily says. Her voice is small, shocked.

"Of course I can make it in one day."

"Wes, please—"

"Or don't you want me?"

"Of course I want you, but the drive will be—"

"Look: do you *really?*"

"Yes, of course, you know that, of course," she says half-angrily, "but you don't want to kill yourself on the road— You do everything so compulsively, you're so—"

"Compulsively! Me! Is Kevin there? Will you put him on the phone?"

"Do the drive in two days. Will you? I don't want Kevin to get his hopes up, I mean about seeing you tonight. . . . He isn't here, he's down on the beach."

"But you *do* want me there," Wes says excitedly.

"Of course, don't be ridiculous, I was going to call, I was going to suggest—but then I thought, you know, your work— You've often said you'd like to be alone for a while— A retreat—"

"Oh, the hell with that, I'll see you tonight."

"Tomorrow. Please."

"I don't know: do you think it's *unreasonable* to drive there in one day? Do you think I would be behaving *unreasonably?*"

"I think so, yes. I really think so. Make the drive in two days, don't wear yourself out, Kevin will be overjoyed, I'll tell him you'll be here tomorrow afternoon, is that about right? Please? Will you listen to me?"

Suddenly he acquiesces, and it gives him an extraordinary sensation of pleasure. "All right. Fine. I will. Two days. Tomorrow. Late morning, maybe. Noon. Do you love me?"

A few things thrown in his canvas suitcase with the zipper that always sticks. Reheated coffee, a stale glazed doughnut, eaten standing by the sink. He runs around to the windows and locks them one by one and adjusts the timer so that the living room light will switch on, automatically, at eight-thirty. Upstairs in his cluttered cubbyhole of a study he gathers papers, notes, the university memo pad he has doodled on night after night, the book he has been trying to review, several other books, including Goldstein's *Inquiries into the Idea of the Good,* shoves them into his briefcase. He must hurry, must hurry.

Backs the car out of the driveway. And there is Gloria McIver weeding her rosebed, looking at him expectantly, and of course he stops to tell her he's driving up to Merrickville. Lily's mother's place. About fifty miles south of Albany, New York. Yes, he will be driving through the Catskills, yes, it should be lovely, but he's in something of a hurry.

. . . He certainly meant to tell the McIvers that he was leaving so that they could watch the house but everything has happened so quickly, it completely slipped his mind. . . .

Have a good drive, Gloria says. Tell Lily to call, will you? We're both invited to something the first week of September, I think she'll be quite interested, I mean intrigued, to discover who the hostess is. . : .

Yes, fine, I'll do that, Wesley says with a nervous grin, clearly anxious to be off.

Long afterward Gloria will tell people: But he looked so happy, he looked so full of life that morning, I just can't . . . I can't bear to think of it. . . .

An eventless drive through Pennsylvania. Too many trucks, too much diesel smoke. But he drives at a steady speed and, as always, lapses into a kind of trance, sifting through things in his mind, weighing, judging, fantasizing, discarding. His mind is a great finely meshed net that casts itself out far, and draws itself in slowly, heavy with people, memories, houses and apartments and rooms he has lived in, stray flashes of class-room situations in which he did marvelously, or not so marvelously, over the years. And there is Lily, always Lily: so close he can barely see her. And Kevin. So close, like one's own face brought up to a mirror, pressed against a mirror.

Pennsylvania, that dismayingly large state. And then New York State. The Thruway system would be easier driving but it isn't the closest way, he will have to content himself with a secondary road, Highway 209 which goes up to Kingston and then joins the Thruway, and then he will be in the homestretch, only a few more hours to Merrickville. Lily will surely forgive him when he arrives tonight, it looks as if he might make it by ten or eleven . . . at least by midnight.

The foothills of the Catskills. A grayish, purplish haze. Pick-up trucks on the highway, going below the speed limit, only two lanes to the road, dangerous to pass, maddening to stay behind; but he is making an effort to be reasonable.

Tiny villages, only a few houses. Boarded-up mills. The look of decay, failure. But their speed limits are posted, the signs are rusted and riddled with bullet holes, sometimes Wesley prudently obeys them and some-times doesn't, what the hell, the villages are so small, he will be in and out before anyone notices, driving at a good pace, between sixty and sixty-five. He glances at his watch, often, calculating. So many miles to

Kingston and the Thruway. And then so many miles to Merrickville.
And the time is now. . . .

His head aches, his eyes water. He realizes suddenly that he has not
eaten since breakfast.

A nuisance to stop, a waste of time. Delay. And Lily, perhaps, is
waiting for him; and Kevin. Perhaps even waiting dinner. . . . But his
head aches, he feels groggy, he's been driving for hours and stopping
only for gas, he must stop to have something to eat, must force something down, it's the reasonable thing to do, the prudent thing, and then
he will feel much better, and the subsequent drive will be simple.
. . . His eyes sting. There is a faint buzzing in his right ear. The humid,
hazy landscape, the mountains like a watercolor wash, amorphous, indis-
tinct, dreamlike. . . . The hypnotic turns of the road. . . .

He stops for a sandwich and two beers at the Runesville Inn. There
is a creek behind the tavern, there is another of the abandoned mills,
perhaps a cider mill, boys are shooting rifles around back of it, the sharp
cracking noises make Wesley's headache worse, he is surprised that no
one else in the tavern—there are a half-dozen men there, of all ages—
is annoyed, or even gives any indication of hearing the shots. But he feels
less giddy now. It was really quite foolish not to have stopped for lunch
hours ago, he couldn't have been at his best, his most alert, driving at
high speeds all those miles, fortunately Lily won't know, she would be
disgusted with him if she knew, he can imagine her expression, that droll
downward twist of her lips, he can almost hear her voice. . . .

As he leaves the tavern he hears shouts. His first thought is: they've
done something to the car.

But his car and the several others in the parking lot are all right. The
commotion is at the mill, where boys—though they are not boys, they
are young men in their twenties—are shooting off not guns but firecrackers—and have evidently just tossed a firecracker at someone—a girl, a
woman in a short black skirt and yellow blouse who is screaming at them.
Wesley shades his eyes, staring, confused. What has happened? Is there
danger?

One of the young men tosses a beer bottle at the side of the tavern
where it smashes into a dozen flying glinting pieces. Wesley ducks his
head; fortunately he hasn't been struck. Another young man jumps
down from the broad sagging doorway of the old mill, yodeling words
Wesley can't interpret. He is a massive hulking creature, in bib overalls
and mud-splattered boots, shirtless, his muscular arms and shoulders and

neck oily with perspiration. He has Indian-black hair, straight and luster-less, falling to his shoulders. A wrestler's body. He must weigh two hundred fifty pounds, two hundred seventy-five. Wesley stares, appalled. The young man is being egged on by his friends, who hoot and tease him, and the girl in the black skirt is backing away, her absurd high heels wobbly in the coarse cinders.

"Go get her! Sic 'er! Sic 'er!"

I must leave, Wesley thinks, feeling faint, I must get to the car and leave before it's too late. . . . His heart is beating quickly and lightly, the beers have gone to his head and he feels weak, faint, giddy, frightened. His knees tremble. He knows the warning signs, he knows them very well, but he cannot move. His bowels feel suddenly loose. He knows, he knows, something is going to happen, he is being propelled toward its happening, he sees now that the advancing young man is slack-lipped and grinning, his enormous hands are loose at his sides, he is obviously retarded, his face is sallow, fat-cheeked, grotesquely dimpled, not ugly so much as simply inhuman. With a neighing sound and a buffoonlike toss of his head he shakes his straight lank hair out of his eyes and giggles.

Wesley finds himself stepping off the porch, despite his trembling knees. He raises a hand. He is about to speak. One blow from that giant's great hard fist could break his jaw, his neck. . . . If he should seize Wesley in his arms in a wrestler's hold, if he should apply pressure, pressure. . . . His sallow grinning face is enormous, he is obviously retarded, a cretin, a monster, an innocent monster. If only the others would not urge him on, whistling and jeering and hooting, if only the girl would turn and run, Wesley would not have to hear his own quavering voice raised suddenly, so frail, so frightened, he hardly recognizes it: "Hey, you — You— Yes, *you*— What the hell do you think you're doing?"

The
Tryst

She was laughing. At first he thought she might be crying, but she was laughing.

Raggedy Ann, she said. You asked about nicknames—I've forgotten about it for years—but Raggedy Ann it was, for a while. They called me Raggedy Ann.

She lay sprawled on her stomach, her face pressed into the damp pillow, one arm loose and gangly, falling over the edge of the bed. Her hair was red-orange and since it had the texture of straw he had thought it was probably dyed. The bed jiggled, she was laughing silently. Her arms and shoulders were freckled and pale, her long legs were unevenly tanned, the flesh of her young body not so soft as it appeared but rather tough, ungiving. She was in an exuberant mood; her laughter was child-like, bright, brittle.

What were you called?—when you were a boy? she asked. Her voice was muffled by the pillow. She did not turn to look at him.

John, he said.

What! John! Never a nickname, never Johnny or Jack or Jackie?

I don't think so, he said.

She found that very funny. She laughed and kicked her legs and gave off an air, an odor, of intense fleshy heat. I won't survive this one, she giggled.

He was one of the adults of the world now. He was in charge of the world.

Sometimes he stood at the bedroom window and surveyed the handsome sloping lawn, the houses of his neighbors and their handsome lawns, his eye moving slowly along the memorized street. Day or night it was memorized. He knew it. The Tilsons . . . the Dwyers . . . the Pitkers . . . the Reddingers . . . the Schells. Like beads on a string were the houses, solid and baronial, each inhabited, each protected. Day or

62

night he knew them and the knowledge made him pleasurably intoxicated.

He was Reddinger. Reddinger, John.

Last Saturday night, late, his wife asked: Why are you standing there, why aren't you undressing? It's after two.

He was not thinking of Annie. That long restless rangy body, that rather angular, bony face, her fingers stained with ink, her fingernails never very clean, the throaty mocking voice: he had pushed her out of his mind. He was breathing the night air and the sharp autumnal odor of pine needles stirred him, moved him deeply. He was in charge of the world but why should he not shiver with delight of the world? For he did love it. He loved it.

I loved it—this—all of you—

He spoke impulsively. She did not hear. Advancing upon him, her elbows raised as she labored to unfasten a hook at the back of her neck, she did not look at him; she spoke with a sleepy absentmindedness, as if they had had this conversation before. Were you drunk, when you were laughing so much? she asked. It wasn't like you. Then, at dinner, you were practically mute. Poor Frances Mason, trying to talk to you! That wasn't like you either, John.

There must have been a party at the Buhls', across the way. Voices lifted. Car doors were slammed. John Reddinger felt his spirit stirred by the acrid smell of the pines and the chilly bright-starred night and his wife's warm, perfumed, familiar closeness. His senses leaped, his eyes blinked rapidly as if he might burst into tears. In the autumn of the year he dwelt upon boyhood and death and pleasures of a harsh, sensual nature, the kind that are torn out of human beings, like cries; he dwelt upon the mystery of his own existence, that teasing riddle. The world itself was an intoxicant to him.

Wasn't it like me? he asked seriously. What am I like, then?

I don't ask you about your family, the girl pointed out. Why should you ask me about other men?

He admired her brusque, comic manner, the tomboyish wag of her foot.

Natural curiosity, he said.

Your wife! Your children!—I don't ask, do I?

They were silent and he had the idea she was waiting for him to speak, to volunteer information. But he was disingenuous. Her frankness made him uncharacteristically passive; for once he was letting a woman take the lead, never quite prepared for what happened. It was a novelty, a delight. It was sometimes unnerving.

You think I'm too proud to ask for money, I mean for a loan—for my rent, Annie said. I'm not, though. I'm not too proud.

Are you asking for it, then?

No. But not because I'm proud or because I'm afraid of altering our relationship. You understand? Because I want you to know I could have asked and I didn't—you understand?

I think so, John said, though in fact he did not.

At Christmas, somehow, they lost contact with each other. Days passed. Twelve days. Fifteen. His widowed mother came to visit them in the big red-brick colonial in Lathrup Park, and his wife's sister and her husband and two young children, and his oldest boy, a freshman at Swarthmore, brought his Japanese roommate home with him; life grew dense, robustly complicated. He telephoned her at the apartment but no one answered. He telephoned the gallery where she worked but the other girl answered and when he said softly and hopefully, Annie? Is that Annie?, the girl told him that it was *not* Annie; and the gallery owner, Mr. Helnutt, disapproved strongly of personal calls. She was certain Annie knew about this policy and surprised that Annie had not told him about it.

He hung up guiltily, like a boy.

A previous autumn, years ago, he had made a terrible mistake. What a blunder!

The worst blunder of my life, he said.

What was it? Annie asked at once.

But his mood changed. A fly was buzzing somewhere in her small, untidy apartment, which smelled of cats. His mood changed. His spirit changed.

He did not reply. After a while Annie yawned. I've never made any really bad mistakes, she said. Unless I've forgotten.

You're perfect, he said.

She laughed, irritated.

. . . Perfect. So beautiful, so confident. . . . So much at home in your body. . . .

He caressed her and forced himself to think of her, only of her. It was
not true that she was beautiful but she was striking—red hair, brown
eyes, a quick tense dancer's body—and he saw how other people looked
at her, women as well as men. It was a fact. He loved her, he was silly
and dizzy and sickened with love for her, and he did not wish to think
of his reckless mistake of that other autumn. It had had its comic
aspects, but it had been humiliating. And dangerous. While on a business trip to Atlanta he had strolled downtown and in a dimly lit bar had
drifted into a conversation with a girl, a beautiful blonde in her twenties,
soft-spoken and sweet and very shy. She agreed to come back with him
to his hotel room for a nightcap, but partway back, on the street, John
sensed something wrong, something terribly wrong, he heard his voice
rattling on about the marvelous view from his room on the twentieth
floor of the hotel and about how fine an impression Atlanta was making
on him—then in midsentence he stopped, staring at the girl's heavily
made-up face and at the blond hair which was certainly a wig—he
stammered that he had made a mistake, he would have to say good night
now; he couldn't bring her back to the room after all. She stared at him
belligerently. She asked what was wrong, just what in hell was wrong?
—her voice cracking slightly so that he knew she wasn't a girl, a woman,
at all. It was a boy of about twenty-five. He backed away and the creature
asked why he had changed his mind, wasn't she good enough for him,
who did he think he was? Bastard! Shouting after John as he hurried
away: *who did he think he was?*

I never think about the past, Annie said lazily. She was smoking in
bed, her long bare legs crossed at the knee. I mean what the hell?—it's
all over with.

He had not loved any of the others as he loved Annie. He was sure
of that.

He thought of her, raking leaves. A lawn crew serviced the Reddingers' immense lawn but he sometimes raked leaves on the weekend, for
the pleasure of it. He worked until his arm and shoulder muscles ached.
Remarkable, he thought. Life, living. In this body. Now.

She crowded out older memories. Ah, she was ruthless! An Amazon,
a Valkyrie maiden. Beautiful. Unpredictable. She obliterated other
women, other sweetly painful memories of women. That was her power.

Remarkable, he murmured.

Daddy!

He looked around. His eleven-year-old daughter, Sally, was screaming at him.

Daddy, I've been calling and calling you from the porch, couldn't you hear me?—Momma wants you for something! A big grin. Amused, she was, at her father's absentmindedness; and she had a certain sly, knowing look as well, as if she could read his thoughts.

But of course that was only his imagination.

He's just a friend of mine, an old friend, Annie said vaguely. He doesn't count.

A friend from where?

From around town.

Meaning—?

From around town.

A girl in a raw, unfinished painting. Like the crude canvases on exhibit at the gallery, that day he had drifted by: something vulgar and exciting about the mere droop of a shoulder, the indifference of a strand of hair blown into her eyes. And the dirt-edged fingernails. And the shoes with the run-over heels. She was raw, unfinished, lazy, slangy, vulgar, crude, mouthing in her cheerful insouciant voice certain words and phrases John Reddinger would never have said aloud, in the presence of a member of the opposite sex; but at the same time it excited him to know that she was highly intelligent, and really well-educated, with a master's degree in art history and a studied, if rather flippant, familiarity with the monstrousness of contemporary art. He could not determine whether she was as impoverished as she appeared or whether it was a pose, an act. Certain items of clothing, he knew, were expensive. A suede leather coat, a pair of knee-high boots, a long skirt of black soft wool. And one of her rings might have been genuine. But much of the time she looked shabby—ratty. She nearly fainted once, at the airport; she had confessed she hadn't eaten for a while, had run out of money that week. In San Francisco, where she spent three days with him, she had eaten hungrily enough and it had pleased him to feed her, to nourish her on so elementary a level.

Who bought you this? he asked, fingering the sleeve of her coat.

What? This? I bought it myself.

Who paid for it?

It's a year old, I bought it myself.

It's very beautiful.

Yes?

He supposed, beforehand, that they would lose contact with each other when Christmas approached. The routine of life was upset, schedules were radically altered, obligations increased. He disliked holidays; yet in a way he liked them, craved them. Something wonderful must happen! Something wonderful must happen soon.

He was going to miss her, he knew.

She chattered about something he wasn't following. A sculptor she knew, his odd relationship with his wife. A friend. A former friend. She paused and he realized it was a conversation and he must reply, must take his turn. What was she talking about? Why did these girls talk so, when he wanted nothing so much as to stare at them, in silence, in pained awe? I don't really have friends any longer, he said slowly. It was a topic he and his wife had discussed recently. She had read an article on the subject in a woman's magazine: American men of middle age, especially in the higher income brackets, tended to have very few close friends, very few indeed. It was sad. It was unfortunate. I had friends in high school and college, he said, but I've lost touch . . . we've lost touch. It doesn't seem to happen afterward, after you grow up. Friendship, I mean.

God, that's sad. That's really sad. She shivered, staring at him. Her eyes were darkly brown and lustrous, at times almost too lustrous. They reminded him of a puppy's eyes.

Yes, I suppose it is, he said absently.

On New Year's Eve, driving from a party in Lathrup Park to another party in Wausau Heights, he happened to see a young woman who resembled Annie—in mink to midcalf, her red hair fastened in a bun, being helped out of a sports car by a young man. That girl! Annie! His senses leaped, though he knew it wasn't Annie.

For some reason the connection between them had broken. He didn't know why. He had had to fly to London; and then it was mid-December and the holiday season; then it was early January. He had tried to telephone two or three times, without success. His feeling for her ebbed. It was curious—other faces got in the way of hers, distracting him. Over the holidays there were innumerable parties: brunches and luncheons and cocktail parties and open houses and formal dinner parties and informal evening parties, a press of people, friends and acquaintances and strangers, all demanding his attention. He meant to telephone her, meant to send a small gift, but time passed quickly and he forgot.

After seeing the girl on New Year's Eve, however, he found himself thinking again of Annie. He lay in bed, sleepless, a little feverish, thinking of her. They had done certain things together and now he tried to picture them, from a distance. How he had adored her! Bold, silly, gawky, beautiful, not afraid to sit slumped in a kitchen chair, naked, pale, her uncombed hair in her eyes, drinking coffee with him as he prepared to leave. Not afraid of him—not afraid of anyone. That had been her power.

His imagination dwelt upon her. The close, stale, half-pleasant odor of her apartment, the messy bed, the lipstick- and mascara-smeared pillows, the ghostly presence of other men, strangers to him, and yet brothers of a kind: brothers. He wondered if any of them knew about *him*. (And what would she say?—what might her words be, describing him?) It excited him to imagine her haphazard, promiscuous life; he knew she was entirely without guilt or shame or self-consciousness, as if, born of a different generation, she were of a different species as well.

At the same time, however, he was slightly jealous. When he thought at length about the situation he was slightly jealous. Perhaps, if he returned to her, he would ask her not to see any of the others.

What have you been doing? What is your life, now?

Why do you want to know?

I miss you—missed you.

Did you really?

In early March he saw her again, but only for lunch. She insisted he return to the gallery to see their current show—ugly, frantic, oversized hunks of sheet metal and aluminum, seemingly thrown at will onto the floor. She was strident, talkative from the several glasses of wine she had had at lunch, a lovely girl, really, whose nearness seemed to constrict his chest, so that he breathed with difficulty. And so tall—five feet ten, at least. With her long red hair and her dark, intense eyes and her habit of raising her chin, as if in a gesture of hostility, she was wonderfully attractive; and she knew it. But she would not allow him to touch her.

I think this is just something you're doing, she said. I mean—something you're watching yourself do.

When can I see you?

I don't know. I don't want to.

What?

I'm afraid.

They talked for a while, pointlessly. He felt his face redden. She was backing away, with that pose of self-confidence, and he could not stop her. But I love you! I love you! Had he said these words aloud? She looked so frightened, he could not be certain.

Afraid! he laughed. Don't be ridiculous.

One day in early summer he came to her, in a new summer suit of pale blue, a lover, his spirit young and gay and light as dandelion seed. She was waiting for him in a downtown square. She rose from the park bench as he appeared, the sun gleaming in her hair, her legs long and elegant in a pair of cream-colored trousers. They smiled. They touched hands. Was it reckless, to meet the girl here, where people might see him?—at midday? He found that he did not care.

We can't go to my apartment.

We can go somewhere else.

He led her to his car. They were both smiling.

Where are we going? she asked.

For the past several weeks a girl cousin of hers had been staying with her in the apartment, so they had been going to motels; the motels around the airport were the most convenient. But today he drove to the expressway and out of the city, out along the lake, through the suburban villages north of the city: Elmwood Farms, Spring Arbor, Wausau Heights, Lathrup Park. He exited at Lathrup Park.

Where are we going? she asked.

He watched her face as he drove along Washburn Lane, which was graveled and tranquil and hilly. Is this—? Do you live—? she asked. He brought her to the big red-brick colonial he had bought nearly fifteen years ago; it seemed to him that the house had never looked more handsome, and the surrounding trees and blossoming shrubs had never looked more beautiful.

Do you like it? he asked.

He watched her face. He was very excited.

But—Where is— Aren't you afraid—?

There's no one home, he said.

He led her through the foyer, into the living room with its thick wine-colored rug, its gleaming furniture, its many windows. He led her through the formal dining room and into the walnut-paneled recreation room where his wife had hung lithographs and had arranged innumerable plants, some of them hanging from the ceiling in clay pots, spidery-leafed, lovely. He saw the girl's eyes dart from place to place.

You live here, she said softly.

In an alcove he kissed her and made them each a drink. He kissed her again. She shook her hair from her eyes and pressed her forehead against his face and made a small convulsive movement—a shudder, or perhaps it was suppressed laughter. He could not tell.

You live here, she said.

What do you mean by that? he asked.

She shrugged her shoulders and moved away. Outside, birds were calling to one another excitedly. It was early summer. It was summer again. The world renewed itself and was beautiful. Annie wore the cream-colored trousers and a red jersey blouse that fitted her tightly and a number of bracelets that jingled as she walked. Her ears were pierced: she wore tiny loop earrings. On her feet, however, were shoes that pleased him less—scruffy sandals, once black, now faded to no color at all.

Give me a little more of this, she said, holding out the glass.

My beauty, he said. My beautiful girl.

She asked him why he had brought her here and he said he didn't know. Why had he taken the risk?—why was he taking it at this moment, still? He said he didn't know, really; he didn't usually analyze his own motives.

Maybe because it's here in this room, in this bed, that I think about you so much, he said.

She was silent for a while. Then she kicked about, and laughed, and chattered. He was sleepy, pleasantly sleepy. He did not mind her chatter, her high spirits. While she spoke of one thing or another—of childhood memories, of nicknames—Raggedy Ann they had called her, and it fitted her, he thought, bright red hair like straw and a certain ungainly but charming manner—what had been the boy's name, the companion to Raggedy Ann?—Andy?—he watched through half-closed eyes the play of shadows on the ceiling, imagining that he could smell the pines, the sunshine, the rich thick grass, remembering himself at the windows of this room not long ago, staring out into the night, moved almost to tears by an emotion he could not have named. You're beautiful, he told

Annie, there's no one like you. No one. He heard his mother's voice:
Arthritis, you don't know what it's like—you don't *know!* A woman
approached him, both hands held out, palms up, appealing to him, the
expanse of bare pale flesh troubling to him because he did not know what
it meant. You don't know, don't *know.* He tried to protest but no words
came to him. Don't know, don't know. Don't *know.* His snoring disturbed him. For an instant he woke, then sank again into a warm grayish
ether. His wife was weeping. The sound of her weeping was angry. You
brought that creature here—that filthy sick thing—you brought her to
our bed to soil it, to soil me—to kill me— Again he wanted to protest.
He raised his hands in a gesture of innocence and helplessness. But
instead of speaking he began to laugh. His torso and belly shook with
laughter. The bed shook. It was mixed suddenly with a gigantic fly that
hovered over the bed, a few inches from his face; then his snoring woke
him again and he sat up.

Annie?

Her things were still lying on the floor. The red blouse lay draped
across a chintz-covered easy chair whose bright red and orange flowers,
glazed, dramatic, seemed to be throbbing with energy. Annie? Are you
in the bathroom?

The bathroom door was ajar, the light was not on. He got up. He saw
that it was after two. A mild sensation of panic rose in his chest, for no
reason. He was safe. They were safe here. No one would be home for
hours—the first person to come home, at about three-thirty, would be
Sally. His wife had driven with several other women to a bridge luncheon
halfway across the state and would not be home, probably, until after
six. The house was silent. It was empty.

He thought: What if she steals something?

But that was ridiculous and cruel. Annie would never do anything like
that.

No one was in this bathroom, which was his wife's. He went to a closet
and got a robe and put it on, and went out into the hallway, calling
Annie?—Honey?—and knew, before he turned the knob to his own
bathroom, that she was in there and that she would not respond. Annie?
What's wrong?

The light switch to the bathroom operated a fan; the fan was on; he
pressed his ear against the door and listened. Had she taken a shower?
He didn't think so. Had not heard any noises. Annie, he said, rattling
the knob, are you in there, is anything wrong? He waited. He heard the

fan whirring. Annie? His voice was edged with impatience. Annie, will you unlock the door? Is anything wrong?

She said something—the words were sharp and unintelligible.

Annie? What? What did you say?

He rattled the knob again, angrily.

What did you say? I couldn't—

Again her high, sharp voice. It sounded like an animal's shriek. But the words were unintelligible.

Annie? Honey? Is something wrong?

He tried to fight his panic. He knew, he knew. Must get the bitch out of there. Out of the house. He knew. But if he smashed the paneling on the door?—how could he explain it? He began to plead with her, in the voice he used on Sally, asking her to please be good, be good, don't make trouble, don't make a fuss, why did she want to ruin everything? Why did she want to worry him?

He heard the lock being turned, suddenly.

He opened the door.

She must have taken the razor blade out of his razor, which she had found in the medicine cabinet. Must have leaned over the sink and made one quick, deft, hard slash with it—cutting the fingers of her right hand also. The razor blade slipped from her then and fell into the sink. There was blood on the powder-blue porcelain of the sink and the toilet, and on the fluffy black rug, and on the mirror, and on the blue-and-white tiled walls. When he opened the door and saw her, she screamed, made a move as if to strike him with her bleeding arm, and for an instant he could not think: could not think: what had happened, what was happening, what had this girl done to him? Her face was wet and distorted. Ugly. She was sobbing, whimpering. There was blood, bright blood, smeared on her breasts and belly and thighs: he had never seen anything so repulsive in his life.

My God—

He was paralyzed. Yet, in the next instant, a part of him came to life. He grabbed a towel and wrapped it around her arm, struggling with her. Stop! Stand still! For God's sake! He held her; she went limp; her head fell forward. He wrapped the towel tight around her arm. Tight, tight. They were both panting.

Why did you do it? Why? Why? You're crazy! You're sick! This is a—this is a terrible, terrible—a terrible thing, a crazy thing—

Her teeth were chattering. She had begun to shiver convulsively.
Did you think you could get away with it? With this? he cried.
I hate you—
Stop, be still!
I hate you—I don't want to live—
She pushed past him, she staggered into the bedroom. The towel
came loose. He ran after her and grabbed her and held the towel against
the wound again, wrapping it tight, so tight she flinched. His brain
reeled. He saw blood, splotches of blood, starlike splashes on the carpet,
on the yellow satin bedspread that had been pulled onto the floor. Stop.
Don't fight. Annie, stop. Goddamn you, stop!
I don't want to live—
You're crazy, you're sick! Shut up!
The towel was soaked. He stooped to get something else—his shirt
—he wrapped that around the outside of the towel, trembling so badly
himself that he could hardly hold it in place. The girl's teeth were
chattering. His own teeth were chattering.
Why did you do it! Oh, you bitch, you bitch!
After some time the bleeding was under control. He got another
towel, from his wife's bathroom, and wrapped it around her arm again.
It stained, but not so quickly. The bleeding was under control; she was
not going to die.
He had forced her to sit down. He crouched over her, breathing hard,
holding her in place. What if she sprang up, what if she ran away?—
through the house? He held her still. She was spiritless, weak. Her eyes
were closed. In a softer voice he said, as if speaking to a child: Poor
Annie, poor sweet girl, why did you do it, why, why did you want to hurt
yourself, why did you do something so ugly . . . ? It was an ugly, ugly
thing to do. . . .
Her head slumped against his arm.

He walked her to the cab, holding her steady. She was white-faced,
haggard, subdued. Beneath the sleeve of her blouse, wound tightly and
expertly, were strips of gauze and adhesive tape. The bleeding had
stopped. The wound was probably not too deep—had probably not
severed an important vein.
Seeing her, the taxi driver got out and offered to help. But there was
no need. John waved him away.
Slide in, he told Annie. Can you make it? Watch out for your head.

He told the driver her address in the city. He gave the man a fifty-dollar bill, folded.

Thanks, the man said gravely.

It was 2:55.

From the living room, behind one of the windows, he watched the cab descend the drive—watched it turn right on Washburn Lane—watched its careful progress along the narrow street. He was still trembling. He watched the blue-and-yellow cab wind its way along Washburn Lane until it was out of sight. Then there was nothing more to see: grass, trees, foliage, blossoms, his neighbors' homes.

Tilsons . . . Dwyers . . . Pitkers . . . Reddingers . . . Schells.

He must have spoken aloud; he heard his own slow dazed voice. But what he had said, what words those were, he did not know.

A Middle-class Education

The New Year was not yet a week old. Twilight had come early on that Thursday—it had been twilight most of the day, in fact—and by 5:45 P.M., when the murder took place, it was quite dark.

How could I have known, Seeley muttered. There were no warnings. Impossible to have. . . . Afterward, he talked to himself when no one was near. If someone came near he cleared his throat and was silent; occasionally he began humming, a cocky bouncy low-pitched tune. But how could I have known, he queried himself in innocence and exasperation, and when it happens again how will I know until it happens? Until it happens again?

He was ill. He lay in bed motionless as a statue, as a figure on the prow of a ship. He even clasped his hands on his chest, in utter peace. His wife telephoned their doctor from another room but he could overhear her tense monosyllabic replies.

Yes, he is. Yes. Right now. . . . No. When? Yes, I think . . . Yes, if . . . But . . . Yes, yes, he is. Thank you. Yes.

The New Year was a week old, then two weeks old. Gradually it was forgotten; it was no longer the New Year. By the end of January it was gone. It was simply January, the end of January, an ordinary midwinter.

It isn't likely to happen again, Seeley scolded himself. Time to rise from bed, time to return to work. So he did arise. He did shower, shave, get dressed. But then he got partly undressed again and put on his bathrobe and sat at his end of the kitchen table drinking Sanka, until it was nine and then nine-thirty and then ten. . . . Don't think I will drive in today, he told his frightened wife; it comforted him, that his voice should sound so calm.

Of course he had heard the horn. Short, sharp taps of an automobile horn. And then one long blaring wail. He had heard, must have heard, crossing the street as he always did, always, on his two-block walk to the parking garage from the Schools Building where he worked. But every morning and every noon and every afternoon at five-thirty he walked out on to the boulevard and he heard so much noise—ordinary traffic noise —and there were, of course, sirens in the background quite often, and the noise of drills and air-hammers, and jet planes overhead; so much harmless noise. He heard but did not hear. He did not listen.

Didn't you hear the car horn and didn't you hear the men arguing, he queried himself, and if so why did you continue to walk right into it . . . ? What a fool!

No one else queried him so mercilessly. The police had been gentle, thoughtful. Not at all what people thought. Of course they had had other witnesses—two other men and one shrill, articulate black woman, identified in the newspapers as a junior-high-school principal in a down-river suburb. They had been gentle with Daniel Seeley because of his condition and because they had other witnesses to the shooting and because the incident was really completed: there were no loose ends. The victim had died of gunshot wounds behind the wheel of his car and the murderer had died of gunshot wounds a few hours later, in the emergency ward of Metropolitan Hospital. So the incident was completed. Over. Bitten off at both ends perfectly. No one interrogated Seeley; at the very most, his colleagues at the radio station asked him how he was. At the *very* most, his wife asked him if he was still upset about what had happened. Did he dream about it? Did he think about it? When he lay awake, sleepless, was he thinking about *it?*

Not all the time, Seeley told her.

He was forty-three. He had been program director of the cultural radio station WMRL-FM for several years and he liked his work very much. He was devoted to his work. On the day he returned in early February he nearly wept, unlocking his office, seeing again his desk and filing cabinet and bookshelves and the little black-and-yellow Navaho Indian rug on the floor. And the framed photographs on the walls, several of which were autographed—pictures of Stravinsky, Benjamin Britten, Bruno Walter, George Szell, Vaughan Williams, and the mezzo-soprano Ursula Arensky, whom he had met at a reception some years ago after her performance with the city's orchestra; he had nearly forgotten the photographs and his eyes filled with tears when he saw them again.

Everything is back to normal, he thought. Everything is normal.

WMRL-FM was a public radio station supported by grants from the State Council on the Arts and contributions from local philanthropists and businessmen and smaller, sporadic, and always disappointing donations from faithful listeners. It had been in existence now for nearly fifteen years. Its offices were on the eleventh floor of the old Schools Building, at the corner of Seventh Avenue and Delaware Boulevard. The neighborhood was still considered a good one. There were professional office buildings, several fine restaurants, a Cadillac showroom, a small theater that showed art films most of the time. This section of Delaware Boulevard was still rather prestigious. It was safe. During the day it was certainly safe. Across Ninth Avenue and beyond the boulevard was deteriorating quite visibly, and down around First and Second it was still a burned-out shambles from the fires of eight years ago —the much-publicized "riots"—but that area was scheduled for renovation in the near future. It was to be razed and rebuilt, restyled completely.

The Schools Building dated back to the early 1900s. It was a fine old place: granite, marble, columns, Latin inscriptions, high ceilings and wide corridors and ornate molding and old-fashioned radiators that were sometimes stone cold and at other times fiercely hot; massive windows, thick walls, a sense of dignity and privacy. Seeley had always loved the building. He loved even its smells: that peculiar odor of freshly oiled wood, a sharp, acrid, pleasant smell that was nearly a taste in one's mouth. A fine old place, everyone said. And the enormous windows which opened so reluctantly—and the comically unpredictable radiators—and the lavatories with their porcelain bowls forever stained: Seeley did not ever want to say goodbye to the Schools Building.

. . . Illness is boring, he joked with his friends. That's the worst thing about being sick.

It certainly is, they agreed. The holiday vacation itself is hard enough to endure!—it's a relief to get back to work, isn't it?

It certainly is, Seeley said, smiling.

He proofread page proofs for the March program guide; he made a number of telephone calls; he set to work answering letters. His wife telephoned around eleven and he told her all was well, all was going beautifully. His hands did not shake. He drank Sanka at his desk, not coffee; never coffee. Never again coffee. Nerves, insomnia, indigestion.

Even before the murder out on the boulevard he had stopped drinking coffee.

. . . It certainly is a relief to be back, he whispered.

From his office window it was not possible to see the alley where the man named Cox had died. Seeley rose from his desk and leaned far over it and even pressed his cheek against the windowpane, looking down and to the left, his heart pounding; but it was not possible to see the alley or even the antique shop nearby. So there was nothing to worry about. There was nothing to see.

He did not sleep very well, yet. But he had always suffered from insomnia, off and on, over the years; as everyone does. He was fairly happy now. He was content. So many murders took place in this city —nearly eight hundred last year—and every day's newspaper included headlines and photographs and stories about murder: sooner or later one would probably witness a murder. Simple statistics. Destiny. Fate.

Bad luck, Seeley muttered.

. . . Sooner or later one would probably witness a murder, living here. Living anywhere, in fact. So he spoke, casual and guarded, himself again, .anxious to assure his friends and colleagues that he had forgotten the incident. Mathematical probability, bad luck, fate. Nothing serious. Nothing permanent. It was not possible, was it, that a fully mature, intelligent, relatively cultured human being could be destroyed by sim- ply having witnessed . . . ? It was not possible. No. He denied it. He was nearly himself again, he had gotten a great deal of rest during his sick leave, and soon the incident would be forgotten. By spring it would be forgotten.

By spring, he promised himself.

The parking garage was two blocks away. Seeley had been parking there for years. He made monthly payments; the several black atten- dants knew him well and seemed to like him. He still parked there but it was necessary for him to walk around the block, a considerable dis- tance out of his way, in order to avoid the alley where the shooting had occurred. If he parked elsewhere he would have an even longer walk.

His second day back, he tried to force himself to take the usual route. It was the obvious route, the sane route. A simple brisk walk of a few minutes. From the parking garage . . . past a diner . . . past a shoe repair

shop . . . then a street, a narrow street . . . he would wait for the light
to change before crossing the street . . . and then the television and radio
repair shop which had not opened after the holidays, with its rusty
grating permanently pulled down . . . and then . . . and then . . . beyond
that he believed there was a vacant store . . . a vacant store with election
posters and advertisements propped up in its show windows, curling and
yellowing with age . . . and then a pawn shop, open for business though
its windows were permanently protected by an iron grating . . . and then
the alley, the alley. . . .

No, he cried.

No. No. No.

Passersby glanced at him. He must have spoken aloud. Was he drunk,
was he insane? They glanced at him and hurried by. He was going to
faint. He could not support the weight of his body. All sense of balance
was gone, his instinct for equilibrium, everything had become clammy
and sick, sickish, blackly sickening. . . . He reeled and nearly fell. The
sidewalk was icy; he wore leather-soled shoes; he should have worn
galoshes. He reeled, staggered back toward the corner, felt his heartbeat
not only in his chest but in his entire body, in his head, in his eyes. No,
he whimpered. No. Please. Don't. Don't let. Please. Please.

His wish was granted: he did not fall.

Sleepless, he lay now in the guest bedroom, lucid, open-eyed, reasonable. He never thought about Cox, who had been shot in the face—the
gun had been held only a few inches from his face—because that would
not have been reasonable; that would have been dangerous. He might
begin to whimper as the dying man had whimpered. . . . No, that was
not reasonable. The man was dead. Many were dead. It did no good.
It was too late. It had always been too late. Seeley must have heard the
tapping of the horn and he must have heard the men's voices but none
of it had registered; he had been hurrying along the sidewalk, his head
bowed against the wind, he had been thinking of something very pleasant . . . what was it? . . . something very, very pleasant . . . some good
news . . . a $3,000 contribution from Healey Brothers . . . earmarked
specially for the station's series of interviews with contemporary American composers, which Seeley himself had started. . . . Good news! Good
news! And the frequent letters of praise that came to the station, and
the telephone calls, and the sense of a job well done! Good! Good news!
. . . It was the obvious route, the most direct route. There was no other.

How simply the universe unfolds once you discover that truth, Seeley marveled: there is no route other than the one you take.

Twilight all day. Midwestern winter. When the sky was clear, it was so starkly and vividly blue that people glanced at it, startled, as if something were amiss. But that day the sky was overcast. There was a light snowfall. Temperature dropping toward zero. Wind from the river a few miles to the north. Twilight. Winter. The New Year. Dangerous hour for travel. Street lights on the boulevard. Darkened shop windows. The antique shop closed, locked. Darkened. A car idling in an alley, another car idling on the street. Blocking the alley. Someone sounding his horn. And again. And then again, a long blaring angry wail. And suddenly Daniel Seeley was standing on the sidewalk as one man shot another, firing first through his windshield and then through his side window; and then it was over. That quickly, it was over. It had happened, had no more than started before it was over, and the young black man who had done the shooting had jumped back into his car and driven away.

No. Please. Why . . . ? Please don't.

He was whimpering in his sleep.

Paula came to sit by him. She turned on the bedside lamp; she sat in the chintz-covered chair; she smiled and smiled. You've been taking too many of those tablets, she said. He told you, didn't he, not to drink if you took them . . . ? He told you.

I only took three, Seeley told her. He groped for his glasses.

Three? All day? Since this morning?

. . . before bed.

Daniel, for God's sake. . . .

It was a terrible thing, he said. I don't know why it happened. Where are my glasses? My glasses slipped off . . . I nearly stepped on them. What if I had stepped on them! What if someone had stepped on them! The police would have had to . . . What if! But the police were very considerate. They're not as bad as people think.

You must have had a nightmare.

I must have had a nightmare. There's no need to sit up with me.

Do you want to talk about it?

. . . No need, really. I don't mind. I'll read for a while and then I'll sleep, like last night. It's nothing.

Daniel, I'm so worried about . . .

No, it's nothing. It really is nothing. It happens every day.

On his night table were several books. He was reading them all, at the same time. He was halfway through a biography of Poulenc and had just begun a fact-crammed history of medieval music; he was also rereading a volume of stories by Chekhov, in an old paperback edition from his college days. He leafed through the book on medieval music till he came to something to show Paula. It had struck him, had moved him deeply. He did not quite understand it but he knew it was true, profoundly true, and when he read it to Paula his voice shook:

> Our pleasance here is all vainglory,
> This false world is but transitory,
> The flesh is bruckle, the Fiend is slee—
> *Timor Mortis conturbat me.*

I'll heat some milk for you, Paula said softly. Would you like some milk? Please.

Yes. Thank you. Please.

Music By Request from 6:00 A.M. to 9:00 A.M. National and Local News. Follow-Up News. Music of the Baroque Period. Profiles of City Leaders: #5 in a Series. Women in the Arts. Contemporary French Composers. Jazz Classics. Senior Citizens Seminar. The Black Community: Music, News, and Interviews. The Polish Heritage. French Conversation. Chamber Music Recital, taped at the University last fall. Young Composers of America. Eastern Indian Music. A taped poetry reading. A taped history lecture. "Theater of Cruelty": a panel discussion rebroadcast from another network. Calendar of local concerts. Art Exhibit Openings. Capsule News. All-Brahms Concert. All-Mozart Concert. Music from Germany Today. Opera House. The Cleveland Orchestra. Works of Wilhelm Furtwängler. Works of Claude Debussy. The Gay Community: News and Interviews. Choral Masterworks.

It was Seeley's birthday, a blank day on the calendar. That blankness was horrible. Vacant dull leaden dead. His forty-fourth birthday. No surprise: he had known it was coming. No surprise. . . . He was arranging for an evening at the Institute of Arts: a Victorian soiree. Local musicians would play Schubert, in Victorian costumes; there would be furniture, period pieces, artwork borrowed from one of the founders' homes, even Victorian refreshments. Tickets were selling slowly but that was always the case; sales would pick up in a week or two. . . . Do you still love me? Seeley asked his wife. I wouldn't blame you if . . .

On his birthday he rewarded himself by not thinking of the murder all day. He went to work early, found a parking place on the street, on the other side of the Schools Building; and entered the building by the east entrance. Of course he was forced to come out again and again, to put dimes in the parking meter. And he ran the risk of being ticketed, since it was illegal to stay in one parking place for so many hours. But it was a fairly satisfactory arrangement and the blank day passed without incident.

I wouldn't blame you, he whispered.

Please don't. She began to cry. She had been crying quite a bit lately, though he rarely cried now.

He found himself standing on the sidewalk, staring. Like a child or an idiot he stared, stared. He was helpless; he could not move. A tall black in his twenties, wearing a handsome tan leather coat that fell below his knees, hatless, gloveless, had sprung out of his car and ran over to confront another black man, still in his car; there were shouts and almost immediately there were gunshots. What was happening? What had happened? The man in the leather coat fired as he shouted. He did not hesitate. He was very, very angry. . . . He had been parked on the street, blocking the alley, and when the other black man had sounded his horn angrily, wanting him to move, he had lost his temper and jumped out of his car and ran to the other car and began shooting. Five shots were fired, they said. Seeley would not have known. He simply stared. His glasses misted over. He was going to faint. He really saw nothing, comprehended nothing. It happened too quickly. There were shouts, gunshots, a shattering of glass, screams and then whimpers from the dying man. What had happened? What was . . . ?

Much later, Seeley recalled an odd sight: the man in the leather coat had backed away from his victim, slightly crouched, the gun still in his hand and the barrel pointed at the dead man. He had raised his narrow shoulders and lowered his head and seemed to be peeping rigidly out at what surrounded him—at the half-dozen people nearby, all of whom had stopped—not turning his head but swinging his eyes from side to side. He did not seem to see anyone, however. Or, if he noticed them, he did not care. He ran back to his car and slammed the door and drove away;

the tires squealed wildly. There was another person in the car with him. But Seeley's glasses were misted over and he was no longer able to support the weight of his body.

How simple the universe is, he thought.

How irrevocable.

Seeley was a poor witness. His hands shook, his teeth chattered. Comic, really. It was kind of them not to laugh. In his early forties, not a doddering old man, solidly built, of medium height, with fair gingery hair and intelligent dark brown eyes and clothes that were perfect for him—a camel's-hair overcoat, a good blue-gray tweed sports coat, gray trousers, a pale blue shirt and a cheerful yellow knit tie. Nicely dressed, nicely groomed. Smooth-shaven. Intelligent, courteous, responsible. Not a killer. Never a killer. They took his wallet from him because his hands were shaking so badly and because his stammering embarrassed them; they did no more than glance at his identification.

. . . Happened so quickly, so quickly, he told the police.

Yes, they said.

. . . Nothing I could . . . nothing I . . . He fired right into the man's face and . . . And then . . .

Yes, they said. That's fine. You can go now.

There was nothing on the front page about the incident. No headlines. The second, the third, the fourth pages: nothing. Seeley leafed through the paper desperately. He did not know what he was looking for. Cox was one name. Cox. And Simpson the other. Cox, Simpson. Simpson, Cox. One of them had killed the other on Delaware Boulevard the previous day, at approximately 5:45; Daniel Seeley had been a witness. . . . Happened so quickly, he said, licking his lips. So quickly. Nothing I could do. The human body is not a good idea; the face especially. Not strong enough. The skull isn't strong enough. Maybe it was a mistake, somehow there was a mistake . . . that we are so precarious in our flesh. . . . How much more cunning, to live in shells! The softness of flesh protected by shells! . . . Cox and Simpson were relegated to page 43, section D. They were not very important. Cox had been thirty-nine years old, an unemployed factory worker; Simpson had been twenty-six years old, a former gas station attendant. His companion, eighteen-year-old Florence Du Bois, was a student at Lenore's Beauty College in the city. She was shaken by the incident but unharmed. Said only that Simpson lost his temper because they had been quarreling and the other man shouldn't have been so impatient but it was too late now. . . . She was glad, she said, to be alive. Police released her after questioning.

Evidently Simpson had driven to the expressway and had been pursued by police for ten excited minutes; had abandoned his car, jumped out, run along a ramp, had been shot down with his gun in his hand. He died not long afterward at Metropolitan Hospital, of gunshot wounds.

. . . Happened so quickly, Seeley said. He could not feel his lips as they moved.

Disequilibrium.

Unbalance.

Timor Mortis, Seeley scolded himself. But I'm an adult man; I know better.

He practiced speeches on the subject. He learned how to chuckle; he had never chuckled in the past. He imitated one of the men at the radio station, a full-bellied, sunny young man who helped with operations and programming. Laughter is the sound of life, Seeley knew. Good health. Sanity. Joy. A kind of music.

Strangely enough, he said to his mirror image, it was not a racial incident at all. Not at all. It was just a . . . just an incident. Nothing human about it.

He chuckled. He had perfected a certain shrug of the shoulders. Fate, destiny, sheer bad luck. But it won't happen again. To make sure it would not happen again, he sometimes parked on the street; when he parked in the usual place, he circled the block and entered the Schools Building by the east entrance. Only once did his scheme cause him distress: one of his co-workers commented on the fact that he had seen him hurrying along Ventura that morning, why was that? And Seeley had blushed and stammered and made a fool of himself. The others were quiet. Grave. *They knew.* He stammered, managed a chuckle, said only that he had business up there . . . nothing important. And then he shrugged his shoulders. He eased away as soon as he could do so politely.

Of course they know, he thought. But they'll have pity. We must all have pity on one another.

. . . I walk everywhere, at any time; I always have. I don't believe in being a helpless woman.

You're anything but helpless, Grace!

Yes, I walk everywhere it's necessary. I mind my own business. I firmly believe that people let you alone if you mind your own business. It's just frightened, hesitant people . . . women who imagine things . . . and then of course something *does* happen to them.

There's truth in that.

Certainly! . . . Some people are born victims, they say. They invite trouble. If you know what you're doing and walk fast and keep to well-lighted streets and mind your own business . . . well, people are likely to respect you and let you alone. I've never been bothered, not in twenty-three years.

Seeley smiled behind his hand. He smiled and smiled. There was perspiration on his forehead. His friend Grace was talking and everyone listened with interest. They all liked Grace. They all liked one another. Grace was a widow, had been a widow for several years, her hair snipped sensibly short, so blond it looked silver; a full-bosomed, full-bodied woman in her late forties. She was athletic—she even went hiking and camping by herself, in the Rockies. Since her husband's death she continued to live in their handsome colonial house on Ashley Place, about half a mile from the Seeleys'. They both liked her. They had liked her husband also. Around the oval table that night were other friends of theirs—the Gordons, and Lou Schmitt. Old friends. Beloved friends. Gordon was a professor of history at the university and Lou Schmitt was first violinist for the symphony orchestra. Seeley was always happy to be with these people. He respected them, he was proud to be one of them, he felt safe and contained when he was with them. Paula was fairly close to Barbara Gordon; they had gone to the University of Minnesota at the same time, had been in the same residence hall. Everyone liked everyone else. Seeley listened attentively to Grace and nodded as the others nodded, smiling tensely behind his hand. He was actually grinning.

. . . also statistics show . . . they tend to shoot their own kind . . . that feature article in last Sunday's paper. . . .

Yes: they tend to shoot members of their own family. Or friends.

. . . People they're already acquainted with. It's a terrible, terrible thing, of course . . . this city's crime rate . . . just terrible . . . but at the same time there's no need for paranoia . . . no need for whites to panic and vote for fascistic police procedures.

I read that article, someone said. It's true, evidently. Most of the killings are within a family . . . or one friend shoots another in a tavern or during a card game. . . .

The danger is very much exaggerated. It's just a political issue.

Seeley listened and though Paula was watching him, he did not choose to look toward her end of the table. He smiled. He smiled broadly. He began to chuckle.

Grace turned to him. Dan . . . ?

Nothing, he said. He chuckled warmly and heartily.

What is . . . ? Is something funny . . . ?

Not at all, he said.

They were silent. Someone poured wine into someone else's empty glass. There was a clock ticking—a grandfather clock—and Seeley forced himself to listen to it, to count the clear, brittle little sounds. His face reddened. He was hot. Perspiration on his forehead: what if his friends noticed? He did not want to lose them. He did not want to lose his wife. He loved these people, he needed them desperately, human beings needed one another desperately but they did not know it. So they were reckless, they were offended by one another as Grace was offended by him. They did not know how desperately they needed one another, how closely their lives were bound together. Precarious lives. Flesh exposed, shell-less. No protection. So very simple!—a single bullet could smash everything.

Grace changed the subject coolly and pointedly. They were talking now of someone's son, living in New York City; his paintings were to be shown in a young artists' exhibit at the Whitney; wasn't that wonderful news . . . ?

A single bullet could smash everything. Seeley stared, stared. He saw. . . . Reaching for his glass, he nearly upset it. He saw, had seen. He knew. Paula was watching him, trying to get his attention. She loved him. They had been married for many years; he could not even remember how many. Most of their lifetimes, it seemed. He loved her, he loved everyone. Desperately. He did not want them to die. He did not want to die. He wanted to be able to walk past the alley again, like a normal man; he wanted to be free, to be happy, to take the most direct route back and forth from the parking garage. A single bullet, he knew, could smash everything. The windshield. The side window. The gaping incredulous face. Eyes enlarged in terror, mouth contorted by a scream: but it was futile. Happened so quickly. No one could see. No one was to blame. A gun could be fired so very easily—evidently—and no one quite understood.

You don't . . . you don't understand, Seeley whispered. Just to *see*, to *know*. . . .

Grace looked at him again. Lou Schmitt looked at him.

Did you say something, Dan? What's wrong?

He shook his head wordlessly. Paula got to her feet. Dan isn't well, she said, Dan's been taking antibiotics. He's had a cold now for weeks . . . an ear infection. . . .

He agreed. Sheepish. His life was bound up with these people, who were staring at him now with tenderness, with pity; even Grace had softened. He must not offend them. Must never offend them. In the past he had enjoyed their discussions—had sometimes argued rather heatedly with Lou, and even with Grace—but all that was changed now. He did not know why, but it was changed. Over the years he and Paula had lost a few close friends, people had drifted away from them or they had drifted away, involuntarily, unconsciously; but now they were suddenly in the middle of their lives and no more friendships could be lost. It was a serious business, now. It was a grim business.

Thought you were looking a little pale, one of them said.

Yes, Seeley said.

. . . Lost a few pounds too, eh? But you look fine.

Yes. Thank you.

Wish I'd lose a few pounds! . . . An ear infection, did you say?

Yes. It's fine. It's all right.

He's all right, Paula said.

Afterward he begged her to have patience with him. He begged her to forgive him for being so weak. . . . Do you still love me? he asked.

Of course. Of course.

They lay in one another's arms, shivering. It was several degrees below zero that night. The roads had been perfectly dry, the air had seemed to crackle. Such cold, such inhuman cold! . . . Seeley burrowed into his wife's arms, he clasped her rather cool body against his and willed himself to feel desire, to feel love; but he was drained of all strength. He was weak, trembling, exhausted. He willed himself to feel lust . . . a spurt of lust, a pinprick of . . . But it was impossible. It was comically impossible. He had not made love to Paula since the shooting and he would not make love to her again, ever. He knew. He cringed in her arms, weeping. Do you love me? he begged. Do you? Please. If you don't . . . If there's no . . . Please. Please. Please. I promise to get well. I promise. . . . If you don't love me, I . . . Do you? Please? Please?

And then, one day in late March, the sickness was over.

He could not trust himself to do it before work, since he might collapse on the street. And he could not trust himself to do it after work, in the crowds of office workers, among people who might recognize him. So he took a cab on a Sunday afternoon, shortly after five-thirty, and got out by the Schools Building. He was dressed as he had been dressed on that day. And he wore galoshes, since the walks were slushy.

The boulevard was quiet. The side streets were quiet. Most of the businesses were closed—the theater and the diner seemed to be open, but there were few people around. No one will see, he thought. No one will know. He carried his briefcase as always; he crossed from the Schools Building to the north side of the boulevard, his head bowed slightly against the wind. He walked slowly. He was in no hurry. When his heartbeat began to accelerate and the sense of terror rose in him he simply stopped; he stopped, panting, his eyes fixed on the alley ahead; he waited until he was fairly normal again. Of course there was no one around. The alley was empty, there was no one at the curb, no one waiting. Only a few cars were parked on the street but they were empty. Their owners were gone. They were not idling, there was nothing dangerous about them. The antique shop seemed to be closed now permanently; its show window was nothing but clutter. Seeley walked along, slowly, not forcing himself. There was no hurry. He would triumph. He had only to walk past the alley, to walk down toward the parking garage, as if nothing had ever happened. He knew he would do it, but he must not force himself. . . . So he stopped again, breathing shallowly. His glasses had misted over. He took them off to wipe them against his coat. Strange, that he should feel so warm. It was winter, still. Late March. But still winter. The New Year had long since disappeared, had blended into the ordinary year. He had survived, however. Hadn't he? He was stronger than people thought; they had no right to laugh at him and pity him.

Yes, he had survived.

He walked forward. A single pedestrian approached him, taking long swift strides. The man was a stranger and his eyes did not meet Seeley's. They passed each other. They came nowhere near each other. . . . Seeley looked around and realized that he was on the other side of the alley now; he had walked past *it*. Half-blinded he had walked past *it*. There was the fire hydrant, there was the place where Simpson had been parked, there, in the gutter, was the same debris Seeley had noticed so long ago. . . . He breathed deeply now. He was all right now. A survivor.

Of course the whole thing had been ridiculous and he chuckled to think of it. But he had done it, after all; and now he was free.

Yes, he was free.

He walked down to the parking garage, just to make sure. But of course he was free. The madness had lifted. He was free, free. Free! He went into a drugstore to telephone a taxi but he was so pleased with himself that he called home instead; he had to tell Paula, who would be worried about him.

Honey? Hello? Yes, this is . . . Yes. Yes, I *did*. I did.

Her thin anxious laughter was distant. But he could hear the relief in it.

Good news! he said. He closed the door of the phone booth so no one could hear. Let's celebrate when I get home, eh? Make me a martini! I'll call a cab after I hang up and I'll be home in half an hour or forty-five —what? Yes! *Yes*. I did. I told you what I had intended to do, didn't I? And I did it. Yes! I did it!

He began to chuckle. He unbuttoned his coat, it was so warm in the telephone booth.

I did it, he said. A sudden heated gaiety seized him, as if he were drunk. But it was good. It was good to feel this way again, good to be alive. He was clear-eyed now and perfectly normal and he would be home in a few minutes and though it was perhaps foolish they could celebrate, the two of them, and perhaps they could make love afterward. . . . Was it foolish? Was he exaggerating? He struck the inside of the booth as if in merriment, or chagrin; he wiped at his eyes with the back of his hand. Paula? Are you still there? Are you listening? Grace was right, she has the right idea, they *do* leave you alone most of the time and anyway it's so exaggerated, it's difficult to—Paula? Are you listening?

Of course I'm listening, she said in a small calm voice. When will you be home?

In
the
Autumn
of
the
Year

One of them was her lover's son. Her dead lover's son. He had turned out curiously: a balding young-old man with hairs in his nostrils, an annoying habit of picking at his fingernails, a quick strained meager smile.

They were absurdly reverential. All this chatter about her comfort displeased her. No, it pleased her: she had grown petty about such things over the years. Is there anything more we can do for you, Miss Gerhardt. Is there anything you would like.

Graciously she smiled and told them no.

Graciously she looked from one to the other to the other, favoring them equally. (She and her former lover's son had, of course, exchanged certain furtive looks—at the airport he had stammered his name, so nervous, so highly wrought, that Eleanor herself had begun to stammer. What folly! But she was, as always, beautifully in control of herself.) When she told them she preferred to rest, since the plane from New York City had been delayed, and the flight tiring, they seemed quite satisfied. Clearly her presence made them uneasy: she was too famous: she was too old.

The dean chattered as they prepared to leave. Was the guest room suitable, had she noticed the antique furniture, if it was cold tonight she might want a fire, the fieldstone fireplace was handsome, wasn't it?— the entire Alumni House a very attractive place. He hoped she would like it here. He hoped the award presentation and the banquet wouldn't be too tiring, he could respect the fact that she did so much of this sort of thing, meeting people, being praised and congratulated and photographed, it must have come to seem rather familiar by now . . . which was why, he said, his face creasing with the effort of his smile, Linden College was especially grateful to her for accepting their invitation.

Though she was not in the least embarrassed, she murmured something that sounded embarrassed. A modest woman. Despite her fame she was modest; she was unpretentious. The dean would tell his wife shortly that the visit wasn't going to be a difficult one after all—Eleanor Gerhardt appeared to be amiable, and approachable, and sober, and she was remarkably attractive for a woman of sixty-three. Her white hair was perfectly groomed, she was slender and light on her feet, her eyes were a fine pale green, calm and good-humored. Her throat was probably quite ravaged, though: she was wearing a pretty little pearl-gray-and-scarlet neck scarf.

"Well," said the dean. "We'll give you a little time to yourself now, Miss Gerhardt. One of us will come by at six to pick you up for dinner. Is that agreeable?"

"Perfectly agreeable," Eleanor said.

As they left, the man who was her lover's son looked back at her, half-smiling, his eyes narrowed as if he were staring into a strong light. Eleanor waved goodbye, wishing to put him at his ease. The poor man appeared to be so uncertain of himself—was it possible that he felt guilt, over his father's behavior?—his father's treatment of her? But it wasn't likely that he knew very much about Eleanor's relationship with Edwin Höller since he had been a mere child at the time.

Now he was chairman of the Music Department at Linden College, and director and conductor of the Ellicott Civic Orchestra. He must have been, Eleanor guessed, in his mid-forties. It had been nearly three decades since they'd seen each other last.

Benjamin, his name was. Would she have remembered it?—probably not.

I don't want to hurt the boy, her lover had said. I don't want to hurt his mother either, but it's the boy I'm most concerned about. He's inherited my neurotic propensity toward making too much of things . . . and his mother's inclination toward despair.

I understand, Eleanor had said.

Sometimes she spoke angrily, sometimes ironically. Sometimes with perfect sincerity. At the end, with a studied lightness which she believed adequately masked her despair. I understand, she said. Stroking his face; pressing herself into his arms. But it wasn't true: she had not really understood.

In the autumn of the year she gave in to certain wearing, sentimental thoughts. She became shameless—allowing herself to dream for long moments of love, and of death, and of her girlhood, and of the only man she had loved: the only man she had seriously loved, that is. (Of course there had been many men.) In the autumn of the year she remembered vividly the emotions that were no longer hers, and the harsh, rich, merciless pleasures of the body. It must have had something to do with the slanted light, the acrid odor of burning leaves, children hurrying to school in the morning. There was an urgency to the days, a sense of quickened meaning that did not include her. Autumn was for other people, for younger people. She did not regret this fact. Her mood became elegiac, she played Beethoven's quartets on the phonograph, she labored over long, loosely constructed poems celebrating the tragic necessity of loss.

It was true that she sometimes wept, unaccountably; she sometimes woke from dreams in which she wept, convulsed by a painful soundless wailing. That she had become an old woman. Old! It was a difficult concept to grasp. But most of the time she rather enjoyed her memories, she rather enjoyed the cleansing tears. Merely transforming certain experiences into language subdued them and allowed her a curious sort of triumph. She was a poet, after all. She was a highly disciplined craftsman in her art. Years ago she had emerged from that disastrous affair with Edwin Höller and had forced herself to survive it without self-pity, and had forced herself to write about the experience. Since that time she had never lost faith in her ability to withstand suffering.

My sincerest congratulations, Edwin had telegraphed, when her *Collected Poems* was awarded the Pulitzer Prize some years ago. *Admiration also. And a certain measure of envy.*

She had laughed, delighted; but had not replied.

In autumn she dwelt upon such memories. Her lover was dead—but still living; it wasn't difficult to hear his voice. Others whom she had loved and who had died—her father, her mother, one of her brothers, a favorite aunt—were dead but still accessible if she gave herself enough time.

For years, foolishly, she had believed she would not survive each winter. She anticipated a winter death—lightning-quick and brilliant as a January morning. She would not have minded; she would not have protested. (Pain frightened her, of course—she had always been a terrible coward about pain.) There was no intelligent reason for her to expect to die shortly, since she was in reasonably good health for a woman of her age, but she had supposed—halfway serious—that since Edwin had died at the age of sixty-two, some ten years ago now, she would probably not live much beyond that. She had even caught herself planning on it, as if such a maudlin gesture would please him. The handsome shingle-board house she had inherited, in Chestnut Hill, Pennsylvania, would go to her niece, a junior-high-school teacher who had been renting the house for years now for a token $75 a month: Sally was a fine, industrious girl, not pretty, not even very charming, but she was Eleanor's favorite niece and she would be enormously grateful for the inheritance. The furnishings in Eleanor's apartment on East Eighty-fifth Street would be sold, most of her books probably given away, and her records, and her motley assortment of clothes; the half-dozen pieces of good jewelry were to be divided among friends; the money in her savings account and in various investments—a considerable amount—was willed to several charities, including the American Cancer Association. At odd, idle times Eleanor found herself going through this list with a sense of satisfaction. She did not want to die, she really did enjoy life immensely, but at the same time . . . at the same time her life had come to seem strangely unreal, this past decade. Whether it was because of Edwin or not, she didn't know. (She hadn't seen the man in how many years?—twenty-nine?—so perhaps it had nothing to do with him at all.)

However . . .

Still, she knew she wasn't superstitious; she might have made a few blunders in her lifetime but she wasn't an ignorant person. She had always taken pride in her intelligence. You know too much, Edwin used to say, laughing, drawing back from her as if frightened; not just about me but about everything—everything! It's a fearful thing.

She investigated the room. Yes, it was attractive. Quite suitable. Silk wallpaper in blues and grays, a lovely old Queen Anne writing table, hardwood floor, Oriental rug, a brass-framed bed. The fieldstone fireplace drew her attention. It was very neat, dustless. There were two small birch logs in it, for show; it didn't look as if the fireplace was ever used. Eleanor had always liked the idea of a fireplace but, living alone, never married, she hadn't had the energy or the inspiration to use one. What if the smoke backed up into the room? She had no idea how a fireplace worked.

On the mantel was a brass hurricane lamp and a Wedgwood vase in blue and white and an oversized book, *A History of Linden College 1894–1964*. At one time in her life, when being honored by colleges,

universities, and various institutions was a novelty, she would have read
through the book, out of respect for her hosts; but no longer.

The bureau mirror reflected the afternoon sunshine so brilliantly
that Eleanor's image was obscured and there was no need for her to
peer anxiously at it. (Had the breeze at the airport disturbed her hair,
were those soft, dark, mournful pouches beneath her eyes more pronounced than usual, was her mouth set in that grim line she sometimes noticed?—none of it mattered, she refused to look, she was
going to remain invisible until they came for her at six.) At the window she stood for a while in utter peace, staring at the unfamiliar
countryside. Where was she?—the northwestern corner of Connecti-
cut? She could not remember if she'd been in this part of the state
before. No matter: it was lovely. The hills were graceful, the foliage
was already turning color, there was an exquisite grave stillness to the
horizon; the eternal solace of beauty without words.

Is there anything we can do for you, the strangers asked. Meaning
only to be courteous. Meaning only to show their ceremonial reverence.
One of them was her lover's son—her lover's child—and she could not
keep from staring at him. He was far slighter than his father, and hadn't
his father's busy, exuberant presence. But the eyes were the same—the
broad forehead the same. She stared, smiling. He had tried to smile in
return. Had the others noticed? Thank you, she said graciously, but I
want to be alone for a while. I need to be alone.

It was now 2:50. Suddenly she was tired: her legs felt the strain and
began to go stiff. Well, it was her age. It was accountable. She drew the
blind, and took off the scarf and her dress and shoes, and lay carefully
on the bed, and closed her eyes. She would rest. She would sleep. She
would prepare herself psychologically for the evening ahead—the fuss,
the hyperbole, the confused affection these good people had for her, a
stranger named Eleanor Gerhardt who seemed to them somehow familiar, perhaps because she was so old, she'd been prominent most of their
adult lives, a likable fixture, a comfortable sort of monument. . . . We
are so grateful for your visit, they would say.

She and Edwin Höller struggled on the narrow horsehair sofa. The
study smelled of dust: of books. Hundreds of books. Somewhere behind
and beneath her, beneath her straining head, a piano sounded—notes
that were sometimes muffled and unclear, and other times remarkably
precise. Two floors below a child practiced piano. For hours he kept at

it, maddeningly patient. Edwin's son Benjamin, ten years old, said to be gifted. Very gifted. Eleanor heard a run of scales, and then fragments of compositions, and then an entire composition from start to finish. (It wasn't until years later that she found out that the piece—slow and beautiful and rather self-conscious—was by Satie.) Notes slid in and out of her hearing. She could not listen. She cried aloud, gone suddenly deaf and blind.

My beauty, Edwin said, delighted. My beautiful girl.

He kissed her hungrily, held her too tight, buried himself in her. Wildly he spoke of love. The very first time she came to his attic study he spoke of love, and even of marriage: of going to Europe together. Wasn't it possible? He half-sobbed, he ground his forehead against hers, he kissed her until her mouth ached. Wet, noisy, childlike, ungovernable. Edwin Höller. He had been born in Munich and he wanted to show her Munich. And then they would go to Turkey, and then to Afghanistan and India. He was writing a book on Bactria—ancient Bactria. The Greeks. A civilization and its destruction, its doom. It would be a great book: the most ambitious and comprehensive book on the subject. He would become famous as a scholar. He would be invited around the world to give lectures, and to be a visiting professor, and she would come with him: his lovely, lovely girl.

Eleanor laughed in despair.

She clutched at him, kissed him. Wasn't it possible?

She had been twenty-nine when they met, thirty-four when they parted. This was in the mid- and late-forties, in Boston. Edwin Höller taught at a women's college and lived in Cambridge and Eleanor met him at a party and shortly afterward came to him, climbing the outside stairs to his attic study, anxious and silly as any bride. Are you shocked, she asked. I'm shocked myself. It must be disconcerting, when a woman is so relentless. . . .

He had not listened. My beauty, he said. My lovely girl.

Professor Höller was a noisy exuberant big-boned man who looked somewhat older than his age. (He was only thirty-eight when Eleanor met him.) He was not handsome. At times he was rather ugly. A broad flat forehead, busy peering eyes, a too-prominent nose. Large, clumsy, stained fingers. A habit of muttering to himself in exasperation or triumph.

Where do the hours go! was his constant refrain.

Life to Edwin was accelerated and melodramatic. He was not afraid to weep—he was not afraid to beg. Reading Eleanor's poetry (which was at that time fashionably difficult, a neometaphysical verse she later repudiated) he was not ashamed to admit that he understood very little of it and that, in a way, her imagination alarmed him.

I don't think I've ever known anyone quite like you, he said.

He had not lied. She was certain he had not lied.

She came to his study and it did not matter to him—amazingly, it did not matter at all—that his wife was in the house, or his young son, or that neighbors might see her climbing the stairs. Of his wife he said nothing except that she was "difficult" and "selfish." They had been married a very, very long time, they'd both been too young, in their early twenties, they had grown apart, who was to blame? He did not think he was to blame. Anyway it did not matter that Eleanor came to him because students and friends dropped in all the time—they climbed the stairs and knocked and if he wasn't there or too absorbed in his work to answer they simply went away again, and came back later, or dropped over in the evening, or saw him at the college. (Several times when they were making love someone had knocked on the door and Eleanor's heart had leapt, not with fear of discovery so much as with simple jealousy. She did not want to share Edwin with anyone else—she did not even want to share his good-natured attention with anyone else.)

So she came to his attic study where it was necessary to make one's way past small mountains of books, and where their love was heightened, perhaps, by the presence of other people in the house—the always-invisible wife, the young son at the piano; or he came to her apartment in a charming old building at the very edge of Beacon Hill, always bringing presents—wine, brandy, roses, snapdragons, a potted azalea, an antique doll in gold brocade, a volume of German poetry, untranslated, by a poet Eleanor had never heard of who Edwin insisted was of "colossal genius." Sometimes they met in a downtown hotel, sometimes they drove in Edwin's station wagon up the coast to Swampscott or Marblehead; a few times they went to New York City together. He was a fussy, old-fashioned lover, self-dramatizing, exaggerated, rather comic.

She believed she was the first woman he had been involved with since his marriage; she was fairly certain she was the first woman he had genuinely loved.

They quarreled and he twisted her wrist to silence her. Good! Do it harder. I deserve it: hurt me. She was capricious, playful, reckless, perhaps a little stupid. At the start of their relationship it was she who appeared to be less involved than he, less passionate; it was her refrain that she did not want to marry, she never wanted to marry, the very idea of marriage struck her as stultifying and absurd. He warned her that she would bitterly regret this attitude. It was unnatural for a woman to want to remain unmarried, she would see. So they quarreled, half-seriously, and were reconciled, and Eleanor went away for several weeks one winter to test her feelings apart from her lover, and Edwin worked twelve and fourteen hours a day on his research, and they came together again, and again quarreled: and Eleanor realized that she was very much in love. She was twenty-nine years old. She was thirty. And then thirty-one.

Should I drown myself? she asked once, impulsively.

She gripped the bridge railing as if to throw herself in, even made a playful move with her leg, of course she wasn't serious, she was only joking, Eleanor Gerhardt would never do such a desperate thing. Nevertheless Edwin reacted as if she were serious. Stop! Are you mad! What is wrong with you! You will regret— The shock and disapproval in his voice made her laugh, for how could he believe his threats might have any meaning to a woman ready to commit suicide?—though of course she wasn't serious and anyone but Edwin Höller would have known that. Afterward in her apartment, in her bed, he told her she would be very sorry for such foolishness—she would remember it when she was an old, old woman and be very embarrassed.

That remark struck her as very curious indeed. He was such a histrionic, silly person, where did he get his ideas from, were they folk sayings, were they part of German legend? She could not stop laughing.

He slapped her, to quiet her.

Yes, that's right!—hurt me. Do whatever you like, you know I deserve it.

She had never felt younger. She was never going to age.

In his arms she was immortal.

Her fingers in his thick, springy hair; his mouth gnawing against hers; the taste of each other's body; the necessary rituals of love. (After they parted, after Eleanor left Boston at the age of thirty-four, she made it a point to seek out other men; especially, for a while, large slovenly good-natured men, and married men; and men who would probably hurt her. She wanted to exorcise his memory, she wanted him gone. She had not forgiven him and never would. She wanted him *dead*. But it was five or six years before she could bring herself to respond sexually to a man —after Edwin her body had gone numb, she was always nervously distracted, preoccupied, embarrassed. That too was his fault and she would never forgive him.)

The Edna and Walter G. Davison Award for Distinction in American Letters carried with it a prize for $1,500, and Eleanor Gerhardt smiled gratefully, as one must, and read the poem of hers about autumn in New England, in an old churchyard, which she knew would please her audience; and she made a brief, graceful speech which was well-received; and the most difficult part of the evening was over.

They crowded about her to congratulate her and to shake her small, frail hand. They backed away so that a photographer could take her picture, standing alongside the smiling young Dean of Humanities.

How honored I am to meet you, voices claimed.

How very honored.

She autographed books, in most cases the paperback edition of her *Collected Poems.* She was quite tired now but of course she didn't show it. If her hand began to tremble, why she had merely to lean against the podium and to steady one hand with another. If her hearing failed occasionally, she had only to smile intently and nod, and the speaker was usually satisfied; if she was forced to ask him to repeat his question it could be attributed to the noise in the auditorium. Fortunately she had been able to sleep for about forty-five minutes at the Alumni House— otherwise she would have been very tired indeed. It was quite possible she might have been unable to complete her little speech and the audience would have been disappointed; moreover, they would have been alarmed, they would have made a fuss. If there was anything Eleanor detested it was fuss.

At the reception in a quaint filigreed parlor called the Founders' Room, she noted, and was grateful, that the dean and his wife and Benjamin Höller stayed close by, to protect her from people who wanted to talk too long, or whose questions were inappropriate, or who might have requests to make of her. (Though in recent years very few young poets asked her to read and comment on their work.) She accepted a Scotch and soda. She heard herself laughing, a melodic girlish laughter. Who were these people? Who were these strangers? It was touching that they should wish to honor her, to single her out for an award. It could not be true, as they asserted, that her poetry meant a great deal to them, and that she had contributed something marvelous to American letters—what *were* American letters, she had always wondered—but it was very decent of them to behave as if this were so. Everywhere she went, in this phase of her life, she encountered good, generous, admiring people. They were all so adamant—so young.

Someone's voice broke through. "Would you like another drink, Miss Gerhardt?"

She turned and it was Edwin's son. Unnecessarily she put a hand on his arm; she squeezed the rough material of his coat. Yes. No. Well, perhaps. It crossed her mind that her pale, slender hand was still attractive—delicately blue-veined, fragile. The star sapphire edged with diamonds was lovely. It had the look of an antique ring, an inheritance, but in fact it was quite new—a gift Eleanor had given herself, whimsically, for her fifty-ninth birthday.

"Yes? Shall I get you another?" Benjamin asked.

"If you don't mind," Eleanor said.

While the dean's wife talked to her about the radical changes at Vassar (which Eleanor and the dean's wife had attended, at different times), Eleanor watched Edwin's son make his way to the bar. She hadn't known, had she, that Benjamin Höller was teaching at Linden . . . ? Or had she known and forgotten? Years ago, years ago, she had spied on the Höllers from a distance and she had known a great deal about them, but after Edwin divorced his wife and moved to California, and remarried, and then divorced again and remarried, and accepted a visiting professorship at the University of Hawaii, and never returned to the States, she had grown confused about what, exactly, she wished to know, and what it might be best for her to forget. Of course she had known that Benjamin Höller was studying music. He had gone to Juilliard, she believed, at a fairly young age—fifteen or sixteen. But by then Edwin had left Boston; his life had changed completely. Her life had changed completely.

For a while she had been bitter. Very badly hurt, and very bitter. He had professed to love her, he had courted her, had appeared to wish to marry her—but when their relationship began to alter, after a few years, and it was evident that Eleanor had become rather dependent upon him, and quite emotional at times, he spoke less of marriage and more of his responsibility to his family: he did not love his wife, of course, but he had a commitment to her and to his son. In those days Eleanor Gerhardt was a striking young woman, outspoken, even a little brazen, known in the Boston area for her piquant good looks and her sarcasm and her poetry, which appeared in magazines fairly often, enviably often; she had a wide circle of acquaintances and had accumulated, she scarcely knew how, a tight little band of detractors. At times she felt almost invincible: she intended to work very, very hard at her craft and she intended to take all the prizes by storm. (Her first book, a modest enough venture called *Nurturings,* had been awarded a prize from the National Council on the Arts and one of the Boston newspapers had published a very flattering interview with her.) At other times, weeping in Edwin's arms, she felt helpless as a child, grotesquely weak, contemptible. She did not want to marry him, but—but perhaps— Wasn't it possible for them to go away for a year, she asked, begged, hadn't he wanted that at the very first, why had he changed his mind . . . ? He didn't love her! He had never loved her! He comforted her, she raged at him, he told her to stop, to be still, she thrust him from her, would have liked to tear at him with her nails. It was obvious that he loved her when they were together. No man could pretend such love, such passion. His cries were torn from him; they were brutal, almost shameful to hear. And she in turn loved him—she could not help herself. (Afterward she recalled that she had been aware of her behavior all along, eerily conscious of herself even when transported by passion or rage. A distraught, weeping, reckless young woman who was nevertheless witnessing herself, as if from a distance, contemplating her own mad excesses. She had been an actress pronouncing certain difficult lines, working against them, laboring to master them, until the point at which the words overtook her and carried her along without her conscious will—and then, of course, it was too late.)

I'll leave, she cried. I'll be the one to go away.

My dear Eleanor, please—

I know what you want: what you've been maneuvering. I'll be the one to go away.

Even then the affair hadn't ended. It had dragged on for another year. There were telephone calls in the night, there were threats of suicide, there were outbursts, periods of lucidity and good humor and optimism, dinners together in Boston, weekends in New York, sessions of desperate love. During the five years of their relationship Edwin had changed very little; he was a little grayer, a little more shaggy; he had gained ten pounds, perhaps. But he had not changed in any substantial way. Eleanor, however, had changed a great deal. She was no longer really young —not *young.* She carried about in her imagination a vision of herself as a striking young girl and when she happened to see herself, mirrored when she did not expect it, the sight was distressing.

He's made me ugly, she said to anyone who would listen. Look what he's done to me.

They laughed at her, and denied that she was ugly, and whispered behind her back. She had many enemies; there was no one she could really trust.

I'll be the one to go away, she threatened.

He held her heated, pale face in his hands and kissed her; kissed her goodbye.

I'll be the one to go away—

They could see that the reception was tiring her, so, though it was only ten, they drove her back to the Alumni House. Benjamin Höller accompanied them, seated beside her in the back seat of the dean's car.

They chattered happily about the lovely autumn weather, the lovely countryside, the college's endowment fund, the fact that the faculty was "young and vigorous and community-minded." Eleanor did not care in the least but she heard her voice with the others, and was pleased that she had acquitted herself so well and that the evening was coming to an end. If she chose, she could recall the admiration with which she had been received; she could hear again the warm, generous applause. But in a week or two the visit to Linden College would begin to fade, and within a month she would be confusing it with a visit to the University of Virginia, where she had been awarded an honorary degree the previous spring. Friendly people, generous applause, handshakes and photographs and a few strong drinks; then the flight home.

Except for Benjamin Höller. She would remember him.

At least it was a genuine love, she wanted to tell him suddenly. Your father and I hurt each other very much, we suffered, we were in misery much of the time—but we were alive, at least. We were driven by passion—by life itself. I hated him for years and wanted him dead and then I stopped hating him and now I think of him with love, I can't help thinking of him with love; it's almost as if no time has passed at all. It's almost as if nothing has changed at all. *I am still his young, greedy, frightened mistress. . . .*

After leaving Boston Eleanor returned to her family's home in Chestnut Hill for a few months, but there were disagreements, misunderstandings, attempts to possess her (always made in the name of love), and many quarrels. She was thirty-five years old. She knew herself to be a wreck, a failure, an ugly haggard creature: whenever she thought of Edwin her throat constricted, as if to prevent her from crying aloud. She had no friends now. She wanted no friends. She moved to New York City, to a partly furnished room on the West Side, and there she lay in bed for days at a time, too lethargic to dress, too fatigued to write. She believed she would never write again—what was the point of it, really? She had done quite well with her poetry; people envied her, resented her modest success; she had worked hard and knew that, if she worked hard again, she might be a very fine poet indeed. But what was the point of it? Edwin had been impressed at first, and then he had lost interest. He had loved her very much at first and then he had stopped loving her. No matter what she wrote, no matter how successful she became, it would not have the power to make him love her again.

Her hatred for Edwin detached itself from him. It floated loose, fouling the air. Once she drew a razor blade lightly across the inside of her arm, simply to see what would happen. She detested herself: she was such a liar, such a coward. The razor blade hurt so of course she dropped it into the sink. Oh Christ, she cried, this is such folly.

The razor blade hurt her sensitive skin, a comb drawn roughly through her hair hurt her scalp, the cold bright ferocious winter air hurt her lungs. This is such degradation, she thought. Surely there is some mistake.

She wanted to telephone him. She wanted to write.

She was reasonably certain that if she approached him he would take her back. He had loved her so much, after all—!

But she did not telephone or write. Instead she began to work: haphazardly at first, with a rather cynical sense of direction. If she loathed herself she might at least make a kind of poetry out of it; it was preferable to love oneself, or to approve of oneself, but if that was out of the question she would have to make do with what was at hand. Months passed and she had nothing to show for her effort except piles of notes. Raw emotions. Words. She began another love affair, fully conscious of the fact that she neither loved the man nor felt desire for him—it was simply that she needed someone between herself and Edwin Höller, so that she would be able to deal with her experience. The emotions had been transmuted into words, and now the words had to be given a certain focus, a certain tone. She would have to create the exact structure to contain these words; if she worked very hard she might force them into perfection.

Two years later *A Season of Love* was published. It was an odd book —less than one hundred pages of brief enigmatic pieces, some of it poetry, some prose, in a terse, elliptical voice that was unlike anything Eleanor Gerhardt had done in the past. It received a very limited attention, like most books of poetry, and Eleanor had not been especially disappointed—she had expected nothing much, after all. She would have liked Edwin to read it, she would have liked him to write to her, perhaps. . . . But he never wrote. It was highly unlikely that he had read the book; possibly he hadn't even heard of it.

And then, several years later, when she was immersed in other things, a director who had read *A Season of Love* and had been very moved by it contacted her, and asked if she would like to fashion the book into a play; if she would like to collaborate with a playwright on it. At first she refused, thinking the idea ludicrous. She knew nothing about the theater and could not bear the thought of working with other people. And wasn't the subject simply too familiar?—a disastrous love affair, a great deal of suffering, a bitter farewell? But the director persisted and in the end Eleanor gave in and the result was a surprisingly successful little play. Since it required virtually no stage settings, and only two actors, it was easy to mount; since it involved a great deal of emotion it interested audiences, especially women; and the language was deft, bitten-off, shrewd, cruelly precise, so that one came away moved by respect for the articulate nature of the lovers, however familiar the situation itself was. Eleanor forced herself to see the play once and was not altogether ashamed. . . . And then the extraordinary thing happened: the play made money, it was taken up by universities and summer stock theaters, there was even an Off-Broadway "revival" in the early sixties. Eleanor Gerhardt, by then an established poet, was lauded as a precursor of the women's movement; she was praised for her unblinking honesty, for the terseness of her language, for the violence with which she condemned received ideas of male domination. She might have written other plays, she might have attempted a novel, but, prudently, she shied away from such risks; she did not want public acclaim, she was perfectly satisfied with poetry. At first she felt guilty about the royalties she received—as a poet, she had grown to believe that one was never paid for one's best work. Then as the years passed and the royalties continued, and the sales of her books, even, increased, she came to take this income for granted: at least she was not disturbed by it.

People who knew Eleanor knew that *A Season of Love* was closely based upon her love affair with a man named Edwin Höller, and they might have known that Höller had published a single book, a scholarly study on some obscure facet of Greek civilization, but they didn't know Höller himself, and had only a mild curiosity about him. Had he minded the play, they asked Eleanor, what might a man feel about the fact that his personality had been publicly analyzed, his behavior as a lover so rigorously assessed? Eleanor said curtly that she hadn't any idea—no idea at all. What about the man's wife?—had she minded? It must have seemed ironic to her, that her husband's former mistress should fashion such a success out of their love affair. But Eleanor knew nothing about Höller's wife. Since she wasn't evidently much of a reader she had probably never heard of the book of poems, and possibly not the play either. She knew nothing about Eleanor herself, after all. She might have suspected something but she hadn't any proof. The woman was said to be a self-centered, vain, limited person, mainly interested in her household and in her son; and in any case she was to lose her husband anyway, a few years after his affair with Eleanor ended—he'd divorced her to marry a woman in her mid-twenties, the wife of one of his colleagues.

I was only the first of his women, Eleanor said. She wondered if this was true. Probably not: but she liked the ironic, stoical sound of the words.

Would he like a cup of coffee? There were facilities in the next room, a small kitchen she could use; it would be no trouble at all to make coffee.

He declined, saying that a single cup would keep him awake all night. He'd always been a poor sleeper.

Eleanor murmured something sympathetic.

They smiled uneasily at each other.

Eleanor had seated herself in a wingback chair beside the fireplace, conscious of sitting rather stiffly. A proper old lady. Her hands clasped in her lap. Benjamin Höller sat in a chintz-covered easy chair facing her. He was very nervous: Eleanor noted that his fingers moved almost constantly, as if picking out keys on the piano, marking a secret rhythm. She wanted to say that he had played beautifully as a child—she would never forget—there were certain melancholy, haunting melodies—she would never forget—

"We might as well—"

"I was thinking—"

They paused. Eleanor began by asking gently how his father had been —had the last years of his life been happy?—he'd been in Hawaii, hadn't he—

"I really wouldn't know," Benjamin said with a small hurt smile. "We didn't keep in contact."

"I'm sorry to hear that," Eleanor said.

"I would have thought that—possibly—he'd have been in contact with *you.*"

"No," Eleanor said, startled. "Not at all."

"I thought—"

"Just a telegram a few years ago—no, it must have been twelve, fourteen years ago— Just a single telegram, nothing more."

Benjamin's fingers moved lightly. "He was always such a bastard, wasn't he," he said.

Taken by surprise Eleanor laughed. But it was a mirthless, choking sound.

"He was a—an exceptional person— He couldn't help—"

"He was a bastard," Benjamin said flatly. Out of his drab tweed coat he drew a manila envelope; for an instant his expression shifted and Eleanor wondered in alarm if he was about to burst into tears. "My mother used to say it was because he hadn't the professional recognition he wanted—the fame he thought he deserved. He was so petty, you know, so jealous, he could be so *vicious*—writing savage reviews of Eliade's books, for instance, and sending them in duplicate to journals —anything to hurt an old friend—anything to get published. I think she was wrong, though. If he'd gotten the attention he wanted he would have been just as miserable—just as much of a bastard."

"Would he?" Eleanor asked, surprised. She stared at Benjamin and could see, now, nothing of her lover in that face: not his eyes, certainly. This intense, balding young man was a complete stranger. "I thought — I— But I thought," she said feebly, "that you loved him—I mean, that you—"

Benjamin laughed harshly. "When?"

"What?"

"*When* did you think that?"

"When did I think—?"

"That I loved him?"

"I—I don't know— When you were a boy, I suppose."

"Yes, but when did *you* think that?"

Eleanor was quite confused. She started to speak, then stopped.

"Did you think that when you were sleeping with him?—or was it afterward, maybe?" Benjamin asked. He was tapping the manila envelope on his knee. Though he spoke harshly Eleanor realized that he was quite nervous. She herself had started to tremble; she felt a little faint. "How many years afterward?" he asked.

"I didn't realize that you knew," Eleanor said weakly.

"Knew *what?*"

"About your father and me— About—"

"Of course I knew. My mother and I both knew. I was ten years old when your affair with him began, and fifteen when it ended. I knew everything. Nearly everything. How could I not have known?" He laughed.

"But—"

"You were both pigs," Benjamin said.

For a few shocked seconds they sat in silence. Eleanor could not look away from him. Something pulsed in her throat, in her ears. Was she going to faint? What had happened? . . . She saw that the young man's lips were moving, she realized he was speaking again. "How could we not have known?" he said. "Everyone knew. It was no secret. One day my father threw a bottle of wine against the wall while we were at the dining room table, he began screaming at my mother, asking why she kept so quiet, why did she pretend nothing was wrong, was she scheming against him—calling her names, pounding on the table like a madman — He made no secret of it, he didn't believe in secrets. He believed in *passion,*" Benjamin said softly.

"I didn't know—"

"Of course you knew."

Eleanor half-closed her eyes. She heard herself denying it, she heard herself begging to be understood. If only this agitated young man would—

"You were both pigs," he said flatly, "but I'm willing to agree that *he* was the worst. He made a fool of you, he intimidated you, used you, it pleased him to taunt my mother with the fact that he had a mistress, a devoted, passionate, highly intelligent young woman—*younger than you,* he used to say, *beautiful while you're ugly*—that sort of thing. He liked to shout, he liked to stamp around the house throwing his arms about. That was passion, that was the way passionate people behaved. Filled with life, you know—that sort of thing. He pretended to worship the instincts. His lectures were filled with that sort of crap. In fact he was in despair because he couldn't publish anything substantial, because ideas slipped through his fingers, he was getting old, he was a failure, he was inferior—he was viciously jealous of his colleagues and afraid they were all laughing at him. So he turned to you. So he tormented my mother and destroyed her life."

"But I wasn't the only woman," Eleanor stammered. "I—I wasn't the first, even— I don't think I was the first—"

"But you were the most faithful," Benjamin said. "You stuck like glue. Even when he wanted to get rid of you he couldn't—and that was pleasing to him too, that you were so idiotically in love with him, wanted to marry him, wanted to help finance a trip to India for him— He used to ask my mother for advice, and friends who dropped over: what was he to do, this unbalanced young woman was so madly in love with him, how was he to extricate himself from her, what was he to *do?* In front of my mother he talked like that. He got drunk, he bawled, he threw his arms about, he pretended to be sorry, to be ashamed. The filthy old bastard. The pig. *My God,* he'd croak, staring at me with this stupid, cruel, operatic expression, *what will happen to Benjamin?—to all of us?* He was afraid you would kill yourself, you see."

"Kill myself?" Eleanor said faintly. "But that's—that's preposterous — I was never going to kill myself— And I never wanted to marry him; I have never wanted to marry anyone. He must have been lying—"

"He wasn't lying," Benjamin interrupted. "He was too stupid to lie. The fact was that you *were* begging him to marry you and you *were* threatening suicide; and everyone knew it. He was frightened but at the same time euphoric—that a young woman should love him so desperately, so shamelessly. And if you *had* committed suicide—"

"This is ridiculous," Eleanor said faintly.

"Here are your letters," Benjamin said, holding the envelope out. "That last winter you wrote a dozen letters and I remember him reading parts of them aloud—to my mother, that is—in their bedroom—I listened at the door, I eavesdropped, I had to be close in case she needed protection; I believe I was ready to kill him if necessary. Yes, you wrote him long deranged letters, you certainly were begging him to marry you —and you *were* threatening suicide. If you don't believe me—"

"I didn't write any letters," Eleanor said. "I never wrote any letters."

"When he moved out he left an attic of books and papers and correspondence—and your letters were in all the mess, in a desk drawer. I wanted to throw everything out and my mother wanted to keep everything, so we kept most of the books, and some of the letters—just left them where they were. I would have liked to burn everything," Benjamin said lightly, "but I didn't get my way. My mother still loved him: that was part of her illness."

Eleanor stared at the manila envelope he was holding. She had written no letters; she was positive she had written no letters. Certainly she had never begged Edwin Höller to marry her—!

"I don't believe this," Eleanor whispered. "Any of this."

Benjamin waved her words aside. "Your beliefs don't interest me, Miss Gerhardt, any more than your emotions interest me. *You* don't interest me, in fact. I realize my father exploited you, you were stupid enough to fall in love with him, and at one time of course I hated you —I hated you very much—but right now, tonight, whatever you think or feel doesn't interest me in the slightest. I suppose you brought me to certain realizations about the nature of life: the two of you allowed me to see how 'passion' and 'freedom' are just words to excuse selfish, slovenly, essentially juvenile behavior, and that if I wanted to live sanely, without injuring myself or others, I would have to find quite different models. Which I did. Without much trouble, really. I set out to love and marry one woman, and to remain faithful to her; remembering my father and his silly platitudes, I've never been seriously tempted to do otherwise. My relationship with my family is an unfashionable sort of relationship, by today's standards, but then so is my contentment unfashionable—and it's something I never talk about, really. Please excuse me for bringing the subject up tonight. The only reason I've intruded upon you, Miss Gerhardt, is to hand these letters over to you."

Eleanor made no move to accept the envelope. Why should she accept the envelope, what had it to do with her. . . . He laid it carefully on the table between them.

He was breathing hard. His expression was queerly bright and contemptuous. "If you had committed suicide I think he would have been pleased—though of course he would have put on a noisy display of grief. It was his *nature,* he used to say, to be demonstrative; he didn't believe in suppressing his emotions. He ruined my life and my mother's and he even liked to berate himself about that—saying he didn't know what to do next, he didn't know where to turn, life was a terrible mystery. My mother was half-crazy with shame, as you can imagine. She was from the Boston area, her father was a Presbyterian minister, she simply didn't know how to handle what was happening. It wasn't just that she loved him—it was also the fact that everyone knew about his betrayal of her. Word got back to her family, even. She was so ashamed, humiliated—she began to drink—she'd say to me *I'm just dirt, trash, I'm no good, I'm nothing*—when I came home from school she'd be in the kitchen, drunk—staggering drunk— I felt so sorry for her and I hated him but I didn't know what to do. I didn't know what to do. She and my father had these terrible fights—he'd scream at her, and after a while she began to scream at him, and they'd throw things at each other, and the next day I'd find her drunk again, and she'd hang onto me and say she was trash, garbage, she should be destroyed like garbage, she should die. What could I do?" Benjamin said sharply. "She had been an intelligent woman at one time—she'd gone to Radcliffe, she had a master's degree in French—but when my father started being unfaithful to her she disintegrated: she lost everything. I don't know why. I wish it had been otherwise. She did something very desperate—I wonder if you knew?—probably not, he would have been embarrassed to tell you. Did you know she got pregnant? At the age of forty-one? Deliberately. To hold him, I think. To impress him with the fact of her femininity."

Eleanor stared. "Pregnant—?" she whispered. It was impossible for her to comprehend: what *was* happening? There had been Edwin whom she loved, and there had been, far to one side, vaporous and insubstantial, the woman who was Edwin's wife. But the woman had never been very real. "Your mother was pregnant?" she said. "But—"

"I suppose my father deluded you into thinking he made love only to *you,*" Benjamin said. "Yes? That was part of his style, his contempt. He made his women feel that only they inspired his prodigious passion. Except for my mother, of course, who knew better. . . . Yes, it's true, the poor woman became pregnant at the age of forty-one. And then she had an abortion. Naturally. She was very sick—I mean with drinking, by this time—she was suicidal. It was necessary to have the abortion— she didn't resist. But that was about the end of her."

"I didn't know—I had no idea," Eleanor said slowly.

"Ah—didn't you know, hadn't you any idea?" Benjamin said, raising his voice slightly in imitation of hers. "Well—I suppose not."

"I simply had no—no idea—"

"Your lover *did* keep things from you, didn't he," Benjamin said.

"Though I suppose that was part of his charm—his mercurial passion—his *Old World* style. I'm sure he was irresistible!"

Eleanor pressed her hands against her face. Something caught in her throat; she could barely breathe. I didn't know, she wanted to cry, I didn't know, why are you saying these things, why don't you let me alone?—I didn't know. I am innocent.

"Never mind," Benjamin Höller said, getting to his feet. "I'll say goodbye now."

She stared wildly at him, cringing. For a moment she thought he was going to strike her.

Then he was leaving, backing away. The visit was over. His words swam and echoed and pulsed in her ears. She could not decipher them. She could not understand. He was leaving without shaking her hand; he did not seem to care for her.

"Good night, Miss Gerhardt," he said.

"But—"

She stared at the door and tried to think where she was. What time it was. He had been so angry, that man—that stranger. It was not her fault, surely. Why had he left without shaking her hand?

"I had no idea," she said shrilly. "I'm not to blame."

The fire flared up brightly. Then died down again.

She prodded it with a letter opener she had found in the writing desk, grunting with the effort. Why didn't it burn, what was wrong? She heard herself sobbing with frustration.

Lining the bureau drawers were sheets of near-transparent paper that crumpled noisily in her hands. She made balls of them and arranged them in the fireplace, close about the letters. Stooping, breathing laboriously, she lit another match and held it against the paper. The flame caught at once; again it flared up, nearly touching her fingers.

She stood before the fireplace, panting, trembling. She stared at the crumpled papers. Unread, the letters were starting to burn. At last they were starting to burn.

Where do the hours go, she wondered.

She brushed at her eyes with the back of one hand, sniffing. She was so tired. So very tired. It was unfair. He had not shaken her hand. He had not praised her poetry. She was innocent, yet the letters burned so sluggishly. What if they did not burn? But they would burn. She had all night if necessary.

A
Sentimental
Education

One

Thinned and distorted by the sea breeze came the voice: "Duncan—Duncan!"

Though he had been half-awaiting it for the past hour he seemed now not to hear. Abruptly, he shifted his weight in the uncomfortable wicker chair, bent over his loose-leaf notebook and the physics text. He was taking notes in his slanted, fastidious hand, frowning as if the effort of writing itself were difficult.

"Duncan," his cousin Antoinette called, now closer. "Where are you? Duncan—come see—"

He could not pretend he didn't hear her, nor did he wish to shout a reply. His hand shook in annoyance.

"Duncan, look what I found! Look—"

She ran up onto the veranda, panting. In her cupped hand lay a small black bird. It appeared to be unconscious. Duncan stared at it, surprised, involuntarily moved by its beauty and its helplessness.

"It was really Lucy and Bonnie who found it but they were afraid to pick it up. I think it's just *hurt*, I think it's just stunned, like the birds that fly into our windows back home, don't you think?—what do you think?"

Duncan prodded it with his pen.

"Oh, but don't hurt it!" Antoinette cried.

"I'm not *hurting* it. Calm down."

"But what if—"

The girl's hand was trembling. Or perhaps it was the bird, quivering with life. It had a small, beautifully shaped black bill and perfectly round eyes, now closed, the eyelid darkly transparent. Duncan stared at it: there was something about that dark, sickish eyelid that disconcerted him.

"It's a beautiful bird, isn't it," Antoinette said softly.

"It has interesting features," Duncan said, turning the bird partway

over with his pen. Its feathers were black, spotted with white on the back
and wings and belly; there was a patch of brown, a very attractive
russet-brown, high on its back. Its rather long legs were pale. "I think
it's a sandpiper."

"It isn't a sandpiper, they're never black."

"It's a shorebird of some kind," Duncan said irritably.

"A plover? A rail?"

"How do I know?"

"You've been coming up here all these years, your mother said last
night, what?—fifteen years—and you don't even know the birds—"

"It's a shorebird," Duncan said, raising his voice slightly. In his round
gold-rimmed glasses, with his pert, prim, rather short upper lip, and his
air of barely controlled impatience, he reminded his cousin of a minister
or a teacher: he was nineteen years old but might have been considerably
older. His fair lusterless brown hair was cut short and neatly combed as
always, parted on the left side; his clothes looked new, as if taken out
of their wrappers just that morning; and they were too white—impracti-
cally white. Antoinette saw for the twentieth time and was surprised as
always that the backs of Duncan's short stubby fingers were covered with
very fine, fair hairs, and that his nails—and his toenails as well—were
not only perfectly clean but perfectly filed. Her own fingernails were
ridged with dirt, one or two were attractively long but the others were
broken short or actually jagged; and she did not dare to glance at her
bare feet because it was hopeless—they got dirty immediately every
morning and the toenails were discolored from one day to the next.
Duncan's feet, so pale as to appear bluish-white, were set side by side
on the veranda floor in their new hand-tooled leather sandals, the ankles
primly touching, and Antoinette's lip curled involuntarily as if she had
seen something embarrassing or amusing. How ridiculous her cousin
was, how stupid that she should run to him like this so often, her
trembling hand proffered!—a wild flower, an almost-ripe blackberry, a
broken seashell, a hurt bird! She blushed angrily and jumped backward
off the veranda while Duncan was still examining the bird.

"That's all right. Never mind. I'll ask Uncle Forrest or the Grizzly
—I'll look it up in my mother's book," she cried. "No point in disturbing
you."

Startled, rather hurt, Duncan stiffened and adjusted his glasses on his
nose, and could not stop himself from completing a little ritualistic
series: first the adjusting of the glasses, then a touch of his curled

forefinger against the left side of his nose, then the forefinger, now opened, pressed against his lips as if to bring them together (for his front teeth were slightly oversized, it was only with a conscious effort that he could completely close his lips), then an abrupt impatient scratching of his neck or jawline. He did all this so quickly that Antoinette was not conscious of it, nor was he altogether conscious of it himself. His room- mate at Johns Hopkins the previous year had noted it after only a week, but he had managed, thoughtfully, to say nothing until mid-November, when he suddenly threw down a book and shouted; "For Christ's sake, stop that! *Stop that!*" When he explained to Duncan what he meant, Duncan had felt, along with his astonishment and anger, a queer sense of guilty satisfaction. So far as he knew, however, he had broken himself of the habit. His roommate had not complained again.

"What do you mean by calling Mr. Gyorgy that name," Duncan said. "It isn't funny. It's insulting and stupid and if he ever hears you— Antoinette! Come back here. Do you want to kill that poor little thing, carrying it around like that? Give it to me—I'll take care of it."

She backed away, shaking her head. "I found it. It was meant for me to take care of it."

"You said Lucy and Bonnie found it."

"I picked it up, it's mine."

Duncan laid his textbook and notebook carefully down, and his ball- point pen carefully between them, and got to his feet. "Antoinette," he said, "give me the bird. It certainly isn't *yours.*"

"I could make a pet of it. I could keep it in the upstairs bathroom and feed it."

"My mother won't allow that."

"I don't give a damn about your mother."

"*Don't* you! Why then— Why— You—"

He broke into laughter, clapping his hands together softly. He was about to say, Why don't you go home, then, you and your pathetic mother and your ugly little sister, why did you ever come here, who wants you?—but of course he said nothing. He was not a child like Antoinette: in fact her childishness had the effect of making him stand rigidly upright, his lips pursed together. His laughter was hoarse and jeering, but he had not smiled.

"I insist that you either give the bird to me, or put it out somewhere on the beach. Or in the marsh grass. Yes, in the marsh grass, hide it so that—"

"I'm going to show Uncle Forrest. If he says I can keep it I will."

"He isn't here, he's in the village—"

"He's here! He's here somewhere!"

"All that shouting is going to hurt the bird," Duncan said in disgust. "Why are you acting so stupidly? Do you *want* it to die? It's unconscious but it hears perfectly well every word we say—"

"Hears perfectly well every word we say," Antoinette mouthed in a high-pitched voice. "What do I care if it does? It's mine."

If Duncan approached her she would continue to back away and in a few yards her feet would start to sink in the drifted sand, and he foresaw that she might be startled and might squeeze the bird; so he stopped where he was. "Aren't you absurd," he said. Her mimicry angered him, and rather hurt him, for it was he who had encouraged this playful, satirical side of his cousin. (He had been agreeably surprised when the Tydemans joined them the other week, to discover Antoinette so much more mature than he had remembered. She was—almost— someone to whom he might talk.) But he saw now that she was little more than an overgrown peevish child. Fourteen years old? Fourteen and a half? His sensitive skin prickled with revulsion of her.

"You wouldn't even take care of it anyway," she said. "You'd throw it away somewhere and let it die. It's nothing to *you.*"

He shrugged his shoulders to show his disdain.

And he did not think her very attractive either: pale blue staring eyes in a suntanned face, curly chaotic brown-blond hair, small breasts loose beneath a soiled red jersey blouse. Like most teenagers on the island she wore shabby jeans cut off at mid-thigh and went barefoot. Her legs were lean and muscular, almost too darkly tanned. A flat, boyish body, an aggressive pouty look to her mouth, something too intense about her eyes. Like everyone on that side of Duncan's mother's family she was disfigured by poverty as if by acne, and it crossed Duncan's mind that he would be justified in ignoring her for the rest of the summer.

"It's nothing to *you,*" she whispered.

"*Sargent.* And Tydeman."

Duncan made this pronouncement in his courteous, neutral voice though the white-haired woman in the post office had already gone to search for his mail.

And then he must endure a conversation of two or three minutes.

The rainy weather these past few days . . . squalls, thunderstorms . . . today's sunshine welcome . . . and how was his family . . . and when was Dr. Sargent coming up, was it sometime in August. . . .

A letter from a White Plains realtor for his Aunt Irene, Antoinette's mother; a postcard for Duncan forwarded from Georgetown; a letter for his mother and him on his father's office stationery, the names and address perfectly typed.

The postcard? He had seen at once that his name and address were merely stamped. And indeed it was a worthless bit of mail, notice of a record sale in a store on Wisconsin Avenue. He ripped it in two and let the pieces fall into a wastebasket.

The letter from his father was addressed to both his mother and himself but he slipped it into his shirt pocket without opening it, along with his aunt's letter.

Along Main Street of Sky Harbor he walked as if he were in a hurry, as if someone were awaiting him, swinging his arms briskly and humming beneath his breath. He carried himself as always with a proud, almost military bearing, his head held very slightly back, the soft fold of skin beneath his chin creased. In his white-and-beige striped sports shirt and his clean white trousers he appeared to be taller than his height of five feet six, and when he drew in his breath as he often did in public —for who knows who might be watching here in the village, he was Dwight Sargent's son, after all, and Forrest Sargent's nephew—he looked rather attractive; his pert, round little stomach was not visible.

There were a few greetings. Brightly clad but nonetheless ghostly presences. Women. His mother's acquaintances, or women who would have liked to be. A boy of about twelve, a neighbor. Duncan did not know his name. He crossed the street, unpaved at this point, to avoid running into the wife of their handyman, Mr. Gyorgy. A few days ago this plump perspiring woman had greeted Duncan on a lane near his house by calling out *Aren't we looking trim and handsome this year!* The Gyorgys had known him since he was an infant and of course they meant no harm, they hardly meant to be crude and insulting, but he was uneasy in their presence just the same—particularly in the woman's presence. She smiled at him as if she were seeing a much younger Duncan, a child, and it pained him to be obliged to smile in return. And she had grown so fat over the years! And one of her lower front teeth was missing. ("What a horrible ugly woman," Antoinette had said, drawing her narrow shoulders up chastely. "Why doesn't she do something about her *teeth.*")

The town was beginning to seem crowded. It was late June now; in another week or two a dozen families would arrive, and more would continue to come well into August. Still, Sky Harbor was a fishing village primarily. The area near the town hall and the Presbyterian Church was given over to newer stores and tourists' boutiques, but the rest of the town had not changed since the forties; some of the older buildings dated back to the 1870s. There was a whaling museum on High Street that the girls and their mother had gone to the other day and had professed to find fascinating. And the wharfs, the fishing sheds, the battered old boats, the piles of lobster traps—none of it had changed in Duncan's memory.

Duncan walked out onto the pier. He shaded his eyes, staring out toward Drum Island. It was not yet altogether clear; the air was misty and wet-looking; the sky was mottled. If it rained again he would stay in his room studying. A half-hour of physics, a half-hour of German. He would avoid the girls. He would avoid his mother and his Aunt Irene and his elderly Uncle Forrest. The house was large enough, fortunately —it could sleep at least twelve people. Except for the master bedroom his own had the clearest view of the ocean and he was quite comfortable there despite the inadequate heating. He preferred it to his room back home, in fact. When he shut the door on the rest of the household and went to stand at the dormer window he could half-close his eyes and see not the Atlantic Ocean but a vast undulating splendid element, by turns silvery and blue and brackish and green, utterly mysterious, utterly impersonal. And when the roughened surface of the ocean was prickled by rain he felt a queer, almost uncontainable excitement, as if his body were about to burst into tears. It was quite different back in Georgetown.

There, his room was on the third floor of his parents' townhouse but it looked out onto a meager green space with a solitary emaciated Russian olive tree and, across the way, the redwood deck and free-form plastic furniture of a junior-grade State Department official who was evidently separated from his wife and who entertained noisily several times a week. One night, very late, Duncan had stood in his undershirt and shorts in his darkened room, gazing over at his neighbor and his guests, and calculated how easy—how grotesquely easy—it would be to pick them off one by one with a rifle. If he had a rifle. And he would not even have needed a telescopic lens.

The ocean was colorless this afternoon. Washing noisily about the rusted hulls of the fishing boats, giving off an odor that was fairly strong but not unpleasant. And yet not really fresh. Duncan glanced down annoyed, to see debris bobbing in the water—fishes' heads, guts. No wonder the gulls were squawking. At a nearby fishing shed several men in hip-length rubber boots were gutting fish. One of them had straight black hair, black as a grackle's wings, yet without any iridescence—an Indian boy of about fifteen or sixteen. Another, turning, revealed himself to be not a man but a husky big-breasted young woman.

Duncan shivered and his eyes watered with the sudden chill.

The time? He had been gone only half an hour.

He strolled back to the heart of the village, in less of a hurry. He noted children on bicycles and felt a vague, brief pull: why didn't he have his own bicycle repaired, why didn't he ride again as he had some years ago? As a boy he had ridden his bicycle all over the island. From the dunes where his family had their home to the westernmost tip of the island, some seven miles away, a small fishing village called Southwest Point that looked over toward Mount Desert Island. He had ridden alone or with companions, though mainly alone. And then one year, abruptly, he had lost interest. Had lost interest even in swimming or crabbing or sailing. . . . He spent the summer reading and taking notes and daydreaming, and it had not occurred to him to be lonely until he overheard a guest inquire of Mrs. Sargent: *But isn't poor Duncan awfully lonely up here without any friends?* His mother had rather haughtily said that of course he wasn't lonely: he had a great deal to do.

A motorbike, irritatingly noisy. Shirtless young man, deeply tanned, wearing a baseball cap. Lout. Followed by another on an equally noisy vehicle.

Duncan stared after them, his lips pursed. He saw with a tinge of satisfaction that the first of the boys nearly collided with a car—a taxi cab on its way from the airport. There was a horn's brief blare, there was a shout or two. And then the boys swerved around the car and disappeared out High Street.

Punishments suitable . . . ?

A sudden violent accident and the tanned bodies streaked with blood and dust. Thrown onto the street. Heavy, helpless. Writhing in pain. Or . . .

But it was best not to think of such things. He had told himself, had instructed himself, last autumn; he had taken a vow.

He was *not* to think of such childish things.

"Duncan, you're such a fool," he murmured. "Such a contemptible fool."

He walked on. Passed the post office again. And the stationer's store and the shoe repair store and the Garden Basket where his mother sent Mrs. May to shop though Mrs. May protested, saying the food at the A & P was just as good and much less expensive. An odor of citrus fruit. His mouth watered, which was a good sign. (His appetite was returning gradually. Had been returning since April. In the meantime, the doctor said, he must simply eat and try to remember what things taste like.) At lunch he hadn't bothered to eat much but the evening before, as if stimulated by his decision not to speak to Antoinette again this summer, and by the girl's swollen pouty look, he had eaten a fair amount—quickly and nervously but without any difficulty in swallowing.

His attention was drawn to a man he had never seen before, strolling along the raised boardwalk across the street. A man of indeterminate age though probably in his fifties or late forties, with gray hair and a dark beard, and pale arms and legs. He was new to the island, evidently. He wore attractive sports clothes—a smart patterned shirt with short sleeves, pressed olive-green shorts, hemp-soled shoes—and oversized sun glasses. There was something about his walk that struck Duncan as peculiar. Was he slightly lame, or . . . He carried one shoulder higher than the other, did he, or was it merely that he was turning at the waist to glance over his shoulder. . . .

The man was staring, Duncan saw, at a young girl who had walked by.

She wore shorts and a halter top, and she was very young, hardly more than a child. At first Duncan thought she might be Bonnie Burkhardt, one of their neighbors' children, but she was no one he knew.

Odd, that the bearded man should look after her.

Duncan thought it very odd indeed.

He watched as the man walked on, pausing in front of the library. The Sky Harbor Public Library was housed in a small clapboard building, formerly a private home; it was set back a little distance from the walk and in its front yard poppies, marigolds, and wild roses were blooming. There was also a glassed-in case where books were displayed and it was this case the bearded man appeared to be examining. Duncan stood in the shade of an awning and watched him, his arms crossed. He was not to be hurried home, he had plenty of time. The sky had partly cleared. There was little danger of rain and anyway he would not mind the rain.

A noisy group of teenagers on bicycles pedaled by. Three boys, two girls in cut-off jeans. They must have been fourteen or fifteen. One of the girls had waist-length red hair: no one Duncan knew. But of course she was too young for him to know. From her manner, also, he guessed that she belonged to the town—she was not one of the summer people —and it was unlikely that he would know her or her family.

He saw the bearded man gaze after the bicyclists, pulling for a moment at his lips.

And then walk onward, slowly.

Duncan crossed the street ahead of him and went to stand, trembling, before a store window. The man was to his right and advancing slowly, slowly. The skin on that side of Duncan's body began to lift itself in tiny goose bumps. His mouth was dry, his lips parted. There was a tiny heartbeat in his tongue. It had crossed his mind that this man might one day—might one day soon—turn to gaze after Antoinette as he had gazed after those other girls. And she was so childlike, so unconscious of herself, provocative without meaning to be . . . exasperating in her ignorance. . . . Duncan stared into the store window. Only vaguely was he aware of a display of some kind: nets and corks and seahorses, archaic maps of the Western hemisphere, a single lobster trap, women's shoes, handbags. The bearded man was approaching him from the right. Duncan could not yet see him in the corner of his eye. Ah, but now: now. Now. His reflection appeared stealthily in the window and passed behind Duncan like a wraith. Duncan remained facing the window, frozen, not daring to move. It was evident that this man whom he had never seen before was on the prowl, a hunter.

Had he glanced at Duncan as he passed . . . ? Or perhaps he had merely glanced into the store window, out of curiosity. He was tall: taller than Duncan's father. A wraith, a pattern in the window, a form moving in the bright sunshine, indefinable. Duncan half-closed his eyes, pressing his nails into his palms. He felt soiled. Defiled. He must go home and shower once again and scrub himself thoroughly. . . . Furtively he glanced after the man, now half a block away. Yes. Him. He was the one. *He*.

"Contemptible fool," Duncan's dry lips mouthed.

III

Through the screen door she stared at him. His hair was neatly combed as always, his profile was fleshy but severe, in his fingers the marking pen moved swiftly and with certainty: so absorbed was her cousin in his reading that Antoinette believed he would not have started had she shouted at him.

But then he turned suddenly, he glanced around.

She stood in her yellow bathing suit, arms and legs awkwardly overlong. The back of her neck itched violently and she could not stop her fingers from scratching.

"That bird," Duncan said slowly.

"Yes?"

He cleared his throat. "That black bird you found out on the beach . . . ?"

"When I went out to check the next day it was gone," she said.

"Gone from where?"

"The marsh."

He gazed at her thoughtfully. She could not see his eyes behind the gold-rimmed lenses but she felt they were kindly and forgiving.

IV

He hiked out past the dunes—a wilderness of great misshapen mounds of sand, intimidating as the landscape of another planet—to his secret cove, the stony stretch of beach he had discovered years ago and taken for his own.

The blinding patches of heat in the dunes gave way abruptly to the chill of the sea breeze. He jumped from a flat rock on which tiny weed flowers of exquisite loveliness grew to the pebbly sand some four or five feet below; he landed with a gentle grunt.

The girl awaited him. Golden-haired, bold. Mute. As in the dark of the night her image floated in his mind's eye, pure and undefiled and of a cameo perfection, so now she stood on her long slender tanned legs, on tiptoe, her hair blowing in the wind, whipping about her face. He dreaded that she might speak and her voice be revealed as rough or vulgar. Or childish.

"I didn't follow you here," he said.

He had to clear his throat and speak in a louder voice, to be heard over the surf.

"I didn't follow you here—I was coming here myself. This is my place. No one knows about this but me."

He stared at her, frowning. She would see that his expression was critical; she would not know the emotion he felt. His nails were pressing into the palms of his hands, there were beads of perspiration on his forehead despite the chilly wind.

"You're lonely," he said. "You're afraid. But you shouldn't be."

Her father had died several years before. It had been a sudden, unexpected death—a cerebral hemorrhage—and though Mr. Tydeman had been involved in finance and had, at one time in his life, been a fairly wealthy man, he had died not only intestate but very much in debt. Without wishing to, Duncan had overheard his mother speaking to his Aunt Irene once about a matter of several thousand dollars Tydeman had borrowed from Duncan's father secretly. Irene had insisted the debt would be repaid when the insurance was straightened out but Duncan's mother had said there was no need: magnanimously, rather bullyingly, she had said there was no need.

"Do you miss your father?" Duncan asked. "Did you love him very much?"

He squatted on his heels. A wave splashed nearby and droplets were flung onto his bare arm; they were quite cold. They stung with cold but were refreshing.

The girl stretched her young slender lovely body. He could see her delicate ribs moving beneath the deeply tanned skin. As if in defiance of him she stretched and yawned and turned away to stare at the ocean. About her the surf broke and sprayed, moisture was illuminated in the sunshine, scintillating in the milder colors of the rainbow. The lenses of his glasses were splattered; he blinked rapidly as if to clear his vision.

"I *didn't* follow you here," he said coquettishly.

After some minutes the muscles of his thighs ached and he tired of the image (for in daylight it could be sustained only by a violent effort of the imagination) and climbed to sit on one of the rocks above the beach, out of the range of the spray. Here he had certain conversations. He rehearsed certain arguments. He might be ten years old, or again twelve, or fifteen. Or eighteen. It might be one of his teachers he quarreled with (Mr. Jensen in ninth grade who had accused him—falsely, as it turned out to the ignorant fool's embarrassment—of plagiarism in an essay for English class), or his mother (when she arrived in Baltimore in March to see why he never wrote, never telephoned, never seemed to be in when she or his father called—arrived to discover that he now roomed alone and that he had stopped attending classes and ate only from a vending machine in the residence hall and was showering six or eight or ten times a day and studying already for the final examinations that would be held in early May since he was terrified of doing poorly in them and couldn't his mother please leave him be, couldn't she *understand* that he was in control, in perfect control, and must be allowed to proceed according to the strategy he had mapped out); it might be a former high school classmate or a former friend; or Mr. Gyorgy—with his iron-gray lamb's-wool hair and his enormous, swollen nose—who spent all day clipping bushes that hardly needed clipping, pushing his wheelbarrow about, fussing with his power tools, digging, hoeing, raking, pinching aphids off Mrs. Sargent's rosebushes by hand, complaining to Mrs. Sargent in his nasal self-righteous whine that something had died over the winter as he had predicted and something else had gotten out of hand and it didn't look good for the creeping zinnia she had wanted in the hanging baskets—until Duncan had to thrust his fingers in his mouth to keep from shouting at the old fool to shut up. And there was Aunt Irene, whose cheerful bustling high-spirited manner depressed him because he knew it was a lie, and his cousin Lucy, and Antoinette herself: Antoinette with the scabby knees and the habit of running her finger nervously beneath her nose as if she needed a handkerchief: Antoinette with her collarbone protruding as she sat at the dining room table in shorts and a halter, brooding over her plate. That Antoinette, the one who ran and shouted and laughed too raucously, like a young boy. He wanted to confront her in this private place and shake her hard. "Why do you make yourself ugly!" he wanted to ask in despair.

The fresh air was making him light-headed. He closed his eyes and felt her lips brush against his. They were picking blackberries as she had insisted and their bare arms were getting scratched. The sun was very hot, it was early afternoon, a cloudless sky, they were sheltered from the ocean, the sun beat down pitilessly and though he foresaw that they would both be sunburned—especially Antoinette, whose shoulders were bare—he was too lazy and too excited at the same time to say anything. Prickles, thistles, flies, mosquitoes. The incessant babble of Lucy and the little Burkhardt girl, picking a few yards away. A branch Duncan released whipped around to slap against Antoinette's face. That almost went in my eye! she said angrily. Her mouth was stained, like his. Bluish-black. Their hands were stained, their forearms, even their bare knees. The sun was hot, the odor of the blackberries was mesmerizing, he was in a stupor, he was drugged, he laughed at her distress merely to annoy her as a brother might, as an older brother might, or a lover—and she responded by jagging a sharp elbow in his ribs as a sister might, or as a childish provocative girl might—and he smelled the warm dry fragrance of her hair and shoulders and it crossed his idle mind that he could easily, so very easily, push her backward so that she lost her balance and fell onto the sandy soil, and they could grapple together like children, exactly like children, he could tickle her beneath her damp arms, he could burrow into her neck, tickling her with his tongue, making her squeal, making her pound against him with her fists. All this might happen easily and innocently enough. . . . In fact she slapped him on the back of the

neck and he turned to slap her like an outraged brother and she thrust
into his face, giggling, her fingers smeared with blood and the broken
body of a mosquito, in explanation. Don't get so *angry*, she said
mildly. I was only protecting you.

V

Difficult to believe this soft-spoken old man had once been despotic and
unpredictable, several times married and several times divorced, terrible-
tempered, unforgiving; difficult to believe, even, that in his prime he had
been a high-ranking government official. A friend of Eisenhower's, Antoinette's mother told her. (Eisenhower? The President? The one who
had had something to do with World War II?) He was rumored to have
been a passionate, obsessive sportsman, and to have tried his hand (not
very successfully) at music—piano, violin, cello. He worked hard at
everything he did and if the results were less than excellent he became
murderously angry: or so Antoinette was told. It seemed difficult to
believe since Uncle Forrest was now content to sit on the veranda, hour
after hour, gazing at the ocean.

She and Lucy were to call him Uncle Forrest though he was not really
their uncle; he was their Uncle Dwight's uncle. He was Duncan's great-
uncle—wouldn't he mind the girls appropriating the old man for themselves? ("Do I have to talk to him," Lucy said, sticking a forefinger in
her mouth. "Do I have to." And Antoinette jumped to her feet, throwing her arms about. "I'm afraid of him! He looks at me so *hard*. And
that Mr. Gyorgy with his hair like something grizzly—like some old
grizzly bear— They look at me so—" Mrs. Tydeman grabbed her by the
wrists to calm her down. To quiet her. Why was she such a *big* child,
why did her voice rise so shrilly? "All that is your imagination, Antoinette. Your imagination as usual. *You know it's your imagination.*")

Though elderly, Uncle Forrest was a big, fleshy man, with a coarse-skinned pinkish face and white eyebrows stiff as wire brushes, and sometimes when his head trembled on his neck he tried to disguise it by leaning his chin onto his fist. His back was slightly twisted, or so it seemed. His pale gray eyes were often rheumy. But Antoinette was surprised at his ability to get about once he heaved himself from his chair. He was old, he was ailing, but he was not *sickly.* And it was a relief, his behavior toward her. After the first day or two he didn't stare at her so strangely and he didn't try to draw her into a conversation—forced and awkward, about her school subjects and her plans for the future and her "boy friends" back home. Instead he smiled warmly, in silence. He smiled and did no more than thank her courteously when she brought him a glass of iced tea, or his lunch on a tray, or a bouquet of wild flowers she had thrown together haphazardly on a walk, thinking the old man might take pleasure from them.

She forgot about him during the day. Sometimes he didn't take his meals with them, so she forgot about him for hours at a time. And then, suddenly, for no reason at all, she would find herself half-dreaming of him in her bed at night. When she would rather, of course, have been thinking of Duncan. Or a boy she'd seen on the beach, the public beach. Or crossing Drum Road, barefoot, fishing gear in hand. And in town, in the drugstore, she had exchanged a look, an uncalculated look, with a boy who might have been seventeen or eighteen, as her mother was chattering away and herding her up the aisle, and she would rather have thought of *him* except his image had faded and she was powerless to call it back because it merged with other faces, other images, and they were crowding, jeering, teasing, so that her heart beat rapidly and her mind gave a snap and she was awake, utterly awake, though she'd fallen into bed an hour earlier, utterly exhausted from the sun and wind and water and all the exercise and the excitement. . . . But it was at such times, at such vulnerable times, that she often found herself thinking of the old man. ("But I must call him Uncle Forrest," she said aloud.) She saw in stark illumination his face, his startled eyes, his trembling chin. Was he close to dying, she wondered in awe and resentment. Was she a person like herself who might even be afraid of dying?

That he might be a person like herself, and not an old man who had always been old—that frightened her.

Her father had died when she'd been eleven. But it had happened suddenly. There was no warning, no time to contemplate it. When the telephone call came from that hospital in Chicago he was already in a coma, already near death: so he hadn't had to think about it ahead of time. Which was the worst, the very worst thing, Antoinette thought, her breath going shorter and shorter as it did when she was about to burst into tears. She had loved her father so much and now he was dead and there was no one to tell it to and even his image, his voice, his way of speaking to her was fading. . . . Am I close to dying, she thought. Sometimes she sat up in bed, terrified that her heart might *stop*. Why not? Couldn't it? What kept it going from one beat to the next? She would have liked to ask Uncle Forrest certain things about being very old and being near to dying, did you think about it all the time or was it something comfortable like going barefoot after a while, was it just something you lived with, wouldn't he laugh at her, wouldn't Duncan laugh if he knew, and only her mother would take her seriously but she would take her too seriously—putting her hand on her forehead, maybe, to see if she had a fever. So she had better keep quiet about it. Had better try to sleep. It was clear that no one could help her.

"Only, dear God, don't let me have to *think* about anything bad ahead of time," she whispered. "I would be such a baby and everyone would be ashamed of me. . . ."

VI

"Are you in love with Antoinette?" Duncan asked. "Are you in love with that ridiculous child?"

He regarded himself in the mirror with amusement.

Washing his hands, lathering them thoroughly, digging beneath the nails to get the invisible dirt out. And then holding them to the light for an unhurried inspection though he was already late for dinner. (His skin was getting chapped but what choice had he?—he couldn't very well sit at the dinner table with filthy hands.)

Downstairs there were loud, gay voices. His mother's. A man's. He wiped his hands fastidiously on the towel that was his and hung it neatly on the rack.

"No," he said. "You don't love anyone. As your mother has said— you're incapable of loving anyone except yourself."

Antoinette in a charming dress, pale blue cotton with embroidered butterflies in yellow. Her hair combed for once. Parted in the center of her head so that her tanned face was framed by twin falls of hair—very charming. He stared and stared. He would have smiled except his lips had gone dry and he did not want to expose his big front teeth to everyone at the table.

It was July 1 and on the evening of June 30 he had brushed against his cousin, not accidentally, during a game of croquet on the side lawn. No one was very serious about the game except Duncan; then, abruptly, he lost interest in it and fell to bickering with Antoinette and during the course of their argument he stepped forward as if he meant simply to walk into her, and she pushed him away in surprise, and he closed his fingers about her wrist. "What are you doing," she whispered. "What are *you* doing," he said. Her wrist was surprisingly small; her skin gave off a warm, moist, lemony odor; he believed he could smell, faintly, the heat of her armpits. He could even see in the fading light how her bare arm was freckled, minutely freckled, and in that instant he wanted to kiss the arm: wanted to draw his tongue crazily up and down it like a puppy desperate for affection.

Wild flowers in a cut crystal bowl on the dining room table, Antoinette's contribution: gentian, Queen Anne's lace, small iris, phlox, Turk's cap lilies. Lovely. And of course everyone admired them and praised Antoinette, who laughed, showing her teeth, half-closing her eyes seductively. It must have been the fact that she was wearing a dress and had combed her hair in a new style; it must have been the fact that Mrs. Sargent had invited guests for dinner. Duncan stared at her quite openly as if challenging her to confront *him* in this guise. But she ignored him. Her dark, bright eyes leapt restlessly about the table but avoided the space where he sat.

That child, Duncan thought. What game is she playing now. . . .

Mrs. Sargent's guests were a middle-aged couple from New York City. The man was a lawyer for a brokerage house and the woman was, like Duncan's mother, an officer in the Sky Harbor Historical Association. They were talking about the proposal a local contractor had made a few days ago to the town council for the construction of a solid-fill marina in the harbor.

"It can't be allowed to go through," Mrs. Sargent said in her throaty, urgent voice. "It would be the death of Sky Harbor."

Duncan smiled at Antoinette, who happened to glance his way.

Her lips parted in amazement. He saw that he had startled her. "Why are you smiling at *me* . . . ?" she seemed to be asking.

He had brushed against her the evening before and it hadn't been an accident. And very deliberately he had taken hold of one of her bony little wrists. Afterward she cried in a voice shrill as a gull's: "Duncan lost at croquet! Duncan lost to Lucy and me at croquet!"

He had lain awake much of the night.

The blue cotton dress fit her rather tightly across the breasts. He saw how she held herself, with what girlish self-consciousness she raised her thin shoulders as she spoke, bold and cringing at once. It was clear that everyone admired her: everyone. That Forrest Sargent might gaze at her with something very much like longing—that old Gyorgy might grin at her and try to make conversation—that strangers along the beach or in town, boys and mature men alike, might gaze after her quite frankly: it should not have been surprising.

When Duncan tried to remember the first time he had seen Antoinette his mind went empty. He simply could not remember. It must have been a number of years ago, it must have been at one of those uncomfortable family reunions at his grandfather's farm in Maryland. Little Antoinette Tydeman. Blond hair, fluffy and chaotic and very pretty. Her mother Irene slender and pale and very pretty also, prettier than Duncan's mother. (She was younger than Duncan's mother by at least five years.) But he had not cared for prettiness, he had been miserably bored, none of his cousins interested him and very few of the grown-ups interested him, he had been an impatient, insolent child, shy and demanding at the same time, quite unpopular. Too intelligent for the others, his mother had said. Was it any wonder he couldn't get along with them, couldn't play their childish games . . . ? He was simply too intelligent and they must learn to respect him, his mother said angrily.

He had been crying. Why? She had comforted him. And then his father came in the room. And there was a quarrel. Why? He could not remember. And where was Antoinette at that time? He could not remember. His mind simply blanked out, there were dismaying patches of white like blank white spaces on a map, and if he struggled to remember—as he had struggled to remember in February and March —the blank white spaces grew and threatened to merge.

When the patches of forgetfulness were most frightening Duncan had no appetite but had to eat just the same. Food was tasteless: he might as well have been eating cardboard. But he was commanded to eat just the same. (He knew without his father's advice that he must eat, for there are ways to nourish someone who has stopped eating normally —tubes in the nose, tubes in the arms, even in the legs. You cannot escape very easily.)

"Aren't you eating tonight, Duncan?" Mrs. Sargent asked.

His most civil smile, his most courteous, neutral manner. "Certainly, Mother."

He forced himself to imitate his cousin, who ate so quickly and effortlessly. And so much! Amazing, that such a slender girl should have such an appetite! His heart tripped foolishly, that he might have something to tease her about when the long meal was over and they could escape the adults' company.

VII

Their first explicit gesture of intimacy—clumsy and hurried, though strangely unembarrassed—came very late on the night of July Fourth when Duncan climbed the stairs, barefoot, bare-chested, to discover Antoinette standing in the upstairs hall in her bathrobe. Burdened by her long limp hair, her face looked narrow; her lips were thin with apprehension; for the first time in many days her skittish dark-bright gaze did not go sliding away from him. "Hey—what are you doing here?" Duncan whispered. She took a step backward. Her robe was made of a cheap but rather attractive synthetic material and there was a tiny pink satin bow at the collar, not tied but pinned with a safety pin, slightly askew.

Was he alarmed at the sight of her, or had he known she would be there, had he half-heard her silent footsteps overhead . . . ? In the dim-lit empty corridor the two of them were secret, insubstantial as shadows. It was night, it was past 3:00 A.M., the disruption of the sleeping house had the effect of throwing everything out of rhythm, off course. Antoinette, frightened, put out her hand to touch Duncan's arm. "What's happening? Who's down there?" she whispered.

"A police officer," Duncan said. "Mother called the police. Did you hear the noise out on the beach?—those firecrackers?—the shouting? Well, Mother called the police. They chased the kids away and now Mother is giving one of the officers hell in the kitchen because there weren't any arrests."

"Police . . . ?" Antoinette whispered.

"Only two officers. Evidently they didn't think Mother's call was very important."

Now they could hear Mrs. Sargent's calm furious voice. It went on and on, uninterrupted. Duncan blushed hotly, staring at his cousin's face. His mother's words were not decipherable but he knew she was accusing the police of willful negligence and dereliction of duty, of incompetence, insubordination, and insolence. She had risen from bed to make the call, she had dressed in haste, but with her usual flair for what was appropriate —a lime-green linen dress, sleeveless and casual but obviously not inexpensive; Italian sandals with a small wooden heel. She had had no time to put on stockings, of course, but the hem of the dress fell below her knee and would shield her pale, rather fleshy legs from the officers' eyes. She was a large moon-faced woman with a short, haughty, pouting upper lip, a magnificent tremulous voice, a full-throated anger. Though of less than average height she gave the impression of being tall by standing very erect with her head back. "You failed to apprehend them? Failed to take down their names? Trespassing on private property—drunkenness—lighting an unauthorized bonfire—setting off firecrackers and what sounded like bombs—and drugs, no doubt there were drugs, there were certainly marijuana cigarettes, and immoral behavior, there was certainly immoral promiscuous behavior— And you failed to apprehend them, Officer? You failed to arrest them?" She had gone very white in the face. Her nose had a pale glowing overheated passion. Not a fat woman, not even plump, but big-boned, solid, somehow quite noble: just so had she stood in Duncan's darkened room in the residence hall at Johns Hopkins, clutching her handbag, her voice throaty and urgent, at first commanding him not to fail and then pleading with him not to fail, not to disappoint his father, and then, when she could not finally elude the realization—heightened by Duncan's dull-eyed silence and his slack baby's mouth—that something was terribly wrong with her son, she had advanced to his bedside and wept desperate oversized tears upon him. And hauled him to his feet. And saved his life.

"She's very angry . . . she sounds so angry . . ." Antoinette whispered. Sleep-dazed, Duncan's cousin struck him as stark and womanly and without guile; her dark eyes were quite wide; her fingers were still touching his forearm, tentative and cool and moist. He had to stoop to hear her words, her voice had gone so soft. ". . . don't know if I heard firecrackers or not, there were so many all evening. . . . I *think* I heard shouting a while ago. Were they trespassing on your mother's beach?"

"She thinks so. Claims so. Actually they were down toward the dunes and I don't think our property extends that far."

"But she sounds so angry," Antoinette said in awe.

"Her anger takes different focuses," Duncan whispered daringly.

"Yes? What?"

"Never mind."

The woman's voice ceased, there was a murmured reply, a brief silence; the sound of a door opening.

Duncan stared at his cousin as if seeing her for the first time. They *were* secret up here, wraithlike and insubstantial, hardly more than nervous quivering waves in the night air. His skin prickled beneath her touch but it was a pleasant sensation. Suppose he stooped to kiss her as he had already kissed her in his imagination, as he had already kissed her or someone, unimpeded, unresisted? She had taken a step backward but went no farther. Her eyelids were sleepy, heavy, unresisting. He saw how long-lashed they were, he saw with astonishment how delicate the bones of her face were: had he, for weeks, for years, misjudged her? She was not a boylike child, elastic and boisterous and jeering, she was not even the long-limbed girl he had believed her, drawing a finger swiftly and surreptitiously beneath her nose, picking at a scab on her knee—she was really a young woman whom he had never taken the time to contemplate.

"She'll be coming upstairs," Antoinette whispered as if about to turn away.

"She has to turn off the lights. Lock the doors," Duncan said.

He took hold of his cousin's shoulders. It was easily done: his hands did it by their own instinct.

"I'm sorry you were frightened," he said.

"I'm not frightened," she said.

Her lower jaw shook as if her teeth were about to chatter.

"Were you asleep?" he whispered.

"No. Yes. I think so."

"You were so exhausted when you went to bed. . . ."

His eyes brimmed suddenly with tears. That he should discover her so delicate, so pretty: so much his own: and yet a nighttime secret no one else would ever know. His blood surged, pulse upon pulse, in waves of clarity. The disruption of the night and of the others' sleep (for he himself had been studying physics in his room, in his undershorts, taking methodical notes in his notebook) had thrown everything off course, off rhythm, so that a new rhythm arose, an exquisite new rhythm arose, pulsing with extraordinary clarity along his veins. He was in command and he knew. His instincts knew. Smelling his cousin's lemony hair, smelling her warm, alarmed body, holding her dark shifty gaze firmly with his own, he knew that he had been assailed by one of his own dreams: and out of the secrecy of a dream the girl had come forth to claim him.

It was not Duncan but a shadow-self who tightened his grip on her shoulders and, unhesitating, supremely unembarrassed, bent to press his warm dry lips lightly upon hers.

Quick, weightless, graceful as a butterfly's movement: and done.

VIII

Duncan and Antoinette and Lucy helped Mr. Gyorgy clean the beach —it was a full hour's work of raking and picking up debris, and the sun was very hot. Smashed beer bottles, crumpled paper bags, half-eaten hotdogs; charcoal, charred wood, and ashes; and even, a few yards higher, in the dune grass, a clot of human excrement which Duncan hid before anyone could see, raking piles of coarse sand over it.

"Pigs. Sons of bitches," Duncan whispered.

His upper lip was sweaty, his back and leg muscles ached (for he was not very accustomed to work of this sort), his forehead furrowed with a patrician contempt, yet he did not really feel angry: his eyes followed Antoinette as she worked with a rake and he felt quite good.

"Was life so simple, so clear, all along?" he wondered.

The Gyorgys lived a half-mile away, inland, along a narrow dirt lane overgrown with scrub bushes. Their shanty seemed to be in a kind of marsh; their front walk was a series of mismatched planks set permanently in mud. They must have been in their late sixties. Mr. Gyorgy had worked for the Sargents for many years, and for one or two other summer residents though he never alluded to them as if, slyly, cagily, he believed the Sargents thought him faithful only to *them;* it was said of him by Mrs. Sargent that he was incorruptible. Which meant, Duncan supposed, that he had not troubled to ask for an increase in his salary in recent years. This morning he appeared to be working with less industry than usual. His leathery face seemed morose; his working cap, soiled and misshapen, was pulled down onto his forehead at an uncomfortable angle. Over the surf they could hear him muttering to himself. *He* was angry, as angry as Mrs. Sargent. Duncan exchanged a look with Antoinette behind his back—an acknowledgment of their kinship and their curious complicity.

She did not giggle as she might have, a day earlier. Her response was a quick furtive smile, a lowering of her eyelids. The week before Antoinette had spoken fancifully of Mr. Gyorgy as one of those old men, those old goats, who lure children into their shacks or out into the dunes, *she* knew the sort, *she* couldn't be fooled, and Duncan had been inexplicably outraged by her performance: it was theatrical, it was blatantly insincere, she must have been imitating someone she knew or a popular entertainer who spun out droll, partly ribald "stories" meant to amuse and disturb. It outraged him, too, that his cousin could awaken in him such childish responses. Not only did he begin bickering with her as a child might—"Mr. Gyorgy isn't like that, you're being ridiculous" he would say, and she would say at once, "He *is,* you don't know, with your nose in a book all the time how would you know," and he would say, "Just shut up before anyone hears," and she would say, "I'm not afraid of anyone hearing: I'll accuse the old goat to his very face!" and he would say, "Antoinette, I never want to hear you say that again," and his entire body would tremble with the desire to slap the girl's silly sullen face—

not only did he feel such violent, humiliating emotions, but he carried them about with him for hours afterward, his heart still pounding, exactly like a child who has been bested in a squabble and plots revenge. What shame he felt, what self-loathing, to be reduced to a bickering child by his cousin, by the Tydeman girl whose father left the family so impoverished, a burden on his own—! He stalked away, infuriated by her laughter. But now, this morning, she did no more than accept his own somewhat mocking look, and continued with her energetic raking as if she were a very good girl and wanted to please Mr. Gyorgy. Duncan saw with pleasure that she was carrying herself, in his presence, with a touching, demure stateliness, an almost maidenly restraint.

Duncan helped Mr. Gyorgy carry the trash can up from the beach. The old man was complaining about worthless young people who lived on the island all year round, who did no work, who wouldn't listen to their parents and defied even the police, did Duncan know that there were some serious things going on, a filling-station robbery back in April and the attendant beaten so badly he was unconscious for a week, drunken driving, vandalism at the high school, garbage dumped in the harbor, a twenty-year-old woman assaulted by three or four young men she'd met at a tavern and unwisely joined for a ride over to Southwest Point—and though there were arrests made and even a conviction or two the trouble just kept increasing year after year.

"Is that so," Duncan said politely.

"It's come to be like the mainland, almost," the old man said with a sour twist of his lips.

Though he had been only half-listening to Mr. Gyorgy, Duncan wasn't surprised when, the next evening, he heard a car speeding along the road, heard its brakes squeal, heard something—rocks, bottles?—thrown against the house.

And the next night, when everyone was in bed, a firecracker was tossed onto the roof and exploded in the gutter outside poor terrified Aunt Irene's room.

Mrs. Sargent called the police again, and again the police drove out. "I want this stopped," she said. "I want arrests. I want justice done for once and lawbreakers not protected—do you realize Forrest Sargent is staying with us, do you realize he's an elderly man and all this excitement might kill him? Will it be necessary for me to appeal to the governor of the state?"

The police were fairly certain that they knew who was involved but unless there were witnesses—

"You can't mean that you'd leave us unprotected," Mrs. Sargent said.

So a guard was posted for Drum Road and the assaults stopped. And when the guard was lifted after a week there was one more foray—this time a half-dozen plastic bags filled with garbage were opened on the Sargents' veranda and front lawn.

"They're just pigs. They're simply animals," Mrs. Sargent said. Duncan noted a peculiar thrill to his mother's voice as if, at the age of forty-five, she had come to a profound realization of some kind, a realization that might be liberating if she could only absorb it fully. "It would be pointless, wouldn't it, to attempt to reason with . . . to attempt to care for . . ."

"Yes," Duncan said. "I suppose so."

This time Mrs. Sargent hired a clean-up crew from town so that Mr. Gyorgy would be spared, and Duncan and the girls and Uncle Forrest and Mrs. Sargent and Mrs. Tydeman drove out to the Lighthouse Inn for brunch. It was a fine, clear, sunny day and Duncan, seated beside Antoinette, felt supremely happy. He brushed his arm against hers; he felt the hairs of their arms meet; it gave him an abrupt, unreasonable joy that she did not move her arm away immediately or nudge him aside as she might once have done. He supposed he did love her. A part of him loved her, a night-self that acted boldly and without shame, even with a sort of prankish good humor. Did she know? Could she guess? They looked at each other and their faces went hot and they found it very difficult to attend to the adults' angry conversation.

"As for the girls," Duncan's mother said, "Antoinette especially—I halfway wonder if they're going to be safe on this island."

IX

On July 12 it began raining shortly after dawn and continued raining all day. By midafternoon Antoinette had dragged herself into her mother's room and lay, in jeans and a gunmetal-gray sweatshirt from the Hanover School, across her mother's bed. She let her head hang over the edge of the bed, fascinated at the way her hair spilled in unpredictable little coils and waves and columns against the hardwood floor. But blood ran into her cheeks and pressed against her eyeballs from the inside and frightened her.

She sat up quickly as if remembering something.

"Honey, don't get the spread dirty with your feet," her mother said in a vague querulous voice.

"My feet aren't even on the bed. They aren't even dirty."

"Lillian said something about the towels in the bathroom—"

"What did she say? That was Lucy."

"She didn't exactly say anything."

"Which bathroom was it?"

"Downstairs."

"That could be anybody," Antoinette said, protesting. "It could be one of her guests."

Irene was turning the pages of the *Financial Post,* a cigarette in her fingers. The polish on one of her nails had begun to chip; the sight of it, the tiny flash of white, went through Antoinette like a knife blade. And why did her mother squint like that, biting her lower lip as if she were calculating something beyond her ability. . . . "It was probably Lucy," Antoinette said. "It might have been Duncan."

"Just be sure your neck is clean," Irene said, distracted. "My sister notices things like that."

"Oh, the hell with her," Antoinette said.

Startled, her mother looked at her. Rain drummed on the roof, the heat wave had broken, why did it smell so stuffy in this room. . . . Antoinette shook her hair out of her face, rolling over heavily onto her back. She expected Irene to scold her but instead she began complaining, as if thinking aloud, about the difficulty with the house in White

141

Plains: the market was bad, there were no buyers, the only buyer in recent months was that manufacturers' representative who had sounded so enthusiastic and optimistic but who had been turned down for a $50,000 mortgage and had consequently backed out of the deal. . . .

"Is life just money? Is that all it is?" Antoinette said.

She sat up, feeling suddenly weak. The blood rushing to her head like that: beating behind her eyes: ugly. Very ugly.

". . . see our way clear for another six months or so," Irene said slowly. "Then there are those bonds, I'm waiting to cash them in until . . . what was it, the first of the year . . . or the first of March. . . ."

Irene, like her sister Lillian, had attended Briarcliff College; she had left in her sophomore year, to marry. It seemed like a very long time ago. She had taken courses in the great world religions and in conversational Spanish, the easiest of the language courses. She had taken a course in algebra but had withdrawn before the first exam. Now she removed her glasses and rubbed the chafed spots on the bridge of her nose and her daughter, pained by her uncharacteristic weariness, did not know whether to be contemptuous or moved.

"Is it still raining?" Irene asked, blinking toward the window.

"What do you think of Duncan," Antoinette said.

"What do I think of Duncan? A brilliant boy."

"But do you like him?"

"I'm not sure he wants to be liked."

"Do you think that's true?" Antoinette said. And then, before her mother could reply, "You just resent him, he's always contradicting you."

"Is he? I don't notice. Whenever I try to talk with him I feel him wanting to escape. . . . He's too intelligent, I suppose. A very complex young man."

"Do you think anyone likes him? Do you think he has any friends?"

"Of course he has friends."

"Where? Not here."

"Back in Georgetown, I suppose. What does it matter to you?"

Duncan had driven through the rain into Sky Harbor after lunch that day and he had not invited her to come with him. The day before, when Mrs. Sargent had asked her for the fifth time whether she wanted to come along swimming at the Reiners' pool down the road, and Antoinette had blushed in embarrassment, shaking her head, she glanced at her cousin's face and had seen, had known, that he understood why she wasn't eager as always to go swimming: and she wondered if he was disgusted. Today the bleeding had just about stopped, today she might very well have been able to go swimming, but it was raining and Duncan was gone without troubling to say goodbye and she had nothing to do and certain vexing thoughts slid in and out of her head with the sinister grace of her mother's cigarette smoke: why had he kissed her only once since that night, why did he seem friendly enough but guarded even when they were alone, did he think she was ugly, did he think she was stupid. . . . He must believe her quite stupid: he had asked her to promise not to mention the kiss to anyone. As if, she thought, there was anyone to whom she might mention it.

He had kissed her on the evening of July 6, down on the beach. With more force than the first time, but with an air of hurry and embarrassment. And then Lucy had come running down and he'd stepped adroitly away. . . .

"What happened to him at college," Antoinette asked.

"Evidently he exhausted himself from overwork and this roommate of his he was tutoring. It's really none of your business, dear."

"Is he going to be a doctor like Uncle Dwight?"

"I think so. I don't know."

"But will they let him back?"

"Lillian says he was allowed to withdraw and he'll take the semester over. The poor boy was quite badly sick, you know. He'd stopped eating, he couldn't go to classes, he was very weak and had lost weight—so Lillian made an arrangement with the dean and he'll be allowed to take his courses over again. But it isn't any of your business, Antoinette. I don't want you gossiping about . . ."

"But he *is* strange," Antoinette said, staring at her toes.

"He's polite and thoughtful. He isn't like other boys his age, that's true—he's more reserved, more mature. He always has been. . . . In what way is he strange, Antoinette?"

Antoinette shrugged her shoulders indifferently.

"The two of you seem to get along well enough. Better than you did before."

". . . How sick was he, exactly? I don't like weak men."

"What an odd thing to say," her mother said sharply.

"Well, I don't."

"But why—?"

"You know why, Mother," Antoinette said coldly.

Irene laid the *Financial Post* down and got to her feet and turned to leave. She wore an attractive outfit—white slacks and a matching jersey blouse—but it looked wrinkled and even soiled in the dreary light.

"Your father was not weak," she said at the door.

"Oh shit."

The words came out in a mumble but they were loud enough for Irene to hear as she left the room.

"Why did you walk out and leave me *here*—this is your room, not mine—" Antoinette cried.

She sprang to her feet. Frightened, she chose to exaggerate her fear. She stood with her arms raised and her fists caught in her hair as if she might tear it from her head. Turning slowly at the waist she could see in a dressing table mirror her narrow, rather flat torso, lean and sexless in the unbecoming gray shirt as a young boy's.

"I don't love you. Or him. Or anyone."

Her voice was unconvincing. She was seized with a near-paroxysm of loathing. Why did it rain, rain, rain, why was she trapped here in the house, why did they box her in with their names for her and their love. . . . Her cousin had taken her by the shoulders and bent to kiss her and she had been too startled to resist. And she foresaw that it would happen again, and again. And that she would not tell anyone. Until, perhaps, he revealed his secret: that secret weakness she detested.

At that moment her small tanned face acquired a look of concentrated pleasure, almost of rapture. Her eyes narrowed involuntarily; her lips curled upward; she seemed little by little to be passing over into something purely abstract, a radiant beauty without consciousness. What did it matter, her glaring face seemed to argue, what did anything matter except such a defiant self-determining existence . . . ? As if in a trance the girl walked to the window and opened it as far as she could and pressed herself forward, against the screen, her cheek against the screen, breathing deeply, almost convulsively. She was not thinking of her father's death, she was not thinking of her mother, or of her cousin whom she loved or wished to love or played at loving—she was thinking of nothing at all save her own being, her own desperate assertion. From the ground, from the wet grass, glimpsed through the slanted silver-gray sheets of rain, her tiny face might have had the power to assemble everything else about it: the expanse of shingleboard, the glistening roof, the slender leafy trees, the invisible sky.

X

Wave motion is not a mechanical phenomenon because a wave is not a material object, but a form. It cannot be assigned a mass. . . . The motion of a wave is vastly different from that undergone by the medium in which it travels; consequently we can have a wave without any movement of matter at all. . . . A wave is a pattern, a form that moves.

Again and again he repeated these simple words to himself. Though transcribed in his notebook, in his meticulous hand, they somehow eluded him: they drifted out of the lighted arena of his consciousness.

A wave is not . . . A wave cannot be assigned . . . We can have a wave without any movement. . . .

His intellect greedily seized upon these words and mastered them. But he did not understand them at all. He did not feel their truth, their inevitability. And he rather doubted that anyone did: those classmates who, like himself, had scored in the upper nineties in preparatory school, his teachers in that school or at the university itself, his own father.

Wasn't it a formality, an empty ritual, the convention of certain "truths" which must be shared. . . .

A giant moth slapped against the screen. Tiny gnats crawled about the peach-colored globe of his lamp, a converted kerosene lamp that must have been an antique. His mother had discovered it years ago at a barn sale south of Bangor. He adjusted his glasses and contemplated the insects. Drawn to light, to warmth. Blindly yet sensibly. Did anything else matter, he wondered. He flicked one of the gnats away with the tip of his pen and did not even feel his customary distaste when the insect blundered against his bare arm.

That evening at dinner he had stared without smiling at the silky tangle of his cousin's hair. And at her dark, animated face. Her lips moved too often and too readily, stretching into smiles, into wide guileless grins, but they were a lovely mulberry shade: he felt them brush against his own lips, he felt a sudden terrible need to press his mouth against them and still them. She said such exasperating things . . . ! He too laughed, like the others he laughed, though he resented her cheapening of herself. ("Why, you're becoming quite witty," Duncan's mother

145

said to Antoinette, half-praising, half-criticizing. "We'll all have to be careful of you, won't we?—otherwise we'll wind up parodied.")

After the garbage had been strewn on the Sargents' veranda and lawn there was no more trouble, but in Sky Harbor the other day a car driven by a long-haired young man in his early twenties braked to a stop near Antoinette and Duncan, who were just coming from the post office, and the driver shouted something, and a shirtless young man in the passenger's seat made an obscene gesture—and in that instant, while Duncan was too startled to comprehend the situation, Antoinette jumped from the walk to pound on the car's hood and stick out her tongue. There was an exchange of shouts, Antoinette cried "Go to hell!" and the young men drove off. All this had taken place within a few seconds, and in full view of Mrs. Sargent, who was waiting for Duncan and Antoinette in her own car parked at a curb across the street. "How could you . . . ? How could you actually *speak* to them," Mrs. Sargent said afterward. "They're simply animals. . . ." Antoinette said brightly that she wasn't afraid: why should she be afraid? Duncan and his mother exchanged a glance. He understood, bitterly, that his mother thought Antoinette common, and silly, and ignorant; and the girl hadn't any awareness of her aunt's disapproval but rather imagined herself daring, a sort of heroine. She even giggled at Duncan's obvious discomfort. "Why should I be afraid of them, I'm not afraid of anyone anymore," she said boastfully.

Kissing her, holding her in his arms, he silenced her and transformed her. Her spirit became pliant at once. Almost austere, abstract. And he too, pressing himself against her, took on an identity that was not altogether familiar to him.

. . . *a pattern, a form that moves.*

The words danced away. He felt the flickerings of panic he had felt in late winter, staring at the overcast featureless sky that, immobile as it was, seemed already to contain his future, his fate. Was it possible that Duncan Sargent, who had been valedictorian of his senior class and who had received four As and one B+ and one C (in physical education) his first semester at Johns Hopkins, had reached the peak of his intellectual life and would now descend, descend, from the day of his nineteenth birthday onward would he simply and helplessly descend into the commonplace, the average, the ordinary, the unexceptional. . . . With his prim, constrained manner and his prematurely furrowed forehead he had not expected to attract young women, nor did he much regret their absence in his life. He overheard his parents discussing, from time to time, the children of their friends who had blundered into disastrous follies—pregnancies that resulted in abortions, love affairs that resulted in venereal disease, squalid sequences of drug-taking, alcoholism, criminal activity—and he sensed his parents' relief that he spent so much time in his own room there on the third floor of the house, utterly absorbed in his studies. He did not care for music. He certainly did not care for television, which he had rejected at the age of six. The fact that his classmates liked television so much and, as they grew older, popular music, seemed to confirm in Duncan's mind the essential vulgarity and pointlessness of these diversions. Whatever the crowd clamors for, he thought with disdain, I will reject.

"Your son is an exceptional young man, he will have a brilliant career. . . ."

"Duncan? Why, I hope you know that he's the outstanding student in my class this year. . . . He's far too modest to tell you himself."

"There's no finer premed program than the one at Johns Hopkins, and since you'd like Duncan to live fairly close to home . . ."

He heard the voices, unmoved. They droned about his head for a while and then faded. A small moth had crawled between the pages of his textbook: he closed the book: squashed the creature. Did it matter, why did it matter, what could possibly matter. . . . If he was not a genius, why then he was nothing. Simple as that. Pudgy, unattractive, nearsighted, cowardly. In his underwear, sitting at the old, handsome desk that had once belonged to his grandfather and had been moved up to his room, he had the look of a mourner, a baffled and heavy-spirited mourner. A roll of pale flesh fell outside the band of his shorts; he pinched it, at first with an abstract disgust, then with some force. And his thighs were fat. Waddled like his mother's—like the lardish-pale quivering flesh of middle-aged women who, not guessing at the contempt of others, of others younger than themselves, strolled along the beach or the streets of Sky Harbor in short dresses or even in shorts or even—horrible to see!—in bathing suits. Duncan saw again the jeering dark-tanned faces of the young men in the car. If he chose he could bring the image back with perfect, merciless clarity: their straggly hair, their eyes, their mouths, their coarse, absolutely self-confident masculinity, their raw young mocking voices. They saw *him*, they saw and knew *him*. They knew him perfectly. If Duncan Sargent was not a genius, why then he was nothing. His thighs waddled like a woman's, that tiny babyish double chin, his small eyes set too close together in his round, stern face. . . .

Perhaps it had been merciful, he thought, and not for the first time, that in his illness he had begun to forget so much. Great vast patches of blank space, like enormous canvases . . . a map the size of a room, dotted with territories that were yet unexplored and consequently dangerous. . . .

He let the heavy book fall from his hand, and with uncharacteristic grace he got to his feet. Barefoot, he was weightless; even the old floorboards did not squeak as he passed out into the hall. It was night, very late. His special time. Like a man certain of his destination because he has gone this way many times before, and because he has always been welcomed, Duncan went to the far end of the corridor to his cousin's room and opened the door. It always surprised him, when he peeked in this room during the day, when no one was around, that the ceiling should slant so strangely and that the room should be so disappointingly small. But she was the daughter of a bankrupt man, after all. And her mother—well, the mother! Untrained, self-pitying, casting about (so Duncan's mother said and who should know better) for another husband to support her. . . . The girls were darling, of course, especially little Lucy, but Irene made one blunder after another in her investments and before long the family would be forced to withdraw their support and then what would she do, what would she do. . . . Duncan stared at his sleeping cousin, who lay on her side, perfectly still. Her hair was a tangle as always. Her face looked unusually pale. The nights were cold and so she slept beneath a woollen blanket, but it had ridden down, past her breasts, and Duncan supposed he should draw it up to her chin. Was she a child, a mere girl, was she helpless as she appeared to be, motionless in sleep, submissive beneath his wondering gaze . . . ? He stooped to pull the cover up. His fingers brushed against her breast.

He bent over her as if weightless. He cradled her head in his arms. She was awake: her bare arms slipped about his neck. He dreaded her crying out *O Duncan what are you doing here, what kind of a game is this* but instead she said nothing, she said nothing, not even his name.

XI

In his presence she found it difficult to keep her rapt worshipful gaze from him. That he was slow-speaking, that his expression was frequently critical and even censorious, that he sometimes glared at her through his gold-rimmed glasses as if in actual dislike—none of this rebuffed her. She loved him, she carried the knowledge of her love for him everywhere. Her mirror image shared her secret and she must have gazed at herself fifty times in a single day, as if seeking confirmation of her love.

He took care not to speak to her intimately, or at great length, when the others were around. They never touched. Never sat beside each other. There were times when she took from him a sense of their brilliant daring and a kind of hilarity, a reckless hilarity, flooded her: she could not control her laughter, as if she were intoxicated. Staring at her Duncan would blush, his lips parted. He broke off in the middle of a sentence and could not think how to conclude.

She studied her mirror image with care and knew that she was pretty. She was very pretty. . . . And then again she saw with a sickening dismay that she was not pretty at all: she was quite plain, even homely. Yellow did not become her skin tone, why had she so many yellow things, what could she have been thinking of. . . . Her hair was drying out from swimming and from the sun. . . . Her legs were not very attractive, the calves seemed to her rather muscular. There were tiny blemishes on her forehead that must be covered by swipes of hair. And while it was necessary that she minimize her height—for what if she grew to be taller than Duncan, and his intermittent interest in her faded—she could not possibly allow herself to become round-shouldered like other girls her age, for there was nothing so ugly. Duncan, with his perfect, effortless posture, would be revulsed.

"Does he love me?" she said aloud. "Does he think about me. . . . What does he think about me . . . ?"

It was a riddle so perplexing, so exhilarating, that she sometimes burst into laughter even when she was alone. And sometimes into tears. And sometimes she discovered herself scratching so hard at a spot on her leg or thigh that she broke the surface of the skin and got blood on her nails.

In her bed she invented dreams to encompass him, her vision jerked about clearly and cunningly beneath her closed lids, her lips twitched with the involuntary mimicry of speech. At meals, even when he was present, she sometimes continued her dream . . . which might run on and on for hours, undisturbed by others' voices, others' demands upon her. . . . She had only to acknowledge these strange shadowy shapes and to appear to acquiesce to them and the sanctity of the dream remained inviolate. (There were times when, oddly, Duncan himself intruded and came to seem a clumsy, blundering stranger—as when he joined Lucy and Antoinette in a game of Chinese checkers, and did not resist teasing Lucy about one thing or another as if his instinct urged him, gracelessly, to play at being an older brother.) It was out in the dunes that she dreamt most lavishly and shamelessly of him, however, since there was something about the loneliness of the place and the irregular mounds of glinting sand and the ceaseless, ceaseless wind that expressed her own emotion, her own inchoate passion. Apart from a few scrub trees and rugosa roses and dune grass, and some shards of glass, and crumpled papers, the dunes were absolutely empty. She could speak aloud here if she wished. She could wander for as long as she could bear the sun, which appeared to be magnified, glinting from an incalculable number of angles, like a fierce all-knowing consciousness. Was it lovely here or was it monstrous, she wondered. Even with sunglasses she blinked continually at the glare. Winds that blew forever from the ocean, trickles of sand that were forever moving, shaping and reshaping the contours of the land . . . sand that drifted like snow but unlike snow would never melt, would never disappear. . . . A vast wilderness like a graveyard, dazzling. Intoxicating. She brushed away the stinging black flies and wandered in the intense heat, seeing in her mind's eye Duncan at her back, some distance away, observing her. Despite the sunshine the dunes struck her as melancholy and her own figure, moving gracefully among them, was a melancholy one. Duncan pitied her because her father had died. It was right for him to pity her, to want to comfort her. Perhaps someday he would come to her room when the others were asleep and, hearing her sobbing, would lean over her and ask what was wrong, what was wrong, what was wrong. . . .

But one day near dusk she wandered into the dunes and like a fool came upon a boy and girl lying on a blanket a few feet from a parked Honda. Though she turned away at once she could see that they were both naked from the waist down and that the boy's buttocks were an astonishing creamy white, in contrast to his tanned back and legs. Her eyes brimmed with tears of shame; she turned and ran out to the beach, stumbling in the sand. How ugly it was, how ugly they looked, was that the girl's arm outflung like that or the boy's, how old were they, had they done it many times before, was it perhaps the first time, was the girl in pain, or was she an older woman, had they noticed Antoinette, were they angry because she had seen them or were they laughing together at her distress, was it all a joke of some kind, was it a nasty joke or was it something very serious. . . .

"Why are you so quiet tonight," her mother asked later, "what are you thinking about?"

"That's my business, isn't it," she said.

XII

Despite his hope that he would remain gentle and kindly and a little detached, he could not control the remarkable beating of his heart as he kissed her. Ah, what was happening! It almost frightened him. And she too was frightened, sitting erect and frozen in his embrace.

Her lips were cool, her fingers quite cold. But it was a revelation, the soft resilient fleshiness of her mouth. Her mute acquiescence, her pale trembling eyelids, the warm fragrance of her skin: all, all were revelations.

What did he whisper to her? Did she hear?

He should stop. But he did not. He could not seem to draw away from her but continued to kiss her eagerly and hungrily, with no sense of caution. If someone should turn the corner and drive up behind them, if a stranger's headlights suddenly flashed into their car. . . .

Her face was like a flower held between his uncertain hands and it seemed to him the most enigmatic thing he had ever seen. What was she thinking, did she love him, did she sense his vulnerability, his obscure sense of shame, his sudden drunken elation. . . . He found himself gripping her tight as if he feared she might escape him. But she was pliant, she was shyly eager, and her thin arms even slid about his neck. As she moved to raise her arms Duncan smelled a faint warm scent, rather like the sea, briny and acrid, and his elation threatened to spill over into laughter; he was so suddenly, so inexplicably happy.

The easiness of their affection startled him. And the gracefulness. He had feared he would offend her, or upset her, stopping in this lonely place; he had feared she might shove him away—might knock his glasses askew on his nose, rendering him a morose comic figure. But she was sweetly submissive, she was utterly silent, pressing forward now to kiss him in return.

Some years ago Duncan had been seized by a giant wave while swimming in the surf not far from where he and Antoinette were now parked. The undertow had sucked him down with such precision, such clinical abruptness, that he had half-thought—despite his precocious intelligence—that it must be deliberate. His flailing arms and legs, his writhing body, his gaping staring astonished being: suddenly of no consequence whatsoever, sucked weightless, soulless, into the eerily cold deeper waters, insignificant as an insect's husk. There must have been tons of water crashing about him. Not liquid but solid: brutally solid: and fired with a sort of instinct or possibly even an intelligence that wished simply to devour him. Somehow he had been rescued. Pulled to shallow water. Half-carried to the beach. A stranger, an older boy, had saved him. But he had felt at the time that his life was so precarious, so fragile, how would he survive . . . how could he escape. . . . It was more than alarming, it was stupefying, the realization that he could so slenderly control his life; he had thought it best to put the memory out of his mind. And to avoid swimming in such waters.

Now, as he kissed Antoinette, the memory returned suddenly. But it was transformed: a rising mist, a gentle cloud, an awareness that he was being carried out of himself in this girl's arms and that he must not resist. He seemed to be swimming. The two of them were swimming together. They were short-breathed, they were agitated, but close to euphoric. Not simply the embrace and the willful passionate kisses but the very circumstances of their alliance pleased them.

They paused to whisper together, like guilty children.

The time? How late? And was anyone waiting up for them. . . .

Antoinette had been invited to a birthday party for a girl in town whose mother was a friend of Mrs. Sargent's, and Duncan had driven her to the party and picked her up afterward. It was now nearly midnight and in another minute he must drive on home but he found it difficult to draw back from Antoinette. She was so unexpectedly sweet, so sweetly submissive! His mother was mistaken about her: she wasn't common or vulgar: she wasn't at all stupid. When he had seen her in the Henleys' living room just now her beauty had pierced him like a knife blade, he had been absurdly proud that she was his cousin and that he was to drive her home, it did not matter in the slightest that she was only fourteen years old and that her family was so poor. . . . He bent to kiss her again. He held her face in his hands, knowing himself master of her feelings, her capricious whimsical emotions. Did he love her, did he want her, could she keep his secret. . . .

Duncan's blood pulsed with a strange keen euphoria. He was certain of something but he did not know what. The girl's arms, tightening about his neck, were a sign of his new luck, his promise. Ah, it was difficult to bring the moment to an end! Like struggling to awake from a dream that holds such intense mesmerizing pleasure that it is disturbing to one's consciousness. . . .

But Antoinette must be exhausted. It was late, she had gone swimming early that morning, before breakfast, and had been in and out of the house all day; he must get her home. He smoothed her hair back from her forehead, he kissed her eyelids, her nose, as if he had been her lover for many months, and the lie—or was it a lie—seemed utterly plausible.

He was certain that his mother would wait up. And possibly Antoinette's mother as well.

He paced about his room, lightly striking his hands together. He was giddy, he was euphoric, his heart continued to pound with joy, he could not quite believe what had happened: yet he knew very well that it had happened and would happen again.

Antoinette hiding her warm flushed face in his neck and whispering to him. . . .

His bold squeezing of her hand just before they stepped into the house. . . .

At his desk he opened one of his notebooks and wrote for several minutes, his lower lip caught in his teeth. *A premise: that life is abso-*

lutely and incontestably simple. And that its celebrated difficulties are illusions, obstacles set in the paths of fools.

He reread what he had written, with satisfaction. Then he crossed out the word *fools* and wrote in its place *the innocent.*

Part of his sickness earlier that year had been his fear that other people would discover the truth about him. His unclean habits, his soiled clothing, his dirty body, his secret thoughts. That he was ungainly and pompous and ugly everyone must know, and his attempts to disguise himself must have been amusing. Why should I feed myself, why should I live, I see no point to it, I've failed and I deserve to fail and my life is over. . . . There were times when he disliked his mother very much and he feared she would guess. There were times when it seemed to him incredible that she should not guess. And that she should not know (and tell his father) every humiliating secret about him: the near-invisible dirt that lodged most stubbornly between his fingers and toes, and on his neck, and on his groin; the vicious thoughts that sometimes careened crazily through his head, like maddened birds.

But all that had been his sickness and it was now behind him.

Since April he had been getting steadily well.

And now it was the end of July, and his appetite had returned, and his ability to concentrate for hours on his work. And his ability to sleep a normal restful sleep. He got along so well with the girls, his mother praised him for it, it was a pleasant surprise after her worries—for he could be abrupt and sarcastic, and Irene's chatter would irritate anyone. How patient he was with Lucy, who was adorable but sometimes bad-tempered, and how generous and kindly he was with Antoinette, who must bore him—! Mrs. Sargent made it a point when she wrote to his father or talked to him on the phone to speak of Duncan's superb good manners with their houseguests and his marvelous *improvement.*

He got slowly to his feet, smiling. It was so simple. What was so simple? The girl's brown blond-streaked hair that fell nearly to her waist. Her dark restless eyes, her breathy laughter, her lips. It was simple, he loved her, he would never need to punish himself again, all that had been part of his sickness and it was now behind him.

He would be in perfect control of both their lives, and from now on he would see the world with the altered vision of an adult, a man. The sick, shameful weakness of a prolonged boyhood was over: he woke from it as from a feverish dream.

Two

From somewhere she had acquired a necklace of amber and carved wooden beads, and it hung down heavily between her breasts when she wore her Indian blouse of white muslin. "Where did you get that, Antoinette?" her mother asked. Antoinette lifted the necklace from her and contemplated it critically, as if she could not quite remember. "I think I bought it somewhere in the village," she said slowly. "The drugstore, maybe. The five-and-ten."

She wore her faded cut-off jeans less often now; it pleased her mother to see her in one or the other of her skirts. But Mrs. Tydeman disliked the Indian blouse because it was cheap and because the material was too thin. On the beach at midday she stared at her daughter's shadowy swaying breasts and wondered that everyone did not stare. The girl's two-piece bathing suit seemed somehow less indecent. In the little halter top Antoinette's breasts looked no larger than a child's fists, and her collarbone was painfully prominent.

"Antoinette is really a very charming girl, a very pretty girl," Lillian said, as if the point had been contested.

"She can be. When she wants to."

"Do you remember when you were that age?"

Irene flicked her cigarette ashes onto the sand. She frowned at Antoinette, who was going to rush past them and into the house with only a mumbled greeting. Behind her was Duncan, carrying a basket. He had grown tan: his hair was even bleached slightly by the sun. But he had clipped a pair of sunglasses over his regular glasses and the effect was distracting.

"No, I really don't. Do you?"

"I was going to say yes but really . . . really I don't. . . . No. I don't."

"Anyway their lives are different from ours," Irene said.

Antoinette flashed her rowdy impertinent grin and bounded into the house. Duncan, panting a little, set a basket of blueberries near his mother's feet. A droplet of perspiration ran off his short, snubbed nose.

"Blueberries!" Lillian said. "Wild ones, aren't they?"

"They seemed to be growing wild, yes," Duncan said.

"Where did you get them, dear . . . ?"

"Down the road."

"Down the road where?"

"They were growing wild, they don't belong to anyone."

"It was very considerate of you and Antoinette to pick them, and so many of them. . . . I suppose they *do* belong to someone even if you think they were growing wild. But it doesn't matter."

She picked up a small handful and considered them closely. Their bright, slightly frosted surface mimicked her frosted nail polish. She rolled them on the palm of her plump hand and bent to bring them to her mouth, frowning.

Duncan was smiling mechanically at his mother. He stood with his arms akimbo, his weight on one foot. The dark green snap-on lenses gave him a remote, rather censorious appearance. He was almost an attractive young man, Irene thought; but she did not like him. She had never liked him. When his gaze shifted to her she felt the familiar force of his disinterest; the boy's mind was elsewhere, he was only forcing himself to be polite, digging his heels into the packed sand and waiting for his mother to release him. In the past few weeks it had come to seem to Irene that Duncan behaved differently toward them all, even toward her sister. He was courteous as always and, as always, his courtesy was qualified by a certain elegant contempt. But he seemed somehow younger, more boyish; more vulnerable. The other evening when the telephone rang just after dinner and Lillian murmured aloud—mistakenly, as it turned out—that the call must be from her husband, Duncan's head had jerked up and he had looked for a moment both hopeful and intimidated. But the call was only from a friend on the island, and Duncan had turned away without a word.

"I'm sure, Mother, that it *doesn't* matter," Duncan was saying coldly.

A big woman, Lillian was careful to eat with impeccable manners; yet with a certain deliberate, critical refinement, as if it were her duty, and as if it were her duty to comment on the quality of what she ate. "These blueberries are a little sour. Do you want to take them in to Mrs. May, dear?"

"What do you want done with them?"

"That's up to you. Ask Antoinette."

"I mean—do you want Mrs. May to fix some sort of dessert, or jelly, or—"

"Ask Antoinette," Lillian said, wiping her hands carefully on a tissue. "If you haven't already asked her."

"She likes anything at all," Irene said. "Pie, tarts, stewed blueberries . . . blueberries with cream. . . . Anything at all."

Duncan turned to her, smiling in his strained perfunctory way. She could not see his eyes. There was a faint mustache on his upper lip that gave him an adult, sober appearance and contrasted with the casual clothes he was wearing—a blue-and-white striped shirt and white shorts that were a little soiled. Was he going to be nineteen years old, Irene wondered, or was he going to be twenty. . . .

He picked the basket up and went inside, careful to keep the screen door from slamming behind him.

". . . different from us, really?" Lillian said slowly. "Their lives are different from what ours were? No, I don't believe it. I really don't. Duncan and I are very much alike: I'd sense the slightest difference."

The sea, the heartbeat of the sea, was in the room with him. It sucked at his ankles. Rose to his chest, and to his lips. To his eyes. He shook his head free in a delirium of anticipation. *I won't hurt you. Be still. Don't cry. Don't.* The girl's presence expanded to fill the room. She was so beautiful, her hair so long and golden and wavy, he could not bear it. And her face—a cameo of exquisite beauty! Her half-closed eyes, her pale eyelids, her tense quivering mouth, her small soft breasts which he touched gently with his tongue: he could not bear it. Antoinette. His cousin, his sister, a child, a girl, a young woman, a stranger. His jaws gripped hard together. *Don't cry. Don't move away. Be still.* He was sick with love of her, his senses were filled to the brim, every part of him sharpened, in anguish, tearful. His entire body was about to burst into tears. *Don't hate me—*

The savagery of the pleasure took him by surprise. He had not remembered it like this: his breath torn from him, his eyes rolling in their sockets, his lips twisted into an ugly grimace.

Don't hate me—

He half-lay against the wall, his face pressed against the steamy bathroom mirror. Sobbing, gasping for breath, he clutched at his slippery body and did not dare draw back from the mirror for fear of seeing himself. Would she hate him if she knew, would she be disgusted if she

knew. . . . He pressed his sweating face hard against the mirror, over-
come by wracking humiliating sobs.

High above the harbor, on the redwood deck of the second floor of
the Sailing Club, Forrest Sargent allowed himself to be drawn out by
his nephew's wife and her guests. He sat at the head of the glass-topped
table, a red bachelor's button in his lapel. His full, heavy face glowed
with the effort of his protracted speech and the pleasure he took in his
listeners' flattering attentiveness.

A long convoluted anecdote involving President Eisenhower and a
naval commander and a certain notorious Washington personality, a
very beautiful woman. . . .

Antoinette stared at the old man, unsmiling. She felt that he was
betraying her. Was he drunk? Why had he allowed Duncan's mother
to fill his wineglass so many times? Those people he kept mentioning,
those names: who were they? No one Antoinette knew. Dead people,
perhaps. The anecdote went on and on, rambling, blundering. Old
dead scandals and old dead people. Who cared for them? Who
wanted to listen? From time to time Uncle Forrest paused to clear his
throat and there was the possibility that he might lose the thread of
his narrative and be unable to continue. But he always recovered himself. His anecdote was punctuated by the refrain *And then, wouldn't
you know . . . !*

If Duncan were here she might turn to him, with her droll sad smile
and her bored expression. They might communicate with each other in
silence; and none of the adults would know.

If Duncan were here, Antoinette thought, poking at a heavy wooden
pepper mill with the tip of her knife, pushing it by sly cautious inches
toward the center of the table, why then everything would be different:
everything would be transformed.

But these old people . . . !

How attentively they listened to the story Uncle Forrest was telling,
as if the people involved were known to them, as if those names had any
meaning at all: an aborted love affair, a near-suicide, a blunder in public
relations, the necessary resignation of an acquaintance of Forrest Sargent's, the ruin of a career. Yet the recitation was presented in a calm
humorous voice. It seemed to call forth ironic chuckles, ironic head-
shakings. Antoinette feared it would evolve, in the end, into a dirty joke.

Her mother, her Aunt Lillian, her Aunt Lillian's friends from Boston.

The green Plexiglas awning gave their faces a vaguely aquatic, anxious look despite their frequent smiles. And how did Antoinette look, she wondered nervously, in this strange light? She tried to see herself in the knife blade but it was too dull, too scarified. Her mother, noticing, frowned. A warning. Antoinette, you were rude the other morning to Lillian, I won't tolerate that sort of behavior up here, not when we're guests, do you understand, do you understand. . . .

Aunt Lillian was quite ebullient this afternoon. She wore an attractive white linen dress that was cut just low enough to show her large, shapely shoulders and arms, which were lightly tanned. Her hair was dark and glossy, fashioned into a stylish bun. She wore a wristwatch decorated with tiny jewels. And a large diamond ring. Her nails were long and polished and her small, plump hands were surprisingly beautiful. Duncan's hands too. Though he seemed to dislike them. The set of the mouth, the small alert gray eyes, the faint line between the eyebrows. . . . But his mother's laughter was full-bodied and unrestrained when she was enjoying herself; and Duncan's was usually subdued, as if it pained him to laugh.

He had gone off hiking up the beach, beyond the dunes. He had left her behind to be dragged off to the Sailing Club for lunch. Aren't you coming, Duncan, she asked in surprise. I thought you said last night you were. . . . Should I stay behind with you?

Don't be ridiculous, he said curtly.

Hiking off toward the northeastern point of the island where there were no beaches, only rocks and torturous inlets and a noisy chilly surf. The German grammar book in his backpack. Was he wearing his swimming trunks beneath his trousers, Antoinette wondered, but did not ask. . . . I could stay behind with you. We could have a picnic lunch.

Don't be ridiculous: what would *they* say?

Irene was staring at the old man, a faint, fond, incredulous smile on her lips. Evidently the anecdote had moved her. Had surprised her. But then of course she was old enough, Antoinette reasoned cruelly, to know who those people were: to care about an old dead scandal. (She would be forty in December. And though she fretted aloud about her age she did nothing to make herself appear younger—she might get her graying hair tinted, as Aunt Lillian did; she might try not to frown like a hag.)

The Rushworths from Boston were an attractive couple in their fifties who had disappointed Antoinette immensely when she learned that they hadn't brought their granddaughter along after all. (Though it hadn't

been altogether certain that the girl would be with them. And at thir-
teen she would probably have been too young, too silly, for Antoinette
to befriend.) The woman was rouged, and wore a diamond ring not
dissimilar from Aunt Lillian's; she seemed astounded by Forrest Sargent's casual revelations. Her husband too was surprised, though as the
anecdote went on he began to smile ironically, and to wink at Antoinette
as if there were an understanding between them.

What would *they* say, Antoinette thought sullenly, looking away.

He had not kissed her, had barely come near her, for several days.
Perhaps he had tired of her. On the stairs that morning she had deliberately brushed against him, she had reached out to pinch him, hard, but
he only laughed nervously—laughed and stepped away.

The luncheon was set for twelve-thirty and Duncan had known about
it well in advance, but at ten he told his mother he wouldn't be going
after all. He had work to do. He wanted to be alone.

Should I stay behind with you, Antoinette begged.

Of course he was right. He was right. If her mother guessed, if Aunt
Lillian guessed. . . . The Tydemans would have to leave Sky Island at
once. Would have to return to White Plains. Antoinette could imagine
her mother's hysteria. She could imagine her aunt's glacial murderous
calm. But we love each other, Antoinette protested, why can't we stay
together. . . .

Love. Love. We love each other.

From another part of the club a popular song drifted out to them.
Picking at the warmed, mealy remains of her avocado salad, Antoinette
shaped the words under her breath. The song was new that month, yet
its melody, its rhythm, its words were somehow familiar. Love, what can
it be but love, love, isn't it always love, what else is it but love, love,
love. . . .

She had pressed the avocado into a sort of mash and though she did
not glance over at her mother she knew Mrs. Tydeman was watching
her; so she laid her fork down at once.

Uncle Forrest was completing his story. His hoarse old-man's voice
was trembling with a sort of triumph, a strange abrasive gloating. Antoinette judged from the adults' chuckles and their wry head-shakings
that the story, with its tragic possibilities, had turned into a dirty joke
after all.

How long had she been crouched up there on the rocks, watching . . . ?

To disguise the helpless raging shame he felt Duncan hurried to his cousin, to help her down. The rocks were wet and slippery, and her sandals were smooth-soled. If she lost her balance she might fall and hurt herself badly.

He reached out for her. He grinned stiffly, as she was grinning.

"This is an ugly place," she said, leaning against him. "All these rocks and that green slime and the way it smells . . . and there's almost no sand. . . . I wondered where you went to, all the time," she said, raising her voice to be heard over the surf. Her small hopeful features quickened with a sort of nervous coquettishness. "Is this a secret place of yours. . . ."

"Of course not," Duncan said. "I have no secret places."

"It's such a long walk and it isn't very nice out here," Antoinette said, shading her eyes. "For a while I couldn't find you. I thought you must have turned back toward the road, there's a narrow little sandy road nobody lives on, do you know what I mean . . . ? I went out there, then I came back this way. I almost *missed* you. It's like a secret cove here, with all these ugly rocks. Why does it smell so strange? Has something died?"

"It's just the ocean," Duncan said.

"It smells like a fish or something that's decaying," Antoinette said, wrinkling her nose.

Duncan heard himself laughing almost gaily. "It's the ocean—the ocean. Nothing but the ocean."

"But why do you come here?" she persisted. "Is it to escape from the rest of us? From me?"

A massive wave crashed noisily against a nearby boulder and threw its spray onto them. It was quite chilly: Antoinette flinched.

"Of course not," Duncan said.

He was angry, he was trembling with shame. But he could not determine from her bright, insouciant manner whether she had been spying on him, or whether she had just appeared at the top of the sea cliff when he happened to turn. He had climbed down only minutes before. Alone amid the familiar noises of the surf and the wind and the gulls, stimulated by the harsh, fresh, tolling air and the fact of his absolute solitude, Duncan had stood facing the ocean with his hands on his hips, breathing deeply and passionately, his eyes half-closed. The lenses of his glasses were splattered but he did not mind. It was part of the turbulence of the cove, its secret power. After a minute or two he would begin to feel slightly disoriented, as if the earth were quivering beneath his feet, shaken by the thunderous surf. Here it was of all the places he knew that everything was thrown off balance, out of rhythm; here he had perfect freedom. He might laugh aloud, defiantly and contemptuously. He might shout after the seabirds like a child, half-expecting them to respond. He might talk to himself, he might imitate the voices of others, he might beg for help, for love, for a release from his anguish.

No one had ever followed him here before. No one had ever discovered him.

"Of course I wasn't trying to escape you," he said, forcing himself to laugh.

The golden-haired image had pursued him through the night. It had risen from the sea with an eerie grace, shrouded in mist. Beautiful, silent, pure and undefiled as marble; a cameo that had the power of expanding to fill the entire cove with a pulse beat more violent than that of the sea itself. When the image arose the stony cacophonous beach came alive as if touched with an animal warmth . . . and Duncan's words of yearning, of desire, had been torn from him as if, locked in the paralysis of sleep, he had had no control over his behavior.

"How can you study here?" Antoinette said. She tugged at the German grammar he carried in his back pocket. "Doesn't the book get wet?"

"If I study I sit up on the rocks. Up there," Duncan said evenly.

"Ah, up there!" Antoinette said, shading her eyes and squinting. "I could sit there too, I could bring something along to read. . . . You said you'd help me with algebra sometime. Then you forgot."

"I didn't forget."

"You don't like me, you've been avoiding me," she said with a small pouty smile. Sunlight, broken by the choppy waves, reflected dizzily on her upturned face; a single droplet of water, like a playful tear, ran down her cheek. Duncan had the urge to lick it with his tongue. "You come all the way out here, all these miles, to avoid me."

"It isn't miles," Duncan said. "It can't be more than a mile and a half. And I haven't been avoiding you; don't be ridiculous."

"*You're* ridiculous," she said, unsmiling.

He had been holding her protectively. Now she pushed him away and jumped down, scrambling to the very edge of the beach, her feet sinking in the wet sand. She shook her hair out of her eyes. Squatting, with a childlike display of utter detachment, she began examining the seashells at her feet. She picked one after another up, studied it, found fault with it, tossed it negligently back into the sea. The surf cracked into thin sheets of spray, wetting her. As Duncan watched, locked in a new paralysis, the girl's tight, very short denim shorts and her thin white blouse became soaked.

"What are you doing!" he shouted irritably. "Come back up here."

She did not glance around. Another sheet of spray covered her and she wiped her face roughly with her forearm. Still selecting shells, bits of glass, pebbles, as if she were utterly alone, and throwing them out into the sea. A gull squawked overhead and she threw a stone at it clumsily.

"Do you want to catch cold? You're being ridiculous," Duncan said. The ocean was so loud, she couldn't hear. Duncan laughed angrily.

"You little bitch, you brattish headstrong little bitch, what are you *doing . . . ?* I'm responsible for you. You have no sense of your own. I don't want you here, this isn't the place for you, I command you to leave here at once. . . . I love you, why are you so stubborn, so perverse? No, I don't love you. I don't love anyone. I command you, Antoinette: *leave here before it's too late.*"

She turned to peer up at him, her expression petulant, prim. Not hearing what he had said she cupped a hand to her ear and shrugged her thin shoulders indifferently.

Duncan climbed down and stood beside her in the wet muddy sand. His glasses streamed with spray. Antoinette straightened, throwing a last clam shell out into the water, shaking her hair out of her face. She was shivering; Duncan saw with a mixture of gratification and pity that her flesh had gathered itself into tiny goose pimples. The wet clothes were stuck to her and the shirt had gone nearly transparent so that he could see her tiny, hard nipples, and even the curve of her ribs.

"Look at you," he said roughly. "Do you want to catch cold? The air isn't warm today, there's a strong breeze. . . ."

"What do you care," Antoinette shouted. "You don't love me."

"What?"

"You don't love me! What do you care about me!"

She pushed at him with an elbow. The gesture was so ungainly, so spontaneous and childlike, that Duncan was moved; he stared at her in astonishment.

After a long moment he said, with a jesting confidence he did not feel, "You know I love you. Isn't it obvious?"

She turned away, frowning.

"Should we go back up?" Duncan said. He hesitated, wondering if he should touch her. She might misunderstand—might slash at him with her elbow again. "It isn't very pleasant here. I can hardly keep my balance. . . . Should we go back up, Antoinette? And sit in the sun until we're dry?"

"Go to hell."

"Antoinette—"

She backed away. He found himself staring at her breasts, at her nipples. How like a child she was, an undeveloped girl, nearly sexless in the wet shirt, shivering with cold. . . . He was touched by her anger though he could not understand it. If there was resentment between them surely it was his, for hadn't she followed him from the house, hadn't she spied on him in his secret cove, hadn't she interrupted his reverie and crowded against him with her shrill ungovernable emotions . . . ? Crouching up there on the rocks she had called down to him, waving and grinning with something close to fear; and now, staring at her, he felt his face twist into an identical grin.

"Come on," he said, grabbing her by the wrist. "We're going back up."

She resisted limply, then surrendered. They climbed together up the rocks, out of the range of spray. At the top Antoinette pulled free of his fingers; she stared at him through her thick damp lashes, her lips tightly pursed. She's insane, Duncan thought. She wants me to . . .

But he could not allow himself so crude a thought.

And anyway he was mistaken, surely.

"This is better, isn't it? Why don't you sit down and dry yourself off," he said nervously.

Since he had first kissed her that night, weeks ago, he had not allowed himself to envision precisely what might happen between them. Even his groggy, hypnotic daydreams became blurred and fragmented as he drew near to her; seen up close, Antoinette's face became any girl's face, her body any girl's body. He could not be blamed, he could not be accused, how was his lust a *personal* affront . . .

"You hate me, don't you?" Antoinette said.

"Why do you say that?"

"Ever since that luncheon—"

"I explained about that. It was my understanding that the Rushworths were bringing their granddaughter so there was no need for *me* to sit through it too."

"You walked away, you didn't even say goodbye, you told me the night before you were going and then you didn't, you just walked away, and since then you avoid me, you're never alone with me. . . . I don't care, really. I really don't. It means nothing to me at all."

"You seem to be exaggerating everything," Duncan said.

"*You* don't exaggerate anything. What you do is just the opposite," she said, stammering slightly. "You—you make things down into nothing. You grind them down fine and then they're nothing and you jeer at them."

"I don't jeer at anything," Duncan said quietly.

He urged her down and they sat close together on a broad, flat rock, facing the ocean. Antoinette was still trembling, so Duncan slid his arm around her shoulders. "You're angry with me for following you," she said, wiping at her nose.

"No."

"This is some sort of secret of yours, this place. . . ."

"No. Forget it, please."

She hid her face in her hands. Her shoulders jerked, and for a moment Duncan thought she must be laughing at him. Then he realized she was crying.

"Antoinette—"

"I don't blame you for hating me," she said. "At school I have a few friends . . . but only because they don't know me, they don't know what I'm really like. I . . . I tell them things. Anything that flies into my head. When my father died, for instance. . . . I don't tell the truth. Sometimes I hate myself so, I know I don't deserve to live. . . ."

Duncan tightened his arm around her shoulders, roughly, and pulled her against him. How could she talk like that! Those were his words, *his*. And he knew they were the words, the very voice, of his sickness.

They must be brushed aside, they must be silenced. They could not be taken seriously.

"I love you. If I love anyone," Duncan whispered.

She wept, not hearing. The waves and the wind and her own sobbing were too loud.

Duncan's heartbeat had accelerated. He held her so tightly against him that she had to resist, drawing back; she raised her shoulders as if in self-defense. Seen so close, her face was startlingly mature—a lovely, stricken, mysterious face for some reason offered to him. He might press his own against it, blindly, hungrily; he might kiss it, or lick at it greedily.

"I don't jeer at anything," he said in a broken, desperate voice.

III

She quarreled with her sister Lucy (over what?—a matter as trivial as a straw purse whose contents had been spilled out onto a bed) so loudly, and at such length, that Mrs. Sargent had to ask the girls to please be still: didn't they know Uncle Forrest was trying to rest, this time of the afternoon? She quarreled with her mother (Irene had seen her, evidently, strolling along Drum Road in the company of several other teenagers, all of them—or so Irene claimed angrily—smoking cigarettes) and burst into tears. At mealtimes she was sullen and overly cheerful by turns, and her politeness toward Mrs. Sargent sometimes struck the woman as impertinent. Was Antoinette laughing at her, behind that pose of respectful attention? Toward Duncan she behaved in an arch, unconsciously provocative way. . . . Like a little slut, Mrs. Sargent thought. But of course she doesn't know what she's doing.

She quarreled with her sister and her mother, and burst into tears, frantic and heartbroken. She locked herself in her room. On that hard unfamiliar mattress she wept and wept, ignoring her mother's timid knock at the door. Her hair tangled in her face, a strand caught in her mouth, she threshed from side to side on the pillow, she tried to embrace herself as Duncan had embraced her. . . . Her own yearning fingers stretched wide on her back, pressing hard into the flesh, into her ribs. "I love you," she whispered. "I love you. No one but you."

He had kissed her, many times. He had touched her breasts through her shirt. Groaning, he had hidden his face in her throat, in a way that had frightened her: he seemed so suddenly blind, so helpless, unable to control himself. In a queer ecstatic terror she had shut her eyes tight. The surf was so thunderous, the wind so strong, so exhausting, it was almost more than she could do to keep herself awake. . . . She yearned to fall asleep, to press herself into Duncan's arms like a child, to give herself up to him. *He* was the stronger, the older. *He* would know what must be done.

In the end he had pushed her away from him, abruptly. He had turned aside as if ashamed.

"Antoinette, are you sick? Is something wrong?"

She shouted for her mother to go away: to leave her alone.

In a detached, still voice she told him about her father, gazing out at the flotilla of sailboats with an interest that must have been feigned, it was so keen, so impenetrable. Duncan stared at her in astonishment. In awe. The others had remained at the table but Antoinette had risen to go to the railing, and Duncan followed her immediately, as if she had whispered to him, "Come along." Only when he went to stand beside her did he wonder if the others had noticed.

She told him about her father in a leisurely conversational manner, all the while watching the colorful sailboats, her expression quite blank. From the start of the evening when Duncan had first seen her, looking so poised, so confident—her hair braided and coiled about her head like a crown so that her long graceful neck was exposed—she had seemed to him indescribably beautiful. It was not his fancy, his imagination: the girl *was* beautiful. At the Sailing Club people looked at her with an interest they did not show to the others in Mrs. Sargent's party; Duncan saw with a thrill of angry despair how men stared at her, even men twenty or thirty years older than she. Of course they could not have guessed she was only fourteen years old. She wore a fashionably long dress of some coarse, burlaplike fabric with very narrow straps so that her tanned shoulders were exposed, and much of her back, and she had looped a number of heavy, chunky necklaces around her slender neck.

For the first time that summer she wore shoes, not sandals: they were white and had a considerable heel so that she was easily his height. When she stood self-consciously erect with her head of heavy elegant hair she might even have appeared, to observers, to be taller than he.

Duncan had found the dinner, the food and the conversation and the very presence of the others, distasteful. He had been restless, he had wanted to interrupt, to contradict, to laugh contemptuously. Antoinette's silence had seemed to him the only important thing: why didn't everyone stop talking and simply stare at her . . . ? From time to time she glanced at him, but she did not smile. He smiled; but she did not. He saw that she was disgusted with him, that she no longer cared for him, and his hand crept to his glasses to adjust them, and then to his nose, his lips, his chin. . . . He could not eat. His mother had talked everyone into ordering lobster, how could they *not* have lobster on Sky Island, and he had been repulsed not only by the strong-tasting rubbery flesh (which he had never liked very much, so why did his mother bully him into ordering it) but by the evident delight of the other diners, who said repeatedly that the meal was delicious, they had never tasted better lobster, weren't the Sargents lucky to come here every summer. . . . The cracking of the lobster shells struck Duncan as intolerable. His nerves tightened; his stomach tightened. He left two-thirds of his dinner untouched and when his mother glanced at him, her eyebrows raised in a wordless question, he did no more than glance at her in return, unsmiling, and turn away.

During the long chatty dinner someone who had been reading about the history of the island said that in the nineteenth century a town law had been passed declaring that a man could not be granted a marriage license unless he had gone out to the northeastern tip of the island, into the dunes, and planted three bushels of grass seed and six young trees and shot a dozen crows. Everyone had laughed, some of them rather uproariously. It had seemed to them utterly mad. A fertility rite of some kind . . . ?

When the imbecilic laughter subsided Duncan cleared his throat and said, in a voice undisturbed by the agitation he really felt: "The law was an attempt, obviously, to preserve the ecology of the island. Though it seems hilarious to us it made perfectly good sense at the time."

His curt, imperial manner sobered them. The issue of the solid-fill marina was brought up. To what extent could conservationists interfere with business expansion, someone said, and at once the others leapt in to challenge him, Duncan's mother most exuberantly of all, and Duncan stopped listening. He sat, leaden and melancholy, staring at his beautiful young cousin who had eaten all her lobster without a qualm, and who had hardly glanced at him all evening.

Now he stood close beside her, wondering if he dared step nearer. She was wearing perfume. She was tall, lovely, slender, an image out of his dreams, untouched by the sweaty delirium of his dreams. The other day he had kissed her and run his hands desperately over her tense, wiry body, and her face, seen so close, had seemed to him not very pretty—as drawn, as fearful, as his own must have been. Now she stood at the railing of the Sailing Club as if she were perfectly at home here amidst the overdressed women and the half-drunken men, tall and graceful and impervious to his lust. She was telling him an astonishing story in a detached, even clipped voice.

". . . the 'stack mocket,' he used to call it. He had all these silly little names and singsong phrases and jokes. I loved him so much. He called me Nettoinannie—you know, my name pronounced backward. It was his secret name for me. . . . I loved him so much, but now I don't care if he's dead. Why should I care. With Mother there's all this pretense, she gets to talking about him to Lucy and me, even to me when we're alone, as if she hadn't told me all about him back then. . . . It's so strange, it makes me wonder if I'm going crazy. Has she forgotten what she told me or is it just a game of some kind . . . am I supposed to wink at her and say Yes, Mother, we'll keep the secret. . . . Sometimes I think *she's* crazy. They all lie. But they can't help it. Your mother too: she must know what happened. . . . He flew to Chicago on business. Then there was this telephone call from the police. He was in a hospital in East Chicago, in intensive care. He was dying but they didn't say that. By the time Mother got there he was dead. Just like that. He was dead. I never saw him again. He said goodbye to me one morning at breakfast and I went to school and he took a cab to the airport and I never saw him again. The police had picked him up, wandering on the street in some awful neighborhood. They were black police, it was a black neighborhood, nobody knew what he was doing there. He was wearing trousers and socks and his suit coat but that was all. His shirt was gone, his underwear, his shoes, his wallet and his money and his identification, he was muttering to himself as if he was drunk or drugged, something about people who had cheated him, there were two or three names he kept repeating but they weren't the names of anyone Mother knew . . . and they weren't our names. So he died. It happened like that, over a weekend. Mother told me about it because she was angry. She hated him, for dying like that. For being found wandering around in a black neighborhood with half his clothes gone and no money and no identification. Also he died broke. Owing money everywhere. People in the family, loan companies in White Plains, a terrible loan company in New York they said was controlled by the Mafia. . . . She hated him so she told me everything. Then after the funeral she seemed to forget. Either she forgot that she'd told me, or she forgot about what had happened itself. The version you know, he died of a cerebral hemorrhage. Maybe that's the clinical explanation. I don't know. I never talk about it to Mother now. Why should I . . . why should I talk about anything with her. She's like your mother. You can tell they're sisters. *Your* father, for instance, the way your mother talks about him it's like . . . it's like the way my mother talks about my father. Isn't it? You know it is. It *is.* But you'd better not question her. . . . What I remember about my father, I remember how nice he was to me, always singing songs and bringing me presents and teasing me, that sort of thing. They never quarreled when Lucy or I were around but we could hear them sometimes. That's why I love him. I used to love him. Then there was this time, I was five or six years old, at the country club Daddy carried me out onto the diving board with him and we jumped off together, and it was so exciting . . . I was so frightened, so excited. . . . He was a little drunk, I suppose. But not bad. He should have told me to hold my nose because a lot of water got up into my head and it hurt and for a long time afterward I wouldn't go into the pool but now it's all right, now I know enough. That was almost ten years ago. As time went on there was some sort of story invented, a myth of some sort, about Daddy and me swimming, diving into the pool together, family shit like that, all made up but nice, and nobody questions it. I don't question it myself, why should I."

Duncan opened his mouth to speak. But he could not speak. His hand raised itself cautiously to his face to adjust his glasses. Beside him his cousin Antoinette stood in her high-heeled shoes, watching the sailboats moving into the harbor, and though he was staring at their colorful sails —one, the most magnificent of all, was an enormous lavender sail flanked by smaller yellow sails—he had not been seeing them for some time.

"Why should anyone question anything," Antoinette said flatly.

IV

A premise, he read, stooped trembling over the notebook, *that life is absolutely and incontestably simple. . . .*

Grinding himself against her as he had, that morning. The surprise of it. His penis swollen and throbbing, her belly hot, hard, shrinking from him. Like a figure he might have glimpsed in a film or a photograph he stood pressed against the girl, his hands on either side of her head, kissing her. She whimpered but he could not determine her meaning. She shrank from him, yet in the next instant clutched him around the neck, kissing him eagerly. Her breath tasted of peppermint. Of toothpaste. Her lips seemed oddly small, her tongue cool and shy. It had happened so quickly there in the hallway that Duncan felt intoxicated with his daring. Downstairs the cleaning woman was vacuuming and there was the outlandish notion that . . . that . . . somehow the noise of the vacuum cleaner would hide them. . . .

As it was, Duncan stepped away from Antoinette only a few seconds before a door opened down the hall and Mrs. Tydeman appeared.

She was dressed for the beach in a one-piece striped bathing suit and a pretty straw hat and wooden clogs that gave her long, rather sinewy legs an almost glamorish appearance. She carried her sunglasses, an enormous towel, and a large straw purse into which a paperback book had been stuck. Her cheerfulness indicated that she had seen nothing and guessed nothing—in a hurry, she did not pause to scold Antoinette for anything, or to remind her of anything, nor did she exchange more than a perfunctory smile with her nephew.

In his room Duncan studied the calendar. How many more days . . . how many more days until Labor Day. . . .

At mealtimes when he could not avoid staring at the girl he consoled himself with the melancholy observation that in less than three weeks the summer would be over, and it was quite likely that he would not see her again for a very long time. He might never see her again. His Aunt Irene might marry and the family might move away. If they came to Sky Island next summer, perhaps he would be elsewhere: attending summer school, or traveling in Europe. If nothing happened between Antoinette and himself over the next several weeks, why then they were both safe, no one would ever know, it would remain a secret between them forever. . . .

There was the possibility, however, that something might happen between them.

Two weeks and five days until Labor Day. Dr. Sargent had intended to fly up on August 15, but one of his patients was unexpectedly ill, and since the man was a high-ranking Pentagon official Dr. Sargent thought it wisest to remain in Washington for another week at least. Two weeks, five days. Studying the calendar Duncan was seized with an almost unbearable desire to weep. It was unfair, unfair. He wanted her and he would have her. It was unfair that he should be denied her since he loved her, he loved her so much, and he was certain that she loved him. . . . And his father would not be flying up until the week of August 22.

"I feel no need to defend myself," Duncan whispered. His adversaries were silent, as if intimidated by his calm, reasonable manner. They glanced at each other, perplexed. What to say? How to react? Duncan was, after all, a brilliant boy. His teachers had declared him brilliant. There was no doubt about it, even his adversaries were proud of him, and would be forced now to admit the justice of his point of view. "Where there is love involved, genuine love. . . . Where two people love each other so much. . . . It's unfair for anyone else to interfere."

Suppose they were thrown together again at Christmas. It was not impossible. Aunt Irene would be lonely, perhaps; Antoinette said her mother was often depressed at holidays. Mrs. Sargent would invite them to Georgetown because she was very fond of her younger sister, and in his room at the top of the house Duncan would embrace Antoinette and they would kiss each other eagerly and . . . Groggily Duncan imagined their lovemaking, on his bed. It would be more easily accomplished there, he reasoned, than here. He didn't know why. The distance, the remoteness in time. . . .

What a pig I am, he thought, revulsed.

He went for days without much appetite, then ate ravenously. His stomach ached. Lucy's shrill voice grated against his nerves, as did the noise of Mr. Gyorgy's power mower. His mother nagged him to eat when food disgusted him, and scolded him mildly for overeating at other times. How strangely he was behaving, she murmured. Which meant, he supposed, a report to his father.

"How is your stomach, dear, these days? You looked so pale at dinner last night, I was sure you must have been suffering from gas pains. . . ."

"I'm perfectly fine, Mother. Will you close the door behind you?"

He leafed through his notebooks. Each was labeled—PHYSICS, GERMAN, BIOLOGY, ENG. LIT.—and each label was protected by a strip of cellophane tape. The pages were numbered. There were even subsidiary numbers, like 17a, 17b. Duncan's handwriting had been fastidious for the first two-thirds of the notes and had then deteriorated somewhat as his health had deteriorated that winter. The notes he had taken this summer, however, were neat and clean and orderly.

Vectors and circles. Acceleration. The simplicity of Newton's laws. . . . He leafed through the pages but could not comprehend what he read. *Angular momentum. Kepler's second law.* He must not panic, for it was obvious that he did understand this material. He had mastered it well enough to receive grades in the high nineties during his first semester, hadn't he, and consequently he would remember it all when required to, just as he would remember the German verb endings, and the structures of the German sentences, and everything else.

He thought again of how brutally, how helplessly, he had rubbed himself against Antoinette that morning. Of how she had meekly backed against the wall like a girl in a film, obedient to his will, mesmerized by what he did. Around the house he heard her singing under her breath, he heard snatches of words, phrases involving *love, love, what else can it be but love,* and while part of him was contemptuous of the simple singsong melody and the brainlessly repetitive lyrics, another part of him quickened in response. He stared after her, smiling foolishly. In a kind of stupor he stared into space. Shaving, he found himself gazing nearsightedly into his own small wondering eyes. What was happening, what were these changes that came over him, why did he want at times to hold his cousin's face gently in his hands and kiss her very, very gently on the lips and tell her not to worry, he would protect her always, he would shield her from all harm, even from the ugly memory of her father and his death and his debts; why did he want at other times to grab her and shake her, hard, and if she resisted he would strike her with his fists, groaning her name, shrieking *Bitch, bitch* until she slumped onto the ground before him, no longer resisting. . . .

Her footsteps on the stairs. On the veranda. In the corridor outside his door. Her voice, her scent, the glimpse of her colorful blouse through a screened window, the flash of her long brown legs. The warm surprise he felt when, one morning, he saw that she had painted her nails—and her toenails as well—a bright pink.

A quick, almost husbandly kiss as they hurried along the side path, through a border of tall bridal wreath, to the car where Mrs. Tydeman was waiting. (They were all going to the movies in Sky Harbor, to see an idiotic suspense film that involved the possible end of the world.)

Her small cool hand squeezing his, the fingers surprisingly hard.

Once, sprawled on the beach, she tickled him with her toe . . . touched him as lazily and idly as if he were a dog or a cat . . . rubbing his ankle. He drew away, blushing. Only a few yards away Lucy and one of her girl friends were playing, and farther up the beach Duncan's mother was chatting with a neighbor.

"Stop that," he whispered.

"What? Can't hear," she said, cupping her hand to her ear because of the surf.

He loved her, he carried her image everywhere with him. In his reveries they were, at times, already married: with no self-consciousness or dread whatsoever they made love as often as they wished, in any room of the house. (But which house? It appeared to be one they had rented, somewhere else on the island.) Antoinette was older. He too was older, in his mid-twenties, and she was nearly the same age. She slid her arms about his neck and giggled and allowed him to kiss her however he wished, and to touch her however he wished. . . . But at times she resisted, she refused. Her face went hard and prim. It was then that he had to discipline her: had to slap her into submission. Once he threw her to the ground and thrust his knee between her legs and when she thrashed from side to side, screaming, he had to strike her again and again until . . . "Don't you ever try to keep yourself from me again," he said afterward. He stood above her, his hands on his hips. She was sobbing, her face was swollen, her lower lip cracked. "You belong to me. You love me. So don't you *ever* play that game again."

Another time he came upon her, alone, in an unfamiliar room in which light fell in latticed slats, smelling of the sea, and something lemony and tart; and he saw that she was sobbing. Because her father was dead. And they had lied about him. She loved him but he was dead. Nettoinannie was dead. No one would love her again, no one would tease and fondle her, and make little jokes. If you didn't love, there were no jokes. "But I will love you," Duncan exclaimed, with as much surprise as if he were saying this for the first time, "don't you understand?—

haven't you guessed? I will love you. I will take care of you. Always and forever. And I won't hurt you. *Nettoinannie.*"

(But in reality—in the real world—in *the* world—he never dared call her that name.)

Laughing and shouting like children they raced all the way to the village together on their bicycles. Sometimes Duncan allowed her to win. It quite astonished him, and pleased him, that he had grown so fit this summer—his legs were strengthening, and the muscles of his shoulders and arms. In the village Antoinette browsed in the boutiques and Kresge's and the drugstore (where, surreptitiously, she could read quickly through magazines that presented, in chaste columns of unexceptional print, information on birth control, having an affair with one's boss, no-fault divorce, plastic surgery for all purposes, apple-and-yogurt diets, yoga exercises, astrological forecasts, fall wardrobes, fall makeup, the ten best girls' schools in the East, various methods of abortion, how to train for the Olympics, how to tell if you're really in love or only infatuated); while Duncan returned books for his mother and aunt at the library, and picked up a few more, or went to have his hair trimmed, seated rather self-consciously in the window of the barbershop. He hated the place. But there he was—his mother couldn't abide straggly hair.

Oblivious of Duncan's boredom the barber chattered about the weather, the crowded weekends, the noisy motorboats and motorcycles, the beer bottles and cans left in the park every night, even strewn onto the street; he was a plump melancholy man in his mid-forties who knew who Duncan was—that is, he knew his father, and knew of his great-uncle—but, out of a sense of courtesy, did not address him by name. Stiffly, aloofly, Duncan murmured in response to his remarks, neither agreeing nor disagreeing. He watched the passersby, dreading that someone who knew him would glance into the window.

Once he believed he saw Antoinette, on the far side of the street, in her short shorts and crimson top. His heart pounded strangely, he felt an urge to leave the barber's chair and follow her. Suppose he spied on her as she had spied on him that day. . . . But of course he remained seated.

A moment later there passed by a man who looked familiar. A friend of his mother's, or a neighbor. . . . Someone his father knew from other summers. . . . The man was bearded and dressed with fashionable taste in white trousers and a sporty navy blue shirt; his walk was brisk; his arms swung at his sides. He passed by the front of the barbershop so quickly that Duncan had not time to see him clearly, but he was certainly someone Duncan knew . . . or had met, briefly . . . at the Sailing Club, perhaps, or at a party last summer. It irritated Duncan that he could not recall the man's name or the context of their meeting. He thought it strange that he should be irritated, for ordinarily he did not care in the slightest for other people, and certainly not for near-strangers. The man had been in his late forties or early fifties, darkly bearded, with graying hair, and quite handsomely tanned arms. He had passed by too quickly, Duncan had not really seen him, yet for some reason the image of his face hovered with a sinister acuity in his mind's eye. Only when Duncan left the barbershop and joined Antoinette in the library did the image fade, and even then a queer sensation of uneasiness remained with him for the rest of the afternoon.

Two years earlier at the age of twelve Antoinette had made an upsetting discovery.

While riding her bicycle one mild June day with two or three other girls, along a pleasant residential street in White Plains, she had happened to overhear the laughter of several black women standing at a bus stop nearby. The laughter had not sounded malicious. There had been no reason for Antoinette to think that it was directed at her or her friends. When she turned to see who was laughing, however, it was one of the shocks of her young life to see Maudie there—full-bodied good-natured Maudie who had been cleaning the Tydemans' house for as long as Antoinette could remember. Had Maudie seen *her,* had Maudie even glanced *her* way . . . ? Or were the black women simply laughing at some silly little white girls in their bleached jeans who were pedaling energetically along, their long straight hair flying out behind them, each girl a replica of the others . . . ?

Most disturbing was the thought, new to Antoinette at the time, that Maudie and her black friends might not have been thinking of anything that had to do with white people at all. Their laughter was their own concern, their own secret. Antoinette would never know what it meant.

And when she let herself into Duncan's room, while he was taking one of his prolonged, innumerable showers, and saw how the room looked without anyone in it—how stark and complete and *secret* it appeared—she was equally disturbed though she could not have said why.

What a surprise it was. . . .

Of course she had been in Duncan's room in the past. Before *that* had happened between them. (By which she meant the surreptitious kiss late on the night of July Fourth.) And she had dawdled in the doorway from time to time afterward, and had wandered in and out, casually, as a sister might have done. But Duncan had always been in the room, previously. He had usually been sitting at his big desk, and with a pleased, startled smile he would swivel himself around and stand . . . though sometimes he would not look quite so pleased. That minute frown would appear between his pale eyebrows as it appeared with tiresome regularity between his mother's eyebrows and Antoinette would know that she was not welcome. But with Duncan in the room it had a center: a certain gravity that contained her.

Now the room was empty. Tiptoeing into it like a thief Antoinette felt her heartbeat accelerate with the daring of what she did. The room, Duncan's room, was empty. Except for some clothes lying on the bed —one of them, a pale blue shirt, still in its wrapper—the room might have been vacant. There were notebooks and textbooks on the desk, and several pens and pencils neatly lined up, but still the room had a stark, queer air of being vacant—unoccupied. Ah, there were Duncan's sandals by the bed! Surely they would smell of the sea, of the beach; surely they would smell of *him*. But was there nothing else? A mahogany bureau, a handsome piece of furniture, each drawer shut tight and the top absolutely clear. . . . A wingbacked chair in a corner, smartly uphol-stered, in which no one ever sat. . . . The walls unadorned except for the beige-and-white striped wallpaper: no mirrors, no pictures.

Delighted and intimidated simultaneously Antoinette sat on the edge of Duncan's bed. His mattress, like hers, was made of horsehair and gave way only reluctantly beneath her weight. So *that* was how the doorway looked to someone who sat here. . . . Antoinette touched Duncan's freshly laundered trousers and his white underclothes and the shirt in the wrapper (which Mrs. Sargent must have bought just the day before in the village), and her sense of daring, of recklessness, increased. How angry he would be to discover her here! How shocked! ("We can't let anyone know about us," he said repeatedly, fussing like an old woman. "We've got to be careful how we even *look* at each other. . . .") He would return from his shower and close the door behind him and see her lying on the bed and his face would register surprise and alarm and reluctant desire. And he would hesitate. And then come to her. Half-lying on the bed, her eyes nearly closed, Antoinette summoned him to her. She had seen him frequently in his green terry-cloth robe and his house slippers, his hair wet, plastered onto his broad forehead, she had been moved by his look of . . . of what? . . . of being less guarded than usual . . . sleek and supple as a water creature of some sort. . . . And when he wasn't wearing his glasses, his eyes were larger than anyone knew. Their gaze, less pointedly focused, seemed to take in hazily all that lay before him.

"Duncan. Come here. You know I love you: come here. No one is around, no one will know. Don't be afraid of hurting me. Come here. Come *here.*"

She lay back impatiently on the bed, her long slim legs bare and gleaming, her arms outspread. And her hair—how did it look? She would have wished it fanned out behind her on Duncan's pillows. Her face was flushed. Her eyes bright. She bit at her lower lip, awaiting him. He had avoided her for two days in a row, and before that he had kissed her only lightly—as a father might have, or a brother—as the two of them hurried together somewhere, awaited by one of their mothers. She wanted more. She *wanted* more. In the village library she had leafed through certain books, standing in a corner, her back to the corner, so that she could see whoever approached . . . she had borrowed magazines from one of the girls who lived farther in, along the beach . . . she had noted the abrupt, sweaty coupling in a recent film. And while such things were hardly new to her (she and her friends had become quite interested in sexual matters, especially in their forbidden aspect, when they were in fifth grade), they struck her now in an altered light as being possibilities, suddenly, for herself.

("I saw you with your boy friend," one of the Sky Harbor girls said with an odd envious smile. "He looked like he was in college or something—how old is he?" And Antoinette had been forced to say that he wasn't her boy friend, only her cousin. "We're staying with him and his mother and he takes me places, that's all. He's my *cousin.*")

She flung her arms out behind her head. She sighed. The pit of her belly stirred. Sometimes, half-asleep, she could feel him *there.* She would touch herself shyly, imagining that it was him. Duncan. Someone. Such sharp wracking pleasure. . . . But it frightened her: she did not like it, really. She would jerk her hand away, she would go to wash her hands, the feeling would fade, die. This afternoon as she lay on Duncan's bed staring at the closed door she could not determine whether she felt sexual desire for him, or whether her excitement was really a kind of terror.

"Duncan, I'm not pretending. I do love you. I will never love anyone else but you. Come here. Don't be afraid of hurting me. *Come here.*"

On that flat slab of rock above the cove he had kissed her, and run his hands over her, and she had been rather frightened. His panting breath, his flushed yearning face, his hard unfriendly hands. . . . Though fairly high above the beach the rock was occasionally washed over by the highest tide and bits of ocean debris were left behind—smashed shells, strips of seaweed, coarse-grained sand. And these things had hurt Antoinette's bare skin. And pressed through her thin blouse. She had wanted to scream for him to stop—to stop!

But he had stopped suddenly, of his own accord. Drawing away from her, his face slick with perspiration, his lips slack and rubbery and stunned.

Afterward, on the way home, he had said little. At first she guessed he must be ashamed of her, and disgusted; gradually she came to see that he was simply very upset. His voice shook when he made a joke of some kind and his eyes blinked rapidly, behind his round glinting glasses.

"You're so slow. You're always taking a shower and washing your hair. I don't love you: you're ridiculous."

Bending her legs sharply at the knee she uncoiled herself and sprang to her feet as she was taught, in gym class, to rise from the mats in one fluid motion. She whistled under her breath. Went to examine the notebooks, opening them carelessly. *Genetic information transferral. Ribonucleic acid, deoxyribonucleic acid.* She frowned and checked the cover of the notebook. Biology. She would be taking biology in tenth grade. Next month. She leafed through another notebook, saw pages of equations, a complicated diagram that looked like a pyramid with many dotted lines, words like *vector, magnetism, tension, motion, waves.* His upright, prissy handwriting! *A wave is a pattern, a form that moves.*

Her mouth contracted sullenly. Of course he did not care for her, he knew everything and she knew nothing. Mrs. Sargent was always boasting of him. Yes, fine, all right: everyone agrees he is a genius. *Duncan Sargent is a genius.* And little Antoinette is stupid. Works as hard as possible to get her wavering precarious average of . . . what was it last term . . . eighty-seven. Higher than just a B but not *quite* B+.

"Of course Antoinette's school is a very strict one," Irene was always saying. "The girls are all bright. It's quite competitive. I know the tuition is absurdly high but my husband wanted both the girls to attend private schools and it would be a betrayal to him if I wrenched them out and into public schools. . . ."

Antoinette pushed the notebooks aside.

Her lover was a genius. Was he. Or was he weak. Had he failed, secretly: flunked out of Johns Hopkins: and the Sargents were keeping it to themselves. He scorned Antoinette's mother. Her family. *Her.* . . . He didn't love her, wanted only to bully her. That day above the cove he'd been rather rough with her. Suppose she told her mother, showing her the bruises on her left thigh. . . .

In the hallway a few seconds later she nearly collided with Duncan as he was leaving the bathroom. He seized her hands impulsively. "What are you doing up here? I thought you were swimming," he said. Antoinette laughed nervously. She stammered and could not speak. Had he seen her come from his room, was he teasing her. . . . Without his glasses he looked impetuous. His hair was damply combed, his face was flushed from the shower, and he smelled of a pleasant astringent odor. "Should you be prowling around here all alone?" he said, smiling strangely.

"I came—I came upstairs—"

"Yes?"

"I came to look for you."

He held her still and kissed her lightly on the lips. They were both quite agitated; they could not keep their mouths from twisting into odd helpless grins.

"Did you? To look for me? When I was in the shower? Really?"

She laughed and pushed him away. He caught at her, she poked him under the arm, she squirmed free, panting.

"I do anything I want to do," she said, wiping a droplet of perspiration off her upper lip.

"Do you, eh? Do you really?"

He advanced upon her, grinning, his face ruddy and his breath short. She squealed, backing away.

In silence they wrestled together at the top of the steps. Duncan held both her wrists in his and she went limp, finally, and bowed her head so that her hair fell forward against him.

"I could come back in your room with you," she whispered.

"Could you? No, you couldn't."

"Nobody is around, they wouldn't know."

"You don't mean it. You're just talking."

"I do mean it—"

"You don't."

"I was in there just now—in your room—waiting for you," she said, raising her eyes to his with the sly calm precision with which she raised them to her own image in the bathroom mirror nearly every day. "But you were too slow. So I left."

"You weren't in there."

"I was—I was in there, waiting."

"You weren't, were you?"

"I was! I was lying on your bed."

"You *weren't.*"

She began laughing. She twisted her arm free and groped for the first step, laughing gaily. Duncan, staring, stood frozen. Then he too laughed as if he could not help himself. They stared at each other as Antoinette backed down the stairs, her fingers closed tight about the railing. From a short distance they might have looked like figures in a stiff, stylized dance: the girl descending slowly, blindly, her head thrust dramatically back and her long wild hair falling nearly to her waist, the young man in his green robe motionless at the top of the stairs, one hand clutching the robe shut at his throat, the other extended hesitantly toward the girl. Their laughter was shrill and convulsive. Their bodies appeared to be taut, tightened, charged with an intensity that must have been nearly unbearable.

"Come to me. Do it. Do it!"

Once, long ago, he had shouted at the roughened, maniacal waves during a rainstorm. No one could hear: he could shout as loudly and as despairingly as he wished.

The sea was a heartbeat gone wild, gigantically wild. The earth trembled with its own heedless, ungovernable life.

Rain pelted at the choppy waves, which broke and crashed and sank back again as if momentarily exhausted. It ran across their turbulent surfaces in sheets. Duncan stared, exhilarated. His throat hurt from shouting. That the surface of the sea, rough as it was, might be pricked by raindrops . . . that it was tormented by fierce hammering raindrops. . . .

"Come to me," he begged. "Come to me."

He was not wearing his bathing trunks but trousers and a shirt, and his hair was plastered onto his forehead, and his glasses streamed rain. His teeth chattered with the cold. But he stared, fascinated, at the storm. At the ceaseless agitation of the sea. Waves were broken in two and dashed sideways onto rocks, and their freezing spray was hurtled into his astonished face.

"Come to me, come to me, come to me, come to me. . . ."

His words were snatched away at once.

How old had he been, fifteen or sixteen? He had half-known then that something might happen to him. Something might rise up in him, ungovernable. And so he must be stopped, he must be destroyed, it was unthinkable that he be allowed to live. . . .

"Why are you holding back? Come to me, *do it!*"

The waves were frenzied. They mocked his noisy despair. Rain, wind, sheets of rain, waves shattered and tormented by raindrops; spray slashing across his face and body as if it meant to knock him down. . . . He slipped on a rock and nearly fell.

Here, at the edge of the ocean, one is responsible for nothing.

The sea has its own heartbeat, the earth its own wild defiant life. One cannot control anything. Images arise and are smashed down onto the

rocks, brutally, ecstatically. They break and nothing remains. New images arise, are borne aloft, and crash down in their turn.

Nothing remains.

He cupped his hands to his mouth and shouted. The veins in his forehead and in his neck stood taut, tense. Ready to burst. There was something in the ocean: a raging animal of some kind: a stallion or a bull. He called at it, jeered at it. Why didn't it rush onto the beach and ram into him, why did it hesitate. . . .

"Come to me! Do it! *Do it!*"

They clutched at each other hungrily.

"I didn't think you were coming," he whispered.

"I almost didn't—I almost changed my mind—"

He groaned, pressing himself against her. Her cold bare arms tightened about his neck. They kissed repeatedly, anxiously. He could not know, could not determine, what she was feeling. Her breath was as short and ragged as his, she appeared to be nearly as excited, but he could not tell—was she capable of feeling anything, was it desire for him she felt, or merely anxiety—a sense of her own recklessness—

He had been waiting for her in the cove, in their secret place, for nearly an hour. His excitement was so great he could barely contain it. Over and over he had muttered her name, calling her to him, commanding her to come. He loved her: he was crazy with love for her. Why did she keep herself from him? His blood pulsed angrily. He took off his glasses to wipe his face, and put them on again immediately, imagining that he'd seen a dab of color along the beach—but it was nothing, only a seabird.

Their shrewd plot: that Duncan (who had complained mildly of an upset stomach the night before) would tell his mother he intended to stay in bed until dinner time; that Antoinette (who had already taken care of these errands) would bicycle into Sky Harbor to return a library book and pick up something at the drugstore. In reality Duncan would leave the house by a side door and go to the cove, where Antoinette would join him within a few minutes. She would bicycle along the rarely used lane and leave her bicycle hidden. They would have the afternoon to themselves—no one would interrupt them, no one would know.

"Jesus, I didn't think you would come," Duncan said, nearly weeping.

The girl was dark-eyed, wild, her hair in a tangle from the wind, her mouth contorted. The blood seemed to have drained out of her face. She tightened her arms almost convulsively about his neck, whimpering. Was she terrified, was she as excited as he. . . . The wind blew at them even in this sheltered place. They were crouched low on one of the slabs of rock, some yards above the surf, about ten feet below the sea cliff.

"Do you love me," she said. "Do you love, love me. . . ."

Their mouths were greedy. They grasped at each other with cold, estranged fingers. The wind had shaken loose the parts of their bodies and they could not summon them back. Duncan heard himself groaning, and laughing, and whimpering like a child. His father would be on the island tomorrow. In less than twenty-four hours. So his hands clutched, clutched, his body pressed itself desperately against the girl's lithe squirming body, eager to claim it for its own.

He pulled up her shirt, then hesitated, frightened.

"I'm not afraid," she said roughly.

Her small cold hands gripped his. She brought them awkwardly to her breasts. Whimpering, he tore at her blouse—fumbled with the buttons —opened it. Her breasts were hard, as if with cold. The nipples stood out bravely.

He tugged at her shorts. She raised herself on one elbow, helped him pull the shorts off, her hair cascading into both their faces.

"I love you—" Duncan cried.

He opened his trousers. Trembling, he tried to kneel above her; but the surface of the rock was uneven, and she was clutching at him desperately, her eyes shut tight, as if she feared he would leave her.

"Don't stop, I'm not afraid. *Don't stop,*" she said.

He lowered himself clumsily onto her. He tried to enter her but the tiny space between her legs could not admit him. She groaned, she whimpered, he did not know if it was with yearning for him or in pain. One of her fingers poked against his eye. A strand of her hair had got caught in his mouth.

She was shouting at him.

He forced himself against her, prodding, jamming. He gripped her bare shoulders and grunted with the fierce, angry effort of what he must do.

And then suddenly he had entered her, had broken through—and in an instant his senses reeled, he experienced a raw blunt spasm of pleasure that was over almost immediately, and he fell on top of her, sobbing.

They were sobbing together, exhausted.

She moaned for him to get off her. Something was wrong, something was bleeding, she could feel it bleeding. . . . She clawed at his face, pushing him away. In astonishment he saw how closed, how ugly, her expression had become.

"Oh you pig— You nasty filthy—"

She pushed him away. She struck at him with her fists. Cringing, naked, she began to scream at him as if she had gone mad.

"Antoinette— Please—"

She screamed words he could not comprehend. Her face was dirty, her eyes were bloodshot, there was a thread of saliva hanging down from her mouth. He knelt on the rock, hunched, staring. Without his glasses he could see her face clearly but on all sides of her the world fell sharply away into a hazy malevolent void.

"I hate you— You're ugly, you're nasty and filthy— I'll tell them what you did—all of them— I'll tell them! *I'll tell them!*"

He tried to quiet her but she did not hear his hoarse, fearful words. He knelt there, partly naked, cringing, wringing his hands like an old woman overwhelmed with grief.

"I don't love you! I never did! You're ugly! Frogbelly ugly! Fat and silly and ugly! Ugly! I'll tell them what you did! Your father and your mother! I'll tell them! All of it! What a pig you are, how nasty and ugly and—"

It was to quiet her that he did it: only to quiet her that he seized her by the shoulders, close to her throat. But she screamed all the more. She began to thresh from side to side, clawing at his hands with her nails, her face white and witchlike and ugly, very ugly. What should he do, how should he quiet her—was she teasing him even now—was it one of her games— He heard his sobbing voice raised but he could not decipher his words. He loved her!—he hadn't meant to hurt her! It had been a mistake! It had been her fault! Hers! To quiet her he straddled her, gasping, his face contorted with the effort of his exertions. Again and again and again—and again— Yanking her frail body up so that he could slam it back down—yanking it up so that he could slam it down against the rock—again and again and again—until her head veered backward and forward crazily, limply, and her eyes had gone white, and the ugly thread of saliva had snapped off her chin—

Three

Thinned and distorted by the sea breeze her husky voice was thrown back at her. "Duncan," she called. "Duncan—"

He stood a hundred yards away, on the beach, his hands in his pockets and his shoulders in the light canvas jacket somewhat slumped. Was he wearing his sandals, or had he put on socks and his thick-soled shoes as she had suggested. . . . Her eyes strained with the effort of seeing although she was farsighted. It was clear, however, that her son's feet were getting wet. He stood woodenly as the surf broke and spread about him, snaking up greedily on both sides of his firm-planted feet.

"Duncan—"

Wrapped in a heavy coarse-knit Italian sweater that was more like a short coat, Mrs. Sargent strode out to her son. Except for her shoes, which she would change, she was dressed for the flight back home. Her glossy black hair had been brushed back severely and fastened at the nape of her neck in a dense, muscular knot; she had been wearing it like this since the morning after the evening of the discovery. . . . And her full, high-colored face was clean of makeup except for a modest shading of her lips. She had wished to look austere and grieving but in fact she looked merely subdued, as if her anger were only temporarily held in check.

"Duncan, I've been calling and calling you. My throat is hoarse! Your father will be back from the police station in another ten minutes and then we'll be leaving and I think you had *better* try to eat something. They say a person is more likely to be airsick on an empty stomach than on a full stomach, do you know that? Duncan?"

He turned, startled, as if he had heard her only now.

"Yes? Mother? What?"

Seeing him so vague, so pale, his frightened eyes blinking rapidly behind his glasses, Mrs. Duncan could only slip her arm through his.

"I didn't mean to upset you, dear. It's just that I've been calling you from the house for the last five minutes. We'll be leaving soon, we're leaving this morning, have you forgotten? Mrs. May and I have put the slipcovers on the furniture and she's going to stay to close things up, she said she doesn't mind in the least packing Irene's and the girls' clothes and mailing them, that's such a burden off me, such a relief, I really don't think I would have been capable of. . . . Not just Antoinette's things but Irene's and Lucy's too. . . ."

Duncan nodded slowly with the ready acquiescence of the deaf.

"Your things are all packed? Did you finish up last night after I went to bed?"

"What? Yes."

"Your books, your notebooks?"

"Yes."

"Everything in your drawers? In the closet?"

"Yes."

"Well—I'll check to make sure. There was that one year, remember, when your father swore he'd double-checked and as soon as we got home he couldn't find some folder, some file, and naturally I was to blame. . . . You did put on socks? Good. Are they as warm and cozy as they look? Yet so lightweight! It's amazing, these synthetic materials . . . though I think according to the label they're partly wool . . . the salesman recommended them but cautioned not to machine-wash them . . . I mean not with the regular laundry . . . the water would be too hot, the socks would shrink. So remember to keep them separate. Can you remember?"

Duncan nodded slowly.

Mrs. Sargent tightened her arm through his and led him back to the house. She did not allow him to see how her eyes filled with tears.

The girl's death had struck Duncan as powerfully as it had struck Mrs. Sargent's sister. He had not gone into hysterics and collapsed as Irene had, but since that evening . . . since the police car had stopped in the drive and two policemen came to the front door with the news . . . (And how curiously subdued they were, the two of them! Mrs. Sargent had known from their faces that the girl had been found but that she was no longer living: she had very nearly known what the exact news would be) why, his mind seemed to have slowed. Stopped. He stared at her as he stared at anything, numbly and unresistingly. Wooden, zombie-like, in a daze, in a trance. There were a half-dozen nicks on his chin, from shaving with an unsteady hand. And his stomach was constantly upset—that she knew without his telling her. (For two days after the discovery of Antoinette's body he had suffered from a violent diarrhea.) His manner was distracted, his voice hollow and without inflection. Exactly as he had been back in April when she had gone to fetch him home.

"Ah, it was a terrible, terrible thing," Mrs. Sargent sighed, holding him tight. "To happen so suddenly like that when we were all so happy. . . . Without any warning. . . . It's Irene I pity the most, I can hardly bear to think of her in that house in White Plains. . . . With just Lucy there she'll be reminded constantly. And she simply hasn't had any luck at all in selling it; the market is so wretched; but I have the idea she's asking too much. She has always had this unrealistic, inflated notion of things. . . . And do you know, that poor child took after her. I don't mean that they looked alike although I think Antoinette *did* resemble her about the eyes . . . I mean in other ways . . . in other ways. . . ."

Duncan stumbled on the first step of the veranda, then murmured a rapid apology.

"You just aren't yourself!" Mrs. Sargent said. Her voice caught, for a terrible instant she was afraid she might begin to cry. But she did not dare break down. "I wonder if the medication your father gave you is really helping or if it isn't making you . . . making you more . . . But in a few hours we'll be home, dear. You'll be in your own room again. Tonight you'll sleep in your own bed and everything will be different. I mean everything will be back to normal. And in a few weeks school will start. Do you remember, last fall, how excited you were? And how much you liked classes? On the phone you went on and on about your courses, there was that course in, what was it in, you respected the professor so much, remember, you were so very excited and stimulated and . . ."

Duncan half-smiled and nodded slowly. But Mrs. Sargent could tell by the slackness of his lips and his vague unfocused gaze that he did not remember at all.

Not forty-five minutes after Antoinette Tydeman was officially reported missing by her family, a Sky Harbor woman telephoned police to say that she had seen a girl answering that description hitchhiking on the highway just west of the village earlier that day. Long brown hair streaked with blond, falling to her waist; about fourteen or fifteen years old; wearing a plain blouse and very short denim shorts, and sandals.

Deeply tanned. A very pretty girl. . . . Yes, she had seen the girl. There was no mistake about it.

And another woman, in fact an acquaintance of Lillian Sargent's, telephoned police to say that she had seen Mrs. Sargent's niece—yes, she knew the girl personally, had been introduced to her once at the club —she had seen her in the company of two young men at about two that afternoon, and at the time it had struck her as strange, and a little upsetting, that so young a girl would be joking with boys so much older than she. (Boys? They must have been in their early twenties. Long-haired, shirtless, darkly tanned, strangers with unidentifiable accents. Not Sky Harbor residents, but not among the summer people who owned property on the island either. "I almost called across the street to her," the woman said. "I don't know why, there was just something about her, the way she was giggling, and the boys too, I think they were high on some sort of drug, there's so much of that going on this summer. . . . I remember thinking: I wonder if Lillian Sargent or the girl's mother knows about her hanging around the public beach like this. But of course I put it out of my mind. I forgot about it entirely until the bulletin came over the radio. And then I *knew*, I just *knew*. . . .")

When Antoinette had failed to return from the village by six Irene Tydeman drove slowly along Drum Road in her sister's rented car, and it seemed to her that each of the half-dozen girls she saw on bicycles was her daughter—might have been her daughter—until she drew closer and saw that the girl was a stranger. Irene did not feel especially upset because it was like Antoinette to be late, to be thoughtless, when she had told her innumerable times to please telephone home if she was delayed, a mere two or three minutes for a telephone call wasn't too much to ask, was it. . . . She was not upset but she was rather angry. On four separate occasions that summer her daughter had embarrassed her in front of her sister. She knows what my nerves are like, Irene thought. She knows how her disobedience hurts me. . . .

Even when it got to be after seven and she was driving slowly about Sky Harbor, peering at the crowds of tourists that jammed the sidewalks, staring at the many young long-haired girls who might have been her daughter but who were not, she was not truly upset: not yet. The first wave of sickening panic would not come for another half-hour.

Shortly after six Mrs. Sargent rapped on Duncan's door. He had been in his room all afternoon; she rapped cautiously, hoping he was not asleep.

"Duncan? May I come in?"

He murmured an unintelligible reply and she opened the door to see him propped up on his bed, in his terry-cloth robe, one of his school notebooks opened on his lap and a textbook beside him on the bed. He must have showered recently because his hair was still damp. He stared at her with that reluctant, distracted courtesy that meant he did not really want to be interrupted.

For a moment Mrs. Sargent could not think why she had disturbed him.

"I'm studying, I'd like to complete this chapter before dinner, Mother," he said. "Is something wrong?"

"What are you studying? Oh—biology—"

Duncan's lips shifted into a half-smile, half-frown. He had met inane but well-intentioned comments from her, and from others, with that very same grimace when he'd been hardly more than a baby—it was perhaps the boy's most characteristic expression.

"I'm making fairly good progress, I think. By the time the fall semester begins I should know the material and the course will be mainly review for me. . . . It shouldn't give me any trouble this time."

"That's fine. That's wonderful news," Mrs. Sargent said. She glanced around the room, drawing in a breath, for some reason quite gratified. There was her sister's daughter Antoinette, and there was her own son Duncan: a remarkable difference. Which reminded her: "Have you seen Antoinette, dear? Irene's furious, she's been away all afternoon and was supposed to be back by five, you know what she's like. . . . I don't suppose you've seen her?"

"Not since lunch," Duncan said.

He turned back to his work, with a sigh that might have been rude had Mrs. Sargent not understood it.

"Well—of course you haven't seen her, how could you have seen her," Mrs. Sargent murmured. "I'm sorry for disturbing you, dear. She's Irene's problem, not ours."

"Will you close the door on your way out, Mother? Thanks."

"I'm sorry to have disturbed you."

"Not at all. Thanks."

The books were packed. The notebooks. In a certain order, so that his limited space was used economically.

Labor Day was next Monday but they were leaving early. They were › leaving unusually early. If it's so hot here in Maine, Duncan thought, what will it be like in Georgetown. . . .

A vision of his room appeared to him, in his mind's eye, but it was curiously simplified. The walls had become immense white patches and one area was gone. Hadn't there been a desk there, or a table of some sort. . . . The little portable television set he'd received for a Christmas present but never used. . . . He half-smiled, to think that he had forgotten what his room looked like. He had lived in that room for years, for years. For most of his life. For years.

The sky was dense with clouds. A low-lying mist nearly obscured Drum Island from sight. And, far to the east, that little island . . . what was it called . . . Gull Island. . . . Or was Gull Island somewhere else. . . .

"Antoinette?" he whispered.

He had been angry, awaiting her. Crouched for so long on that misshapen rock, his leg muscles aching with the strain and the humiliation. "Antoinette? Antoinette?" His voice rose, at first shrilly and then, as the minutes passed, with a dull idle repetitiveness, as if his words had no more meaning than the crashing of the waves. They were pointless, as the waves were pointless, yet charged with an irresistible clarity.

Droplets of spray were flung high up the rocks, across his flushed face. He had to take off his glasses to polish the lenses several times. It was remarkable that the surf could reach so far, halfway up the sea cliff. In his ironic state he halfway thought that the ocean was mimicking his distress, scattering mock teardrops on his cheeks. "Well, of course she won't come," he said in a matter-of-fact voice, "wouldn't come, never planned on coming. Of course. Aren't you Duncan Sargent, haven't you always been Duncan Sargent. . . ." He waited. He knelt on the edge of the rock until his knees ached, then he sat, clasping his legs, waiting, waiting patiently, as the sky gradually lost its color and clotted gray-green clouds moved overhead from the east. For the third time—or was it the fourth—his glasses were splattered and he took them off, wearily, and polished the lenses on his shirt. While he had the glasses in his hand he saw a movement out of the corner of his eye, a sudden dab of color, and his heart leapt with the certainty that it was Antoinette—but when he put the glasses on, hastily, clumsily, he saw that it was nothing, nothing at all, not even a seabird.

Nothing.

The first day after the child's grotesque death, and the second, and finally the third.

Simply endure it, Mrs. Sargent instructed herself, as she had in the past instructed herself during other times of disruption. There had been unexpected deaths in the family before and while none had been so violent as this, and so ugly, they had all brought with them a queer suspension of time so that the very second hand of her watch appeared to slow, to come near stopping. But of course it had not stopped in the past and it would not stop now.

She would not have guessed that the child would be found murdered but she did guess—silently, involuntarily—the details of the murder, once the fact of the death had been revealed.

Rape? And the back of her skull smashed from repeated blows? Her poor thin body scratched and bruised and broken?

Staring critically at her red-rimmed eyes in the bathroom mirror Mrs. Sargent confessed to herself that she was not surprised, not really. Not surprised. If the child was to die—why, there was no other plausible death for her.

Irene had collapsed and so *she* had to answer the innumerable questions.

Plainclothes detectives who were sorry for her, and as soft-spoken and methodical as her husband's accountants. Had she any idea who the two young men were who were reported to have been talking to Antoinette a few hours before her death . . . did she know any of the girl's friends or acquaintances on the island . . . did she know how the girl customarily spent her time when she was away from the house. . . .

She, and Duncan, and even Lucy. Poor frightened asthmatic Lucy. "I don't know. I really don't know," she said repeatedly.

Perhaps it was to support her that Duncan was so strong at the very first. Only as the hours passed, and she regained her composure, did he begin to realize what had happened to his cousin.

She followed him upstairs. In the doorway of his room he stood as if paralyzed, his knuckles pressed against his mouth.

"Duncan? Why don't you let yourself go, why don't you cry if you want to. . . . They don't have any more questions for you, why don't you let yourself go. . . ."

But he could not cry. So far as she knew, he could not cry.

Pale, stunned, haggard, looking much older than his age: sharing,

⸮⸮⸮⸮ Sargent's worn elderly manner. Side by side they sat on

⸮ at the sea. Something to eat? Just a light snack?

sea, immobile. Only Duncan's peremptory gesture

⸮d that he had heard.

questioning suspects, the body had been shipped

ucy were gone, and now the slipcovers were on the

⸮itcases and valises packed and they were waiting for

⸮rn from town; and then they would be flying in a

⸮ashington.

sed for the trip in a freshly laundered sports shirt and

⸮hite trousers that fitted him, so Mrs. Sargent noted,

t the waist. He had lost about twenty pounds back

l, and then he had regained much of it, and in the

had lost at least eight pounds. His hair was neatly

⸮ion was blank and frozen. If he spoke—and he would

e questioned him—his voice was dull, without inflec-

He sat with his shoulders erect, as if he were at attention. By the fixedness of his gaze and the almost imperceptible quivering of his lips Mrs. Sargent judged that he was trying to sort out something in his mind —trying to remember, to arrange—as he had when he'd been ill and there were areas in his memory that had gone blank, whitely blank. Like empty spots on a map, he had said, wonderingly, trying to describe to Mrs. Sargent what he saw. Or like tiny fires, white flames, burning in isolated patches but eager to come together, ravenous to come together, in one single obliterating blaze.

Her heart contracted with pity for him. He had been fonder of the girl than he knew, or than anyone could have known—with the exception of Mrs. Sargent herself, who had noted shrewdly and without comment her son's frequent distracted manner in the girl's presence.

"Ah, there's the car," Mrs. Sargent said, standing. "There he is. Now do we have everything, is everything set? Your father won't want to dawdle here any longer than necessary."

Duncan got to his feet stiffly. He glanced at his hands, as if surprised to find them empty.

"Once we get back home and things return to normal you'll feel much better," Mrs. Sargent said, half-scolding. "You'll regain your appetite. You'll be able to sleep. Wait and see."

Duncan paused. He was waiting for his father's car to turn in the driveway and for a moment Mrs. Sargent did not think he intended to speak. Then he said in a soft, distinct, rather dignified voice: "I don't think so, Mother."

The following is a list of Obelisk titles now available, each chosen as an example of excellent prose:

A *Different Woman* by Jane Howard

Living Well Is the Best Revenge by Calvin Tomkins

Pomp and Circumstance by Nöel Coward

A *Presence with Secrets* by W. M. Spackman
Introduction by Edmund White

A *Sentimental Education* by Joyce Carol Oates

Sixty Stories by Donald Barthelme